KEEP THIS
FOR ME

ALSO BY JENNIFER FAWCETT

Beneath the Stairs

KEEP THIS FOR ME

JENNIFER FAWCETT

ATRIA BOOKS

New York   Amsterdam/Antwerp   London
Toronto   Sydney/Melbourne   New Delhi

ATRIA
BOOKS

An Imprint of Simon & Schuster, LLC
1230 Avenue of the Americas
New York, NY 10020

For my parents

This book is inspired by a true story. A broken-down car in the time before cell phones, a young couple on the side of the road, an unlucky encounter with someone who had done this before and would do it again. It's a story so familiar, it seems like B-movie trope. But for their families, it wasn't a cliché; it was a detonation. This is my attempt to imagine what came after.

ANA

August 29, 1993

1:30 A.M.

The lake is the great devourer; the giver and taker of life. It has its own weather system; its water circulates up into the bluest blue summer sky, gathers into the fat-bellied purple clouds, then slams down into itself with glee. On the surface, the living splash, their pleasure boats tear up the calm water, their fishing poles dip in to feed. They think they own the lake, but it is only letting them play. When it decides, it will swallow them whole. Ask the ones below. Ask the sailors who lie in their broken beds with undelivered boxes of coal, of wool, of rum, and buttons. They sleep where the water moves slow and dark and holds its secrets.

The young woman who swims now, trailing blood from a gash on her leg, believes the lake will save her. She loves this water and has swum in all its moods. But if she gets too weak, she too will slip under and join the sleeping ones on the bottom.

It's night and there's a summer storm, the sudden electric kind that rips a hole in the sky and then is gone just as quickly. On the shore of the nearby campground, the families huddle in their tents and listen to the rain and wind. They hear the waves crashing, but none of them know about the young woman out in that churning darkness, swimming for her life. They will learn soon. A shoe in the sand, a purse in the grass; these are what remain. In the coming days, they will watch the news and say, "We were camping so close when he killed her." They will shiver with the glee of voyeurs.

And the lake will go on.

The rain will fall, the waves will hit the beach.

And below the surface, the dead will keep their secrets.

CHAPTER 1

FIONA

Now

The lake was a promise. As soon as it started to peek through the trees, no matter what book I had been lost in or what thought had been tumbling on repeat in my mind—the ever-shifting politics of kids in my class, my current crush—all of it disappeared with that first sighting of the water. I'd roll the window down all the way and stick my nose out like a dog. Any other time, my dad's rule was windows up on the highway, but the lake affected him too, and soon all the windows would be down, the radio volume up, and the car would fill with the smell of summer.

Every summer, my father and I went to my grandparents' cottage on the southeast shore of Lake Ontario, just outside a little town called St. Rose. The minute the final school bell rang, Dad would be outside the school, car packed to the roof. My aunts and uncles would arrive at the cottage soon after we did, each bringing their own growing pack of kids, and all summer long there would be a steady flow of cousins, friends of cousins, family members many times removed, the cottage full to bursting but we could always fit more.

My dad had been going to that cottage every summer of his life. My grandparents bought it the year he was born and as the family grew, they kept adding to it, so by the time I was twelve, it looked nothing like the humble shack it had once been. Instead, it was a patched-together hodgepodge forever decorated with drying beach towels and bathing suits like a chorus of flags. On the other side of the peninsula, the cottages were concrete-and-glass monoliths, but on our side, they were old and worn, paint faded from summer sun and winter storms, the walls and roofs held together with love and duct tape. Each cottage told the story of morning swims and evening bonfires; of dayslong games of Monopoly and multifamily beach volleyball tournaments, of sand in your sheets and your hair and between the pages of your book, and always the joyful yells of kids who knew the true freedom of the lake in summer.

As soon as we pulled into the shared parking area, my best friend, David, would sprint up the stairs to the car. His family's cottage was next to mine, and we'd spent our summers together since we were babies. The two of us would fly down those worn wood stairs, across the lawn, and over the sand, shedding school clothes for the swimsuits we wore underneath like a secret identity that could only be revealed when summer officially began. We would grab the bag my grandma left for us at the water's edge—Grape Crush in glass bottles, peanut butter sandwiches, and homemade cookies—and we'd wade out to the floating dock, the bag of food and comic books held high over our heads, and stay out there until the adults called us in for supper. On that first evening, the summer stretched as endlessly before us as the water.

 "Did you ever think about not coming back because of Mom?" I asked my dad once.

"No, never," he said. My mom grew up in St. Rose and had loved the lake just as much as he did. She'd been a long-distance swimmer and had swum across the entire thing when she was only fifteen. "She wouldn't want us to stop coming here." I had believed him. He said we'd never stop going to the lake.

Until we did.

Until he felt he had no other choice to keep us safe.

I lean my head against the airplane window and look down. Now, the lake is a vast expanse of freezing darkness thousands of feet below me. It's waiting for me, calling to me, even after twenty years.

Instinctually, my hand goes to my necklace. I can feel the small bumps under my sweater. Two halves of a heart, broken apart in a zigzag, one new and one old. The older half used to be gold-colored but the cheap metal tarnished years ago. I've had to replace the chain twice, but I always wear it. My mother had the other half. My dad told me she wasn't a sentimental person, but I like to imagine her, young, pregnant, and broke, finding it in some little trinket store. Maybe she was with a girlfriend, or maybe she was by herself, but on a whim, she bought it and had it engraved with our names: *Ana & Fiona*. I picture her tucking one half into the old dresser, daydreaming about when she would give it to me.

Of course, I can't be sure of any of this. Like so much about my mother, any ideas of her are gauzy and insubstantial, made more of dreams than memory. All I do know is that my father found my half and gave it to me when I turned six, and I've created stories about it—about her—ever since.

Everything I know about my mother has come through stories. Stories from my dad; stories from my paternal grandparents, the Greens; a precious few from my mother's parents; and the stories I've found in newspaper articles, crime blogs, and the police and court transcripts. Those ones make up what I know of my mother's final night. It goes like this:

On August 28, 1993, my parents went to a party, leaving me in the care of my grandparents at the cottage where we had all spent the summer. I was two and a half years old. The party was a long way away and on the drive home, their car broke down and they were picked up by a truck driver named Eddie Ward. He said he'd take them to a pay phone, but instead he attacked my dad, left him for dead on the side of the road, and took off with my mother. My dad was found unconscious the next morning and when he woke up in the hospital two days later, he was able to tell the police enough that they eventually tracked down Eddie Ward and his truck many states away. He lived in the next town, St. Thomas, and had been almost back home when he'd picked my parents up. The police searched his house and discovered seven bodies buried in his backyard, but my mother wasn't one of them. All he told the cops was that he took her to the lake, to the state park that's just a few miles past St. Rose; only a few miles past our cottage. Dogs found her shoe half buried on the beach and her purse tossed into the long grass. Hundreds of people searched, but her body was never found, which means her story has no ending.

When I was pregnant with my daughter, Zoe, I bought a necklace just like the one my mom had chosen and now I wear two halved hearts. I thought becoming a mother would be a chance to start a new story, one that didn't hold all the loss of my past. I envisioned giving my daughter her half heart when she was old enough to understand it. Maybe on her sixth birthday, like me. But after she was born, everything changed.

No, I changed. Or maybe, becoming a mother revealed what had been broken all along.

When David's name came up on my call display yesterday, I had two reactions at once. One was that sudden leap of joy to see his name, the boy I'd once thought I might marry in that hazy way you think about the future when you're young. To my twelve-year-old mind, it was a way to make every day like summer. But the sick nervous feeling came just as quickly: David was still in St. Rose and now on the police force, just like his dad had been. That meant he was calling from the place of my mother's murder, a place I have not been back to in twenty years since my dad moved us far away. David and I always communicate by text or email. A phone call meant urgency. I let it ring four times but then, just before it went to voicemail, I picked up.

As soon as I answered, I could hear the noises of the police station behind him.

"Eddie Ward is dying," he said.

Eddie Ward.

A name my family never says. Eddie Ward has been rotting in a prison cell for over thirty years, but despite being locked away, his name unspoken, he is still with us, while each year my mother fades further into the past.

"But," David continued, "he's started talking. And he's talking about your mother."

"Talking—?"

"This guy I know, Jory, is a CO at Grady State. He overheard Ward talking to his son about your mom and—"

He paused, and in that half-second silence, I knew everything was about to change. What had been memory, history, the fabric of my mother's unfinished story, was about to unravel.

"—and he said he didn't kill her."

"What?"

"Fi, you have to understand, he's doped up on morphine. It might not be real."

"But it's real enough that you're calling me."

"Yeah." He sighed, acknowledging this. "Ward's a braggart—you know that. But Jory said he didn't sound like he was bragging."

It was like a hand was wrapped around my throat. "But then what happened to her?"

"He took her to the lake, that part happened. But then—"

"But then what? Where is she?"

"She went into the water but then she disappeared. Ward said she disappeared *in* the water."

"But he didn't kill her."

"No."

What happens when the world cracks open? It seems like there should be some kind of a shift. Your heart should beat faster or stop altogether. Your skin should feel different. David's call came when I was at the ocean conservancy office where I work. The people around me continued what they'd been doing a moment before; the November drizzle continued to fall, my heart continued to beat.

David was still talking. "He's still living in St. Thomas, if you can believe that."

"Wait, who lives in St. Thomas?" I asked.

"His son, Jason. That's who he was talking to. Jason Ward's never visited, as far as my buddy knows. He must have gone in because his old man's dying."

My mother's shoe and purse were found in a part of the sprawling state park that no one ever went to. The police had scoured the park with dogs, helicopters, and hundreds of volunteers. Partial tire treads found on the park service road matched the ones they'd pulled from where my parents' car had broken down, and the ones from where my dad was found. Enough evidence to tell part of a story, but one without an end. The only explanation, for all these years, has been that Eddie Ward had drowned her and carried her out to bury her somewhere else. During the trial, he refused to say what he'd done with her. It was assumed he thought the lack of a body would throw off the prosecution, but there was enough other evidence against him that he's been serving multiple life sentences. My family thought it was his sick way of holding something over us.

"I need to talk to him."

"He's barely coherent," David said. "He doesn't have much time left."

"I don't care. If he can talk to his son, he can talk to me."

"Are you sure you're up for that?"

"Yes. I don't know what the process is for a visit but can you—?"

"He'll have to agree to it."

The thought of Eddie Ward getting to decide if I can come and speak to him was enough to push the nervous feelings away with anger.

"There's a security process but I'll see if I can get things moving quickly, given the circumstances," David said, and then his voice lost the official cop sound and I could hear the boy he'd once been. "So, you're really coming back to St. Rose?"

"I'm coming back. I'll be there tomorrow."

We've moved over land again and I can feel the plane starting its descent. Far below, I see the lights of a single car moving along the winding road that connects the lakeside towns.

My mother got away.

My mother got away, but she didn't come back.

These two thoughts now run in a continuous loop in my mind.

Somewhere in the vast darkness below is the ending to the story that has defined my life. My hand goes back to my necklace, those two half hearts, connected by a thin chain. It's enough to bring me back, back to St. Rose, to my grandparents' cottage. Back to the lake.

CHAPTER 2

FIONA

Now

The moment before I enter the arrivals area, I realize I'm nervous. David and I have sent the occasional picture over the years; he sent one of his first patrol car, and I sent a video of a humpback whale breaching when I got my new job. There have been a few group shots and my grandparents have always shared the Connor family holiday card, sent without fail each year by David's mom, but we haven't shared any photos that really show who we are now. I'm not on social media. My father's old fear of being found—the reason why he took us away from here in the first place—has made privacy a habit. So, despite the holiday cards and occasional group shot, in my mind David is still the thirteen-year-old boy I said goodbye to on the last day of the summer twenty years ago. I told him I could rent a car but he insisted on picking me up, which I'm grateful for. I don't know what I'm walking into here; despite the time that's passed, David is safe and familiar.

When I come around the corner, I see him a second before he sees me. He'd started his growth spurt in our last summer together and now he's over six feet tall and towers above the other people in the small waiting area. The skinny boy with hair flopping in his eyes is gone. Now he's got broad shoulders, his hair is cut short, and there's a shadow of coppery stubble across his face. Instead of a uniform, he is in dress slacks and a tie and standing ramrod straight with his hands behind his back, so he sticks out in the small crowd of sweatshirts and flannel. But his formality disappears as soon as he sees me. He grins and I see the boy he was again. He steps forward, arms held out.

"Oh my God, you came back. You're *back*." Our hug is immediate and tight, but just as quickly, we let go and step apart putting a small, polite distance between us. He grabs my suitcase and says, "Is that all you've got? Come on, there's someone I want you to meet."

Girlfriend? Child? There's so much about him I don't know. That goes both ways. I never told him about Zoe. I had planned to send him baby pictures but nothing about those early months had gone as planned and each time I'd thought about reaching out, I stopped myself. To tell him about Zoe, I'd have to tell him about what was happening to me. I've never been able to lie to David, so instead, I chose omission.

As soon as we walk out of the airport I start to shiver. "They say we may get snow before Thanksgiving," he says. "Did you bring a heavier coat?"

"I don't know if I'll be here that long," I say.

He glances at me. "Ah, I hope you'll stay for a bit. My mother won't forgive me if you don't visit." He taps his key fob and the hatch of his SUV opens. A gangly German shepherd bounds out and comes over to us, tail wagging.

"This is Tucker," David says. "Tuck, this is my oldest friend, Fiona."

"Hi, Tucker," I say. I hold out my hand for him to sniff and he immediately goes into play pose, front legs sprawled out, his butt in the air.

"He's an excellent judge of character," David says.

"Is he a police dog?"

"Nah, he was kicked out of the K-9 program."

"Poor guy. Don't make him feel bad."

David laughs. "He never officially started. He has a kidney issue. It's not a big deal, but it means he isn't fit for police work. I have a buddy down in San Antonio who brought him up to me."

Tucker is sniffing my suitcase. His ears are too big for his head and he trips over his long legs in his excitement. "He doesn't look quite as fierce as police dogs usually do," I say.

"Give him time," David says and points to the back of the car. On cue, Tucker jumps back in. "He's in his awkward adolescent phase. But he's become the unofficial station mascot." To this, Tucker's tongue lolls out the side of his mouth.

"You're too cute to scare the bad guys, aren't you boy," I say to him and give him a scratch behind the ears.

David keeps the radio playing at a low murmur for the hour-long drive to St. Rose and he fills me in on what's changed in the area, though I'm only half listening. I'm booked to go to the penitentiary early tomorrow morning and the reality of being face-to-face with Eddie Ward is hitting me now that I'm here. I had begged David to come with me, but his father was one of the first officers on my mother's case and testified during the trial. There are pretty good odds, he thought, that Ward might hold that against him and clam up.

"You okay?" he asks, and I realize I've zoned out. "Weird to be back?"

"It probably will be tomorrow," I say. Outside the window is pitch-black. I'd forgotten how complete the darkness is out here in northern New York, far away from any big cities. If I could see anything out the window, all there would be is trees and fields. "I can't believe I'm going to actually meet him." A shiver runs down my back just thinking about it. "None of this feels real."

David doesn't say anything. He probably hates the idea of me being in the same room as Eddie Ward, but I appreciate that he's keeping his opinion to himself.

"Do you want to grab a drink or something?" I ask as we come to the outskirts of St. Rose. "Is there any place that would still have their kitchen open?"

"I'd love to," he says, "but I have to work tonight. You must be starving. There's a pizza place on Main that'll have slices."

"No, I'm fine. I have a granola bar in my bag," I say. Food wasn't really the point. "So, that explains the tie."

"I'm still getting used to wearing one," he says, adjusting it at his neck. "As soon as I made detective, Mom went out and bought me a whole set. One for every day of the week. The other guys just wear polo shirts, but I wanted to impress you." He grins and reaches out to pat me on the leg, but then just as quickly pulls his hand back and replaces it on the steering wheel.

"Detectives still have to work the night shift?"

"We got a couple of people out with the flu, so I said I'd cover. Sorry, bad timing. I figured you'd be exhausted."

"I'm on West Coast time. It's fine. Tomorrow's going to be early anyway."

We pull into the parking area up the hill from my grandparents' cottage and he turns the car off. Below us, the waves are crashing onto the little beach that runs in front of all the cottages. Just hearing the water, I let out a breath I didn't know I was holding.

"I stocked a pile of firewood and I can bring over more," he says. "I don't know when the chimney was last cleaned though. Your grandparents haven't been here the past few summers so the maintenance has become a little spotty."

"I thought my aunts and uncles were still using it."

"Yeah . . . I'd just get the chimney cleaned if you're going to be using the wood stove a lot. To be safe."

"Thanks for taking care of this for so long."

He shrugs. "I'm here anyway."

David has become the de facto overseer of the cottage because he's local. No one in the family wants to sell it, but no one's willing to commit the amount of time to it that my grandparents did. I always thought my cousins were taking advantage of his kindness but maybe I've been just as bad. Have I really been staying away all this time just because my dad thought we were in danger twenty years ago, or has it become habit? A way to numb myself?

"Before I forget." David hands me a car key. "It's right over there." I'm using my cousin Jaimie's Jeep she has stored here while she's overseas.

I squint in the direction he's pointing. His headlights just catch it through the rain that's started to fall. "Oh my God, is it purple?"

"It is. I think she had it custom painted. It's four-wheel drive but you don't have snow tires, so be careful." Then in a rush he says, "For Christ's sake, Fi, just stay at my place. You can have the bed—I'll sleep on the couch. Or let me bring you to a hotel. I hate the thought of you out here alone."

It's a relief having him say it. I don't know how much has changed between us in the time that has passed. It's not like we can pick up where we left off; we were children the last time we saw each other. But I desperately want it to be easy like it used to be; to feel that familiarity again. When we were little, we'd have sleepovers all the time, usually me sleeping over at his cottage and loving the respite from all my younger cousins. But our last summer together, it was discouraged. Maybe the adults saw what we didn't, how in a few years our friendship would become something more.

"I'm only a few miles from town," I say. "And it's winterized."

"But there's no one around." He gestures into the darkness beyond the window. "If there's an early snow storm, you could be stuck. They don't plow these back roads."

"I'll be fine." I try to make it sound convincing.

"I would have offered you to stay at my place earlier but I didn't know if you were coming alone, or . . ."

"Nope. Just me."

"There was that guy . . . what was his name?"

"Aaron. That was a few years ago now. We're just friends. He's actually married now and expecting a child."

I have to tell him about Zoe, but where do I begin? I'm exhausted just thinking about it. Instead, I say, "And what about you? Is there someone—?"

He makes a little sound that is probably supposed to be a laugh but doesn't come out quite right. "It's not exactly a hopping social scene up here."

I take a breath. *I'm not with Aaron, but we have a kid. Surprise!* My hand has wandered up to the necklace again. "David, there's something—" I start to say, but at the same time he says, "Look, I don't want you to get your hopes up about what Ward's going to say to you. Guys like him want power. Even when they have none, they'll do anything to get it. If he thinks he has anything over you, even the smallest thing—"

"There's nothing else he can take from me."

"He's still a monster, even though he's old and dying. You have to be careful."

"I know. I will be."

We sit side by side for a moment, listening to the rain and the waves. I know I'm keeping him from work but I don't want to get out of the car yet. I don't want to be alone.

"A few years after we moved away, my grandparents—my mom's parents, not my dad's—Grandma and Grandpa Lukas. Did you meet them?"

"I think so."

"Well, they wanted to put up a cenotaph for my mom. My dad tried to fight it at first. But then he stopped. It's not like he thought she was alive, it was just making this ending where there wasn't one. But then I think he did start to believe it. He met Juliet, got married, had my sister. And I should've been generous enough to let him move on, but . . . All those milestones, you know? And my friends all had their moms there for them and I didn't. And for what? For something as stupid as being in the wrong place at the wrong time? For a fluke? If they'd left the party ten minutes later, or ten minutes earlier; if they hadn't gone, or if the car hadn't broken down at that exact time. It just feels like if something is going to hurt so many people, it shouldn't be random. There has to be a reason."

"But he never gave a reason for any of it," he says. "If he didn't give one during the trial—"

"I need him to look me in the eye and . . . just tell me *why*. There's nothing that can justify what he did, but I still want to hear it."

We have talked about this a thousand times before. For David, maybe it's being a cop and being the son of a cop, having Ward in prison for life is the end. But for me, if I can't have my mother back, then I need a reason. Something big enough to fill the hole she left.

He helps me get my bags from the back and we hug awkwardly, then I watch his taillights bounce along the rough road until they disappear around the bend. Now, I just need to climb down the old wood steps, unlock the door, and reenter my childhood. David's right; a hotel would have been much more comfortable than this cold and lonely cottage, but this was home for me in St. Rose all those years ago. If I'm going to learn the ending of my mother's story, then I need to be here, because this is where it started.

CHAPTER 3

JASON

1984-1995

Jason Ward's collection started with a snow globe. When he was little, his dad, Eddie, had worked locally and the kid had just clung to Mommy. That wormed into his father's head and made him mad. So, Eddie went back to long-haul trucking. He'd be gone for weeks and when he came home, Jason would be shy around him, but the little boy would watch him, fascinated, and after a few hours he'd start following him around. When his mom came to take him for his bath, he'd push her away and Eddie would be pleased, more pleased than he'd ever admit. It worked like a charm for a few years, anyway. But then Jason started getting less excited when he came home. He took his daddy for granted.

At a truck stop on the Pennsylvania–New York border, Eddie had seen the snow globe and, on a whim, he bought it. Its bottom was blue foil and in the center was a little island that rose up with plastic pine trees sticking out of it. When he got home, he gave it to his son. Like any five-year-old, he was excited to get a present, but he didn't know what it was.

"Give it a shake," Eddie said.

Jason shook it and it was like he'd just seen his first magic trick.

"It's snowing! It's snowing! Look, Mommy, I made it snow!"

The joy on his face even got Carole out of her sour mood.

But the next morning, the snow globe sat ignored on the kitchen table while the kid watched cartoons. When his dad told him to switch it to news, he got pissy and said Mommy always let him watch TV.

Eddie switched the channel anyway because he was the man of the house and the kid had to learn that. He told him to go find something else to do but Jason complained that there wasn't anything.

Eddie looked at him. "Nothing to do. You sure about that?"

The boy just stared at him. He'd forgotten that fast. After only one day he'd forgotten his present. It was like he'd forgotten his father. That was wrong. That was an important, necessary lesson to learn.

Eddie got up, went over and picked up the snow globe sitting on the kitchen table where Jason had left it. He walked outside with the boy following, running now.

"No, Daddy, stop," he cried out. "That's mine. It's special."

"Not special enough," Eddie said, and he lifted up the snow globe and smashed it on one of the rocks that lined Carole's pathetic little flower garden. The shell splintered and tiny plastic flakes of snow, the foil lake, and the plastic island fell onto the dirt, now nothing more than junk. Eddie wiped his hands on his pants and walked back into the house.

Jason didn't move. He could feel his lip quivering and knew he was going to cry. He opened his mouth to call to his mother, but then a new feeling started growing in his stomach, taking over the sad one. His daddy was teaching him a lesson and if he was taking the time to teach him, then it had to be important. And his mom babying him, that's how his dad put it, that was just keeping him a baby. Very carefully, he picked up the pieces of the snow globe and cradled them in his hands like he'd seen his mom hold a bird once. He wasn't going to be able to fix the shattered case, but the plastic rock and trees were okay and maybe his mom would give him some glue to attach them to the foil base. And he'd put it on his shelf so he could look at it every day, and then his daddy would know that he understood how to treat something special.

Eddie left the next day for another haul and when he came back a few weeks later, he gave him another snow globe. This one had a cactus and said "Arizona" with a little lizard sitting on the A. Jason had cleared off a shelf in his room—stuffed toys that were too babyish for him now—and he put the new snow globe next to the plastic rock and pine trees. It looked pretty empty with just two things sitting on it, but that didn't bother him. Later, when his dad came into his room, he said, "You going to play with those or just look at them?"

"Just look at them," Jason said. "It's my special collection."

His dad didn't say anything else, but he nodded and left the room and Jason knew that this time, he'd done the right thing.

Over the years, the collection grew. At first, it was things his dad bought at truck stops. There were a few more snow globes, a little statue of Mount Rushmore, an alligator key chain from Florida, a teddy bear wearing a T-shirt that said "I ♥ NOLA." Then, he brought him a key chain bottle opener that said "Missoula Tigers, State Cup '82."

"You hold this for me," his dad said. "Keep it safe."

Who were the Missoula Tigers? It didn't matter. His dad was asking him to help. Maybe that meant the collection belonged to both of them now. That made Jason feel good. His dad trusted him and he would be worthy of that trust.

The next time his dad came home, he gave him a pink and yellow coin purse that had hair bands and barrettes in it. Strands of long blond hair were wrapped around some of the bands. Jason didn't complain about it being a girl's; that wasn't the point. He put it on the shelf next to the other things.

And so, it went on. With every item he added to his collection, he felt closer to his dad because somewhere out there, a person was wondering how they'd lost their engraved lighter (Kentucky haul), or their favorite pair of sunglasses (New England route), or the commemorative coin that had initials on it that looked military (Texas Panhandle). Maybe they were still looking for these things but they would never find them because they were in Jason Ward's bedroom. He would always have them and could look at them whenever he wanted, and they never could.

Later, he realized it wasn't just lost things sitting on his shelf; it was lost people too.

His mom knew not to touch the collection but once, at Christmas, he found his cousin Kylie in his room. She was holding the NOLA bear and a little carved dog his dad had brought back from California. There was still sand ground into the cracks. The carving was rough, it had obviously been done by hand, and the eyes were crooked, which made it look demented. She was making them talk to each other because Kylie was seven and still played baby games. She was a pudgy girl and tall for her age, so even though Jason was a year and a half older, they probably weighed the same, but he was angry and she was too distracted by her game to notice him coming up behind her. He pushed her hard and her face smacked into the shelf causing parts of his collection to fall over. She screamed and blood spurted from her nose all over his stuff. Seeing the mess only made him angrier and he went to push her again but she was quicker than he thought and she dodged him. He crashed into the shelves and the end of one fell off the bracket and his collection slid onto the floor. Kylie scrambled out of the room into the hallway. She was holding her hands over her bleeding face and ran straight into Eddie, who was coming to see what the commotion was. For a second, everything stopped. Eddie looked down at the two of them.

Chubby Kylie blubbering in front of him, blood and snot running off her face, and behind her, Jason, hands balled into fists, his collection scattered all over the floor.

Kylie probably thought that his dad would take her side but before she could get a word out, he grabbed her arm, bent down, and said in a low voice, "You touch that again, you get hurt. Next time, it'll be worse."

He released her and she staggered back. It only took her a second to recover. She ran down the hallway into the bathroom, slamming the door behind her. Eddie looked at his son and then he said, "Clean it up," and walked away. Even though it was Christmas, Jason spent the rest of the night in his room, cleaning up the mess his cousin had made. He heard Kylie sniveling and whining to her parents but no adult came to talk to him. His mom's sister, Annie, and her husband, Pete, left early the next morning. If Kylie told them what happened, they didn't say anything about it and his mom knew enough to stay out of it.

After that, Jason put a sign that said STAY OUT (OR ELSE) on his door and kept it closed. He didn't need to worry. It's not like anyone ever came to visit.

The collection grew.

And then the police came.

One September afternoon the year he was eleven, he arrived home from school to find three cops crowded into the front doorway with two cars parked outside. He could already see the neighbors poking their heads between closed curtains to watch. He went in through the kitchen, ran straight to his room, and pressed his ear against the door. His mom sounded upset and even though he couldn't hear exactly what they were saying, he knew it was about his dad. At first, he thought there had been an accident—his dad had been gone for longer than usual—but then more police arrived and they came into the house. His mother was yelling at them to be careful, but he heard them say "search warrant" and he'd watched enough television to know that only happened if there'd been a crime.

"You hold this for me. Keep it safe."

In that moment, even though he couldn't say exactly why, Jason knew what he had to do. He dumped his school bag on the floor and swept the entire collection into it. He pushed the bag under his bed, but that was too obvious. He opened his window as wide as he could to throw the bag into the backyard, but then a cop came through the gate. He had a crowbar in his hand and was going to the shed. Quickly, Jason shut the window and jammed his school books back inside his backpack on top of the collection. He hoped that nothing was getting broken but there was no time to be precious. He opened his bedroom door, the bag heavy on his back, just as a female police officer was coming down the hall. She escorted him and his mom to a police car outside and took them to the station.

They were there for hours. First, they were together as the policewoman and another guy asked Jason questions about his dad. He cried once during that interview, not because he was scared but because he was so mad and confused and he'd told them a hundred times that his dad hadn't done anything wrong. No, he'd never hurt him or his mom. He barely even raised his voice at them, but it was like the cops didn't want to hear it because they kept asking him over and over. They took him into a separate room and brought in a shrink to talk to him. She asked him all the same questions but by then he was so tired he just stopped talking.

His mom was in for a lot longer. When they finally got to leave, the cops drove them to a motel because they couldn't go back to their house. All the next day, his mom was back with the police and he was stuck waiting in a stuffy room at the back of the police station. They let him keep his school bag with him but he didn't dare open it. Finally, someone gave him an old comic book—a discard from some other kid—and he read it front to back three times, just to break the loop of fear and questions cycling through his head.

That second night his house was on the news. He saw it on the crappy black-and-white TV in the motel. A cordon had been marked around it and there was a crowd of neighbors and journalists. The cops had brought in dogs and then machines and dug up the backyard. They had to tear down part of the fence his dad had built to get their machines in and they didn't even care about the mess they made because of what they'd found behind the house.

Now he knew what his dad had done. Everyone knew. The lawyer his mom got came to the motel a lot but even he didn't seem to question that his dad was guilty.

Through all of this, the collection stayed in his bag and he never let that bag out of his sight. He knew he was risking kid-jail by not telling anyone about it, but he'd made a promise and he was going to prove to his dad that he could keep his word.

But as the weeks and then months passed—when Thanksgiving and Christmas and his birthday came and went like they didn't even exist; when it seemed the only people who talked to them were lawyers or journalists, everyone wanting to take something but no one wanting to give; when they moved into the trailer because their house was trashed, first by the police and then by vandals, and his mother refused to go near it, and when he finally had to go back to school and even the teachers treated him like a freak; when for all this time he continued to protect the collection and keep his promise—he began to wonder if he was doing the right thing.

Jason wasn't stupid. He knew it was evidence. If he handed it in, he would be condemning his father, so he'd hidden it in a box, now stuffed in the back of his closet. And his mother, for all her ranting against his dad, stayed silent.

Would his dad protect him the same way if he could? He tried to push that thought way down deep where it could whither. He'd turn his music up real loud or start a fight at school or do push-ups until he wanted to puke just to get it out of his head. That was a disloyal cowardly question. That was a total piece of shit way of thinking. But still, the question persisted.

It took two years for the case to come to trial. Each day the courtroom was packed. Jason sat wedged between his mom and her lawyer, who stank of coffee and mothballs. He kept facing forward but he could feel the eyes of the victims' families on him, demanding he return what had been taken from them. His dad was up front. Jason hadn't seen him in two years, not since that last night; that final hurried addition to his collection stuffed into his hand before his dad went back to his truck and never returned. He wanted to tell him, *I kept it safe, every piece. I kept my promise.* But his father never looked at him. Not once.

And that's when he realized that the collection had become wholly his. He'd thought it was his father's attempt to share something with him; a father's need to give something to his son. But no, that collection meant there had once been a time when his dad had needed *him*. Even if that time had passed, it had once been real. And so, he kept it.

CHAPTER 4

FIONA

Now

It's still dark out when the phone rings, jarring me out of sleep. The fire has gone out and the cottage is freezing. The phone has wedged itself down between the couch cushions and it takes multiple rings for my fingers to find it.

"Fiona?" It's David. He sounds harried. "Good, I was worried I'd miss you."

"What time is it? Am I late?" I'd set my alarm for six but maybe I slept through it.

"It's five-thirty. Ward's dead. My buddy at Grady State just told me. He died yesterday."

I don't understand. My brain is too sluggish to work properly.

"He's dead?"

I can hear people talking, phones ringing. The police station is busy this early.

"Look, I gotta go. I'm so sorry you've come all the way out here. I knew he was sick, but I thought there'd be a little more time. I'll call you later, okay?"

And he's gone.

I hurl my phone across the room. Even in his death, that monster takes from me.

When I wake up again, weak midmorning sun is coming through the gingham curtains, illuminating the dust that hovers in the air. I've stirred everything up by being here. Outside, pine trees are bending in the wind blowing off the lake. Seasons in this part of the world enter on the wind. Winter is moving in.

I retrieve my phone. No messages from David. I text him to see if he's around, but he's probably sleeping off his night shift. My suitcase is on the floor, clothes and toiletries spewed out around it. I should just go home. This whole frantic trip back here was just me scrounging for crumbs. I bet Ward agreed to the visit just so he could watch me beg for information—information he shouldn't be allowed to have. And I would have done it. Because this was my chance to finally face him. Every kid has a monster who lurks just beyond their sight, but mine was real. I came back to look him in the eye. And now, he's taken that from me too.

If I can't talk to the father, why not talk to the son. I text David.

I want to talk to Jason Ward.

His answer is immediate, so he's clearly not sleeping.

Bad idea. Why?

Isn't it obvious?

Do you have his number???

He starts to type something but then the three blinking dots disappear. Then they appear again, and disappear. I'm about to just call him when he finally writes, Still at work. Later.

Later what? Later he'll give me the number? Later he'll tell me why he won't? I call but it goes to voicemail. I'm sure this is just David being protective, like when we were kids, but I'm not twelve anymore. Just because he has a badge now, he doesn't get to control this.

I weave the Jeep back through the rabbits' warren of dirt roads that lead to the cottages, working on instinct since the only signs are hand-painted family names that have been nailed to the trees since the seventies. On the main road I turn right, away from the town of St. Rose. Three miles along is the entrance to the state park. It's on a large peninsula that juts into Lake Ontario, curving eastward like a hooked finger. The camp sites and beach are at the tip of the peninsula, which is also where the ranger's station is, but the rest of the park is just forest. That's how Eddie Ward was able to drive a transport truck into here without being noticed. On this side there's a thin strip of rocky shore and then open water as far as the eye can see.

When I was a kid, we never came here, for obvious reasons. I've studied maps of this park, traced with my finger how close she was to our cottage, to other people. On a map, it's only a matter of inches. It's a different experience being here. Unmarked service roads branch off the main paved road and I pick one randomly, my tires bumping onto the gravel. It's rutted with potholes and I'm grateful for the Jeep's suspension. The road is narrow and the trees close in around me. I can imagine the sound of their branches scraping over the truck as he bumped along in the darkness. And then the road ends and the lake is straight ahead. It's restless with whitecaps churning under the low gray sky. She would have heard these waves too. Even if she was blindfolded, she would know that sound. Maybe, *maybe* that's when she knew she could escape because the lake was always my mother's place.

When I open the door, the wind hits me full force and my thin coat is immediately damp. I step onto the narrow beach that runs the length of the peninsula. It feels like I'm on the edge of civilization.

At this time of year, the park is empty, but on that August night the campground was full. All those hundreds of people just a mile up the shore huddled in their tents and trailers because of the storm. And our cottage only a few miles to the west; my whole family asleep, oblivious to the nightmare we were about to enter.

One reason why Eddie Ward was able to kill for so long was because he didn't have a pattern. At least not one they were able to discover. The people he killed—the ones we know about, though it's assumed there were more—were from all over the country. They didn't share any traits. The Seven, that's how I think of them. No one knows where they died or what their final moments were. For the families, like mine, we assume they were filled with terror. We only know where they ended up, unlucky siblings of bad luck, hidden in Ward's backyard grave. I've tried to learn what I can about them as if they are my long-lost relatives.

Carolyn was the first that we know of, going by the approximate date of her disappearance. She was eighteen when she went missing from southeast Iowa, but where she crossed paths with him, no one knows. Her parents' farm was nestled between fields of corn and soy, miles from any road a truck would have taken.

The next was Stacey. She was twenty-two, trying to get to New York from Montana by Greyhound, but someone was hassling her. When the bus stopped at a diner in Dickinson, North Dakota, she decided to hitch a ride for the next leg of the route. She had a key chain she was playing with as she sat at the counter. She said it was her brother's. She told the waitress that he was a baseball player and could have gone pro. Then she'd started talking to one of the truckers who also used the diner. When the passengers got back on the bus, she left with him. The waitress never clearly saw the trucker's face because he'd kept his cap pulled low.

Chrissy was nineteen when she dropped her daughter off at her mom's house in Fort Myers, Florida, and never came back to pick her up. Chrissy and her daughter both had long blond hair. People thought they were sisters because she'd been only fifteen when she had her. Her mom assumed she'd gone off to score a hit, which might have been the case. There was a motel just off the interstate that was known as a place where you could get high any way you wanted. She'd been seen going in but never coming out.

Mei was on her way to Hollywood. A modeling scout had seen her in a mall and told her she should go. Jasmine was a runaway from an outer suburb of Phoenix. Both were sixteen when last seen.

Then there was Liam. He was only fifteen, but he was tall and thin and wore his hair long. It's thought he'd hitched rides all the way from his home in Alaska. His family didn't know he was dead until the police found his body. He had long fingers and played the piano beautifully, but had quit when he was fourteen and everything in his life started changing. A pamphlet for a youth group in Vermont was still crushed in his pocket when the police exhumed him.

And Rita was the oldest at twenty-six. When she was a girl, she wanted to be a pilot. She was an Air Force brat from Texas and even though the Air Force had rejected her, she never stopped wanting to fly. Her baby sister had just made Second Lieutenant and started her own flight training when the paper had interviewed her about finding Rita's body.

I know these things because I have spent hours digging through the internet and reading court transcripts. Eddie Ward didn't even know their names.

With my parents, he changed what discernable habits he had. He'd never picked up a couple. He'd never killed so close to his home. And why, when he was a short drive away from that macabre collection in his backyard, why did he bring her here?

These questions are habitual now, mental pathways so worn that I don't have to even consciously follow them; my mind automatically clicks through the questions like fingers on rosary beads. How long was she held in his truck? Was she hurt? Did she beg? Did she tell him that she had a child at home?

Did she say my name?

For all these years, we thought this was where she died. Somewhere on this lonely beach where no one could hear her cries for help over the sound of the waves and the storm. One of the dogs found her shoe buried in the sand; another found her purse, her wallet still in it. The horror of a violent death, of knowing she was alone, knowing no one could help her, reduced to these few objects held in an evidence bag.

But she got away.

If she ran into the park, they would have found her. If she ran along the beach, they would have found her. She must have gone into the lake, and it swallowed her whole.

The waves crash onto the shore. Their monotony is a constant reminder of how small we are; how insignificant our stories, even the ones without endings. I open my mouth and scream, and the wind curls around the sound and shoves it back down my throat.

CHAPTER 5

FIONA

Now

The woman at the front desk of the St. Rose police station looks like she's been here as long as the building. As soon as I say who I am and who I'm here to see, she breaks into a smile.

"Fiona Green? You're all grown up." When I blink at her, clearly not making the connection, she says, "Marva Wright. Oh sure, you don't remember me. That was ages ago."

"No, I-I do remember you," I say.

David and I used to come into the station when we biked into town as a break from the heat. We'd mooch spare quarters—from her, I realize now—and use them in the ancient vending machine that sold sodas for prices that hadn't been changed since the seventies. She'd always seemed more like a kindergarten teacher with her pillowy body, the kind that small children feel safe with, not the front line of a police force, even if it is a small town one.

"I'm just helping out here part-time now. Gotta stay busy so they keep me around."

"I can't believe you remember me," I say.

"I never forget a face." She taps her head. "Comes in handy working here."

But that's not why she remembers me. My mother's disappearance is still the biggest case this police force has ever dealt with. It put St. Rose in national news, and even years later random strangers would come up and start talking to me and my dad when we came into town. They'd tell us about volunteering in the search or manning the tip line and then the conversation would grow awkward because what else could any of us say? It was like a never-ending wake.

"What brings you back to St. Rose?" Marva asks. I know she's just being conversational, but my guard is instantly up.

"Just a quick visit. Is David around? I need to talk to him for a moment."

"He's been in and out all morning with this case he's working on." She tsks. "So sad. This is why I always tell my grandkids, don't travel alone. Especially in bad weather. It doesn't take much, you know? And GPS is not reliable, not up here. Well, I'm sure you know that. Always carry a paper map, that's what I say. They look at me like I'm speaking another language."

"Was there a car accident?"

"No, dear. It's that young woman who's missing."

My stomach drops, an automatic response. "Missing?"

But she doesn't say more. Instead, she leans back in her rolling chair and rests her hands contentedly on her middle. Clearly, whatever urgency is happening in the room behind her is not impacting the front desk. "Now, you and your father moved away, didn't you? Was it California? How is he doing? And how are Mr. and Mrs. Green, senior? I used to see them every summer with the whole family. Are they well?"

"They're fine. My dad and I are in B.C."

"Oh my, that is far. I bet it's pretty though. My Ryan moved out to San Diego years ago and all my grandkids are out there still. But you've come back since then, no?"

"No, first time."

"That's a long time to be away."

I nod, trying not to seem impatient. I'm not sure if she's purposely stalling me from talking to David, or if this is just small-town gossip mining.

"I can't blame your other grandparents for moving away either," she continues when I don't elaborate. "How could they stay when such a thing had happened here. I know you were just a baby but Adele Lukas—I was in school with her—we'd known each other for years and after what happened to your mother—well, I just didn't recognize her. I don't think she recognized herself." She leans toward me and instinctively I mirror her movement. "Between you, me, and the lamppost, mistakes were made."

"Mistakes?"

"I don't mean disrespect to Chief Connor, and certainly not to young David, but I always thought he held a little too tightly to the case. He should have been reaching out for help sooner than he did. The police here just didn't have that kind of experience. Well, how would they? It's no mark on you to know when you're out of your depth and bring in the experts. I know they got him in the end but it took so long. That was just agony for your family—for the whole town, really. It's a blessing you were too young to know, dear."

I have no idea what to say to this. Even if you don't understand why, having your mother suddenly disappear is a nightmare for a young child.

She's still nodding, seemingly to herself, and then, having said what she needed to say, picks up the phone. "Detective, you have a visitor."

David comes out quickly, but when he sees it's me, he looks disappointed. "Hey," he says. He looks exhausted. "Thanks, Marva," then to me, "What's up?"

"I know you're busy," I say. I don't want to talk about this here with an audience. "I thought if there's no other reason for me to stay, maybe I should head back. See if I can get a flight. I'll get an Uber."

He sighs and then glances at Marva, who is watching us with no attempt to hide the fact that she's listening. "Do you have a couple of minutes? I have to go grab Tucker before he eats the couch. Come with me."

We drive the four blocks to his apartment and I wait in the car as David grabs Tucker. When he gets back in, I assume we're going back to the station but instead, he heads out of town. Everything about him is different from last night. He looks exhausted and the well-pressed shirt is now wrinkled, the tie gone. His movements are sharper and as we drive out of town, he keeps glancing at his phone.

We drive for about ten minutes in silence. I don't know the roads around here well enough to know where we are and when he pulls over, it seems like the middle of nowhere.

"What's going on?" I ask as the tires crunch over the gravel shoulder and we come to stop.

"This is where I've been all morning. The techs have towed the car, so it's fine for us to be here."

"This is that missing woman?"

"Yeah. Angela Ramirez." He looks around at the empty road and fields, as if she's going to suddenly appear, walking toward us. "This is where we assume she was picked up."

"What was she doing out here?" We're not on a major road. And no one comes to this part of the world in November. In the summer it makes sense but now the roads and fields, even St. Rose itself, all seem abandoned.

"She was coming from a bridal weekend in Canada. She'd called her sister after she crossed the border. That was around ten-thirty.

I guess Angela thought she'd drive through the night because she didn't want to miss work. She was trying to get to Albany, but the weather got bad."

"Yeah, I remember."

"She got off the interstate near here. Exit's about a mile that way." He points up the road. "Her gas tank was empty but it looks like her gauge is broken cause it's still reading half. There used to be a Mobil station near here, but it closed last year."

"The one we drove past?"

He nods. "Sign's still on the highway though, so we're assuming that's why she got off here. She was supposed to check in with her sister every hour, but she never called and didn't respond to texts or calls, which is apparently unusual. Around two this morning, her sister starting contacting the hospitals and the state troopers but got nothing. Then, a little after five, someone called us about an abandoned vehicle and when we ran the plates we discovered it was Angela's car. When I got out here, the car was locked and there was no purse or phone, so we assume wherever she went, she took them with her."

"She didn't call Triple A?"

"She didn't have a card. Not unusual for someone her age. She texted her girlfriend up in Canada who told her to call anyway. Seems like Angela was worried about money. We've talked to the friend. She said she was on the phone with her trying to convince her to just put it on a credit card when Angela saw headlights and got off the phone. She was going to try to wave someone down. That was a little past midnight."

David hesitates for a beat. "Jason Ward . . . might be a suspect in this case."

"Shit."

"I said he might," he adds quickly. "And he might not. It's just routine to clear the perps."

"Is he? A perp, I mean?"

"Not officially, but I need to make sure. According to his boss, he's on a route out west right now." Off my look he says, "Yeah, like father, like son. I'm hoping the similarity ends there. Anyway, we're waiting to get something back from Oregon to prove he's out there."

"You think he knows his father's dead?"

"I assume he does. The timing is . . . odd. That's why I didn't want to give you his number yet. I'm not saying you can't talk to him. But with his dad dying he might be, I don't know . . ."

"Were they close?"

"My buddy said Jason had never gone in to visit him besides that one time, but he was only at Grady State for a few years. And if they wrote or talked on the phone, he wouldn't necessarily know."

Outside, a gust of wind blows across the empty field, picking up old bits of cornstalks and sending them cartwheeling across the road. In the middle of the night, it must have been pitch-black. What a horrible place to break down.

"Has Jason Ward ever shown any signs he was becoming like his father?"

"My dad watched him pretty close. Especially after what happened that last summer you were here." He looks directly at me now. "Did your dad ever tell you?"

"He claimed we were leaving to get away from him, but he never gave me any proof the guy was dangerous. I thought we left because he wanted to get away from all of it. I was such a shit to him after. For years."

"But he never told you the real reason?" I shake my head. "Jason Ward was targeting you."

"What? Why?"

"He broke into your cottage one night when you were all there. Left some kind of message."

"What'd it say?"

"He threatened you. Not you, specifically, but your family."

"But what was he going to do?"

"I don't know. We figured he blamed your father for why his dad was caught. He's a pretty angry guy. Definitely capable of it. It was right around when we'd seen him in the boat by your cottage. You remember that?"

I nod but memories of that summer seem so far away they're barely real.

"So, what did your dad say about you coming back here?"

"I didn't tell him."

He starts to say something but then, tactfully, stops himself.

My father and I have finally gotten past those horrible years when I wanted to punish him, but we did it by not talking about it. He's married now, and I love my stepmother and half sister, and it feels like staying quiet about the past is a cost we're each willing to pay so we can have our relationship now. It was all working out fine until I had Zoe and all the darkness inside me roared up again.

"Your father refused to file a restraining order. I don't think he trusted that would be enough. It might have just pushed Jason farther." He looks down at his lap. "And, maybe he didn't trust my dad to protect you."

We're both keeping our focus outside the car right now. Neither of us wants to look at the other. I wish I could brush this off, to say no, of course your dad would have kept us safe, but I can't.

David's father was slowly but relentlessly destroyed by his inability to solve my mother's disappearance. We both know the story, how Chief Connor—Jeff, as my family knew him—stood in the living room of my grandparents' cottage a few days after my mother disappeared. My dad was just home from the hospital and the police were still weeks from finding Eddie Ward. I can picture the whole family gathered around the chief as he stood in the center of the room, hat in his hand, and promised—*promised*—he would not rest until my mother was found. How he personally was going to find her. I've been told he went for over fifty hours not sleeping so he could lead the search.

Jeff Connor was a big man—tall, muscular, like his son is now. He'd known my dad's family for years and had been like an older brother to my dad and his brothers. He was the youngest person to have been named chief and was a local celebrity because of it. Good-looking, smart, driven. And all of that got sucked away. By the time David and I were old enough to notice, he'd lose the thread of conversations. I'd see him sometimes staring out at nothing for minutes at a time. His body softened and chronic pain started. David's parents divorced shortly after my dad and I moved away. Chief Connor would get angry and it would come out at home, or with the officers under him, and once I heard he got too rough with some guy he'd pulled over.

Maybe it's a cliché, but when you watch your father break apart trying to do something, there are two ways to deal with it: you either head the other way as far and fast as you can, or you put your head down and run straight into it. It was always obvious what David's choice would be.

"What about this woman's phone?" I say to change the subject. "I mean, that's what the police usually trace, isn't it? Like on TV?"

"It's off. The last tower it pinged was the one near here."

"Where's her car now?"

"It's at the crime lab in Syracuse."

"It's odd she wouldn't call her sister."

"I'm having trouble getting a full story, but it sounds like they were having an argument. Big sister didn't think she should be trying to drive all night, bad weather, old car, you know. Little sister trying to prove she's independent, knowing she'd freak out her family if they knew. Maybe she tried to walk to a gas station."

"I hope not."

"All we know is she saw a car coming, not if it stopped. This road connects St. Rose to St. Thomas, so there is traffic. Not a lot, but some. It was a woman on her way to work early this morning who called in the abandoned vehicle. Unfortunately, if there were tire tracks from this other car, she also destroyed those."

"Are you allowed to be telling me this?" I ask.

"I haven't told you anything that isn't going to be on the news tonight. I've been staring at this for ten hours. It's helpful to talk it out, you know?"

I nod.

"The family's on their way up. I've got nothing to tell them. Less than twenty-four hours in and I'm already hitting walls." He sighs and runs his hand through his hair, which makes it stick up in different directions. "I'm missing something. I know it. We're talking to everyone who was at the bridal weekend, people who she works with, we're combing through her social media. This woman put everything online. I know it's normal for people her age, but why make yourself a target?"

I know what he means, even if it's not how it came out, but it's like a switch gets triggered. "What's that have to do with her car breaking down?"

"Well, we have to look at everything."

"But the focus is all on her. Like she's the suspect."

"She's the known quantity. You start with what you know. What—?"

"Nothing."

I should go to the airport. Neither of us is in a good place for a reunion right now.

"I need air," I say and get out of the car. The bite of the wind feels good. It reminds me that the world has teeth.

David's door slams and he walks over to me. "What is it?"

I still don't want to look at him. "When it was my parents, my dad was treated as a suspect."

"That's just procedure. Like I said, you look at everything."

He doesn't get it. How easily the lines between victim and suspect get blurred. "I've seen the notes. I've read everything. There was a whole line of thinking that my dad somehow arranged for it to happen. Like because he was going back to school and told people about getting his life back on track, he thought that if he got rid of my mom, it would make it easier for him. It was such bullshit."

"Look, I'm pretty sure Angela Ramirez didn't plan to run out of gas in the middle of nowhere. She told her friend she was going to try to hitch a ride. So, ninety-nine percent chance, that's what happened. But what if it's not? I have to look at every possibility."

"To poke holes."

"Yeah, to poke holes. And to close them up. So something important doesn't escape through them."

"You just said she made herself a target. So, you're implying—"

"Okay. Bad choice of words. I'm sorry. It's not personal."

I turn and face him directly. "What's more personal than being attacked? You know, someone at that party my parents went to told the police that my mom was wearing a really short dress. Like it was her fault he picked them up." I've never said these things to anyone but I've felt them. For years. Roiling under the surface. Acid in my mouth.

"I know," he says quietly.

"You know?"

"I've read all the notes too. People say a lot of stupid shit. No one blamed your mother for what happened. And your father was cleared really quickly. And I promise, I am not blaming Angela Ramirez for whatever happened here last night. I'm just trying to do this right."

We stand there on the side of a desolate road, wind whipping hair into my face. My god, I think, who are these two strangers? Where are the two kids who knew what was up with the other just by the way their breathing changed?

David breaks the silence first. "We should get back."

I nod and get back into the car. Tucker whines and leans as far into the front as his leash will allow him. David reaches back and puts a hand on his head. "It's okay, buddy. Everyone's okay."

We drive in silence for a few minutes, each lost in our own thoughts, then he says, "Are you serious about leaving right away?"

"I haven't got a ticket. I figured I'd fly standby."

"You have to get back for work?"

"No. I'm doing stuff remotely. They're pretty flexible."

"Boyfriend? Partner?"

"Nope."

He raises an eyebrow waiting for me to provide the reason for my rush back. This is the opportunity for me to tell him about Zoe, about what is scheduled to happen in a few weeks, but just like last night, I can't. It's too complicated. Especially now.

"I get it if you want to head back home. And now, I'm going to be pretty tied up with this. But if you don't have to rush back, it would be good to have you here."

"It's not like I can help you with the case."

"I just meant as a friend." He looks shy all of a sudden. "This is my first big one. Of all the cases I could have gotten. I just want to do right by it."

We pull into the police station and he kills the engine, but neither of us moves to get out.

"Look, I know the whole reason you came back was to talk to him."

"It wasn't the whole reason."

"No?"

"Of course it wasn't."

He points to himself and raises his eyebrows in a mock gesture of surprise.

"Of course I wanted to see you, dumbass. That woman, Marva, was right. It's been too long to be away."

He smiles, but it's a sad smile. "It wasn't the same without you. The summer after you left, I begged my parents to let me go to a sleepaway camp for the entire break. It was better than being here without you."

"I can stay for a bit," I say. "The cottage needs some work. My dad and I haven't exactly been keeping up our part of it for the past twenty years. Maybe I can chop wood or something."

He looks skeptical.

"What, you think I can't chop wood? B.C. is all lumberjacks. They teach us wood chopping in school."

"Sounds useful." He grins. "Be warned. I told my mom you're back. I talked her down from throwing a full-on party, but she's definitely going to make you dinner."

It is a relief thinking I don't have to rush home yet. I can't stay away from the decision that awaits me there forever, but maybe for a few more days.

"I just wish I could swim," I say as we get out of the car. He lets Tucker out and he bounds over to the door of the police station and presses his nose to the glass. It's clearly his second home. "I swim every day at home. It keeps me sane."

"Use the high school pool," he says. "They have public hours but they're really early in the morning before the swim team practices. Just call the school. Your mom's picture is still up in the Athletic Department, by the way. They've got all their star athletes up there from decades back."

Swimming in the same pool my mother trained in. There's something about that that feels right. I can't go to the house where she grew up because my grandparents sold it years ago, but I could drive by it. I wonder if there are other pieces of her left here. David must be able to tell what I'm thinking because he says, "And I'll try to think of some other people you could talk to."

"Like who?"

"People who knew her in high school. I'm sure there are people around." He gets a strange look on his face. "Hm. What about Eddie Ward's ex-wife?"

"She always claimed she didn't know anything."

He shrugs. "It's been thirty years, and he's dead now. Maybe she'll have something more to say."

CHAPTER 6

FIONA

Now

I call Carole Dunn, Eddie Ward's ex-wife, as soon as David sends me her number, before I lose my nerve. She doesn't answer, which is a relief. I leave her a message, telling her who I am and making it clear I'm not a journalist. I'm sure she'll never call back. Once again, I'm waiting to be given permission to ask the questions that should be my right to demand. It leaves a sick feeling in my stomach.

I have another restless night ahead of me with nothing to do but pace the cottage. The rabbit ears on the ancient TV remarkably still pick up the local station and at nine o'clock, the Angela Ramirez story makes the news.

The segment is titled "Road Side Disappearance." As the anchor gives the intro, the screen shows a photo of Angela Ramirez. She looks young. Her hair is up in a ponytail, she's laughing, and someone's arm is draped around her shoulder but they've been cut out of the picture.

The image switches to outside the St. Rose police station. It must be live because it's raining there, like it is here. Standing next to the police chief are three people huddled together who I'm guessing are the family. A woman, who looks like a slightly older and more heavyset version of Angela, steps forward. The mother keeps her head down but the father stares, unblinking, into the camera as the woman speaks.

"I talk to my sister every day." Under her face, the banner reads VERONICA RAMIREZ, SISTER. "So as soon as she didn't call when she said she would, I knew something had happened."

The father says something too quiet for the mic to pick up. She nods at him and then continues.

"Ángela loved her job. She's a paralegal at McCluskey and Associates. She is a very good person. We don't know what's happened but if someone has her—" Her voice catches for a moment but she continues. "Please just let her go. And Ángela, if you are listening, *Vamos a encontrarte. Mantente fuerte. Te queremos.*"

A number flashes across the screen and the camera moves to the reporter, who is clearly freezing but trying not to show it. "With the sudden drop in temperature, police say that time is of the essence. Now Kim," she continues, "as many of our viewers will know, St. Rose was where the last known victim of the 'Terror Trucker,' Edward Ward, died in 1993. While his victims came from across the country, Ward lived in a nearby town and buried seven of them in his backyard, and his last victim was local. While no official statement has been made about any possible connection, the memory of what happened here thirty-one years ago is still fresh. For the residents of St. Rose, this kind of disappearance has an all too familiar ring to it."

How can there be any connection between this and what happened to my mother? When David said it, I thought it might be possible, but listening to this reporter make the connection it's so obvious that she's just doing it for the tabloid titillation of it to boost ratings. I've seen it my whole life. As soon as you say "serial killer," everyone starts drooling for details. I spent years trying to carefully avoid it whenever I met new people, awkwardly dancing around seemingly benign questions about my family. And then, inevitably, someone would find out something and soon everyone would know my mother was the victim of a serial killer and that would be all they'd want to talk about. Now that Eddie Ward has died, I'm half expecting to get an email or a phone call from a journalist as soon as the news is made public.

The story cuts back to the anchor. "Just to clarify, Moira, have the police made a connection to these earlier cases?"

"Not officially, no," the reporter says, looking grim. "But I spoke to one person who wishes to remain anonymous, who did confirm that the police are considering the copycat quality of this."

I turn the volume down to a low mutter but keep the television on for the noise. I never knew how desolate this cottage could feel without the rest of my family here. I've got all the blankets I can find piled on top of me. When I was a child, I always slept in the attic with the rest of my cousins while the adults and youngest children slept in the bedrooms. I have my choice of beds now, but like Goldilocks, I tried a few and none were right. Plus, it's warmest here in the main room with the wood stove going. I sink back into the couch with the reporter's words echoing in my head: "For the residents of St. Rose, this kind of disappearance has an all-too-familiar ring . . ."

Memories are slippery things. If you try too hard to hold on, they'll slide away and never come back. You have to let them come to you like skittish animals. Be still and don't look at them directly and if you're lucky, they'll sidle up beside you.

Memories are everywhere here: the sagging couches on the porch, the huge table with its mismatched chairs, the pulpy paperbacks my aunts had read, yellow with age, sand forever stuck between their pages. I'm not asleep exactly but I'm drifting. My mind is sending out feelers, sifting through what has been stirred up by my return. What comes is too faint to be a memory—more of an impression, a footprint in wet sand.

I am digging for shells and dropping them into a red plastic beach bucket. I must be on the little strip of beach in front of the cottage. I can imagine the wet grit between my fingers. My mother rises out of the water and walks toward me. I can't see her face if I look at it straight on, so I keep my head down and focus on the shells in my hand.

She squats down beside me. Her skin is wet and cold from her swim.

"What have you found?"

Did she ask this? I can't hear her voice, so it may just be my logical mind filling in pieces. The only time I was ever here with my mother was the summer of 1993, when I was two and a half. I probably played on that beach every day. My mother swam every morning and was teaching me how to swim.

"What have you found?"

How desperately I want her to see the shells like I do, to understand why each one is special. This one is pink, this one is broken but its edges are smooth, this one is so tiny, this one, this one . . .

I will read anything I can find about memory development in young children, anything that will give me proof that the memories of her are in me, somewhere, even if I can't access them. But everything I read says these memories aren't recorded because a young child's brain is too busy learning and growing. Unless there is trauma. Trauma can imprint memories that would otherwise be lost, but these memories are disorganized, their triggers unknowable and unpredictable.

"What have you found?"

My mother swam every morning while I played on the beach, and so it goes that one of those mornings was the last. Even though there is no way to prove it, I choose to believe that a part of my toddler's mind knew to hold on tight. Or maybe in the days that came after, when my mother didn't come home, maybe my brain knew to tuck this memory away before it was lost forever and now that I'm here in this place, I am finally finding it again.

What about my daughter? Zoe's younger than I was but will she remember me crying beside her crib? Even if she doesn't have words for it, surely her young brain can sense the darkness that wraps around me in those moments. Will she remember that day on the beach last March, the man calling out, the dogs barking? What I almost did to us—?

No. She wasn't there. I have to keep reminding myself of this. I strapped the baby carrier to my chest but she wasn't in it.

I shake my head violently and sit up, blankets falling off. The cold of the room helps to snap me into the present. I am not going to let my daughter have memories of how broken her mother is. That's why she is with her father and stepmother now. That's why I am going to sign those adoption papers to keep her safe. From me. That's how I will protect her.

Outside, the wind has picked up again. The wind and the waves make me feel small. My phone buzzes with a voicemail. When I hit play, Carole Dunn's scratchy voice comes into my ear.

"Fine. We can talk." She gives me an address and tells me to come the next evening. No niceties, but no refusal either. I feel a flutter of excitement. I don't know how, but something about this makes it feel like for the first time ever, I'm moving closer.

CHAPTER 7

ANA

August 28, 1993

7:30 P.M.

In her high school senior English class, Ana read *Hamlet.* She was good at English, good at getting the meaning out of stories, but she hadn't understood the women in that play. There were only two: Gertrude and Ophelia, and Ophelia made no sense. The teacher said Ophelia was probably only fifteen; that would have been typical "back then." She wasn't mature enough to take the hits that came at her so quickly: a brutal and humiliating rejection and then the murder of her father. But still, Ana had argued, madness? Just like that? Sane one day and nutzo the next? Shakespeare didn't *get* women, that was her final estimation. He only put two in the play, after all, and they were only defined by their relationships to men. Look at how quickly Hamlet writes off both the women in his life as interested in only sex and deception. "*Frailty, thy name is woman*—fuck you." That had got a laugh from the rest of the class, she remembered. She'd talked for a long time. She didn't even know where the words were coming from, just that this anger suddenly poured out of her. And the teacher— she couldn't remember her name now but she was young and she let them swear—she was looking at her like she hadn't before, like she was actually saying something important, or maybe she was just happy that someone was passionate enough to give more than a one-sentence response. After, Ana had felt the blood rushing to her face. She seemed a little dizzy, and everything was brighter and sharper.

That was only a few years ago but it felt like a story that happened to someone else. Who was that person?

In the first months of motherhood, the bad thoughts came in those floating hours in the middle of the night, the part that's farthest from light, farthest from the rhythms of the world. She did not have to think these thoughts, they just appeared. Like they'd been there all this time and if she let her guard down even slightly, they filled her mind like smoke. All the ways she could hurt this child. Car accidents, the sound of metal collapsing like a hand crushing a soda can. Her daughter's little body slipping out of her hands when she lifted her out of a bath. Or the two of them falling down the apartment stairs as she tried to carry her, the bags, the stroller. There were so many ways for a baby to get hurt, and all of them would be her fault. Every mundane action of parenthood had its horrifying double. The first few times, she could get out of its grip if she focused on something tactile, something right in front of her, like cleaning a dirty plate, or counting the cars that passed. But then that stopped working. The "what if" became more than just a passing vision. It held on, and the longer it lasted, the more sure she was it was *going* to happen. If she picked up her crying daughter, she *would* drop her. If she took her for a walk, she *would* lose control of the stroller. She'd freeze in that space between real and not real. Time would pass. Sometimes, a lot of time. And then she'd "wake" and try to fix or calm or clean up whatever mess her daughter had made while Ana was lost in The Blank.

Those days, Ben would come home and find her still in pajamas on the couch at five o'clock, toys scattered everywhere, breakfast, laundry, and dishes all half-finished. She knew it pissed him off, but she couldn't tell him why it was safer to just hold still. She finally got up the nerve to tell her doctor. "Baby blues," he said. "Totally normal, though they don't usually last this long." He prescribed Prozac and told her to get more sleep. But Ana had read about the "baby blues" and that didn't seem like what she was experiencing, plus she didn't know if she could breastfeed while taking it, so she tucked the pills away and at the next visit she told him she was fine.

And now, this morning, it happened again.

Ana shook her head. Squeezed her eyes shut and opened them again, focusing on the landscape moving past them outside the car window.

"You okay?" Ben asked. If she told him she wasn't feeling well, he'd turn around. But she couldn't do that to him and maybe going to this party would help get her out of her head.

"I'm good," she said. She gave him a little smile, then turned back to looking out the window.

Early evening of another perfect August day. Far out over the horizon there was a band of blue-gray clouds, but here the sky was as clear as it had been all week. In breaks between the trees the lake flashed gold. Ben was driving quickly, the way he drove before he became a father. When Fiona was in the car he was cautious, always five miles under the speed limit with a line of cars building behind him. But now he was relaxed, one hand on the steering wheel, the other resting on his leg. He was leaning back, smiling. He looked good— carefree, confident, the way he'd been at school, before. His hair was still damp from the shower and the sun had lightened it to a blondish brown. His freckles peeked through the tan on his face. Would Fiona have freckles too?

He must have felt her glance toward him because he reached out and put his hand on her leg for a moment. Her skin was sticky because their air-conditioning was broken. The car was a piece of shit, as Ben's brothers loved to point out to him on a regular basis. The lack of air-conditioning was just one of its problems, but car repairs were far down on the list of priorities these days. Ana knew she should put her hand on his, an acknowledgment of the contact, but she didn't. She looked at her hands, sitting in her lap. They didn't look like hers. Ben took his hand back. When did all of their tiny movements get so layered with meaning? It was exhausting.

The party was at a professor's lake house. Years ago, the guy had sold a patent for something and been rolling in dough ever since. This party was *the* event of the summer, open only to engineering majors and grad students, and it marked the unofficial kickoff into the school year. Ben was going back to school and saw this invitation as a sign that he was finally back on track. He thought this party would get Ana excited about going back to school too, not that he'd admit it.

"You need to be back in the world again," he said when she'd suggested he go without her.

"I am in the world," she had told him. "Having a kid is a lot more real-life than academia."

"You know what I mean."

She closed her eyes, but that just made the images from this morning stronger. She opened them again. Better to focus on what was outside the window. Name all the things: *green car, Illinois license plate, pine trees, motel sign, blue sign, blue shirt—Ben's blue shirt, missing button—*

"The button. I forgot," she said, breaking the silence of the car.

This morning, when he'd pulled the shirt out of the closet, she had told him she'd fix the missing button while he was at work. She hadn't forgotten, not really, the day had just become something else.

"Mom gave me a safety pin," he said. "You can't even notice it."

They had moved into Ben's family cottage for the summer. She avoided going into St. Rose so she didn't run into people she knew who would be sure to ask about college and swimming, and be disappointed by her dropping out of both. Her parents were spending the summer overseas on one of her mom's research trips, so Ana had used that as an excuse to stay close to the cottage, not that she'd have been spending time with them even if they were there. Fiona had even made a friend, a little boy who lived next door and was just a few months older, David. Ana watched his mother with him. She seemed so at ease with motherhood but then again, she was ten years older. She was friendly enough, but all she wanted to talk about were developmental milestones: Did Fiona understand colors? What about animal names? How long did she nap for? Mrs. Connor was like the other mothers at the park or the library reading time, the way they chatted to each other like they'd known how to raise a human for years. The secret mother's society. They'd smile at her, silently noting how young she was, like "mistake" was tattooed across her forehead.

But still, it had been good to be back at the lake. It took some getting used to having all the extra people around—Ben's younger siblings with their loud friends, and his parents who were so, *so* eager to help—but being around all these people prevented her from getting so lost in her head. And swimming every day meant her body had started feeling like its old self. And all of that had caused her to let her guard down this morning.

Her eyes were heavy. Ben had turned the radio on low and he was humming along to the song. She used to know all the songs . . .

This morning.

This morning, she had gone for her swim. Fiona was playing on the beach with her grandma sitting behind her. As usual, Ben had left for work early and the rest of the family was still asleep. When she'd come in from the swim, Fiona wanted to show her some shells she had found, her newest fascination. Normally, she would wait to take Fiona for a swim in the afternoon when the water was warmer, but it had felt so good to be in the lake and she wanted her daughter to feel that too. Ben's mom went back up into the cottage to make breakfast, so no one was around. They blew bubbles and Fiona practiced floating on her back. Her pudgy toddler feet glowed pale in the dark water. Then she practiced her kicking and moving her arms with Ana's hand lightly under her belly. She wanted to see if there were shells on the bottom.

"First you try swimming to me and then we'll look for shells," Ana had said to her.

She held her out in her arms and then let go and the little girl started kicking and moving her arms the way she had been practicing, and then—

—movement farther out in the lake caught her eye, a gull with wings outstretched, its feet skimming the water making ripples on the surface, how far would they go? And then—?

The vision came. Like the ones from when Fiona was a baby, so sudden and clear it had to be prescient: Fiona in the water, not moving. Her lips blue. Floating just under the surface, fine hair fanned out around her head like seaweed, her eyes wide open, lifeless—

Ana had gasped, blinked. *Not real, not real, not real.* Her old coping technique.

She looked at the water in front of her. Blinked again.

The water in front of her—the place where her daughter had been just a moment ago—just a second—a breath—a heartbeat ago—

The water was empty.

"Fiona? Fiona!" Why could no one hear her? Why was no one coming running?

Then, bubbles rising to the surface. Movement under the water.

Ana dove under but the water was murky with the loose silt her feet had churned up. She couldn't see anything. She waved her arms frantically in all directions and came up gasping. The cottage, the blue morning sky, the lake—everything exactly the way it had been just a second ago. She looked for the pale glow of her daughter's skin under the surface, the pink bathing suit. How could she have disappeared in less than a second unless time had skipped? What if she had been under for minutes? What if right now Fiona was being pulled out into the deeper part of the lake? She dove back under, arms whipping around her, calling for her daughter, but all that came out were bubbles. And then her fingers touched a hand. She pulled her child into her chest and up out of the water. Fiona coughed and sputtered and as soon as she got enough air back into her body, she started crying.

"I've got you. I've got you, sweetheart, I've got you." She would never let her go again.

Up at the cabin, Mrs. Green stuck her head out the screen door. "Everything okay?"

Her throat was too tight to answer. She couldn't let her know. She couldn't let anyone know. She raised her hand to give a wave and her mother-in-law went back inside. Fiona had been within arm's reach and disappeared. The only way that could have happened was if Ana had blanked.

So, it was happening again. The Blanks were back. Were they seconds? Minutes? She could never tell. All she knew was that when she went into a blank, her daughter was at risk.

When she got to the beach, she had wrapped a towel tight around Fiona and they sat on the warm sand for a long time. She would not let her go. She couldn't stop her mind from spinning out into a hundred different horrifying scenarios.

"Squishy, Mommy," her daughter had finally said, pushing against her. She wanted to look for shells again. Her red bucket was floating away, but Ana didn't dare go after it.

And then she remembered that high school English class and had another word for it: madness. Ophelia. How she disappeared into it and never came out. There was a famous mad scene in the play, but it was just flowers and songs. Typical, she thought, make it all cliché and girly. That wasn't madness. When Gertrude described Ophelia's death, she said it had started as an accident, that she'd slipped and fallen into the water but then she stayed there. She hadn't fought, she let herself get pulled down into it. Madness was in those blanks and it was pulling her toward it.

After she'd changed Fiona out of her damp bathing suit, Ana checked that she had packed the pills. She'd stuck them in her suitcase at the last second, just in case. They were two years old, but the label didn't say anything about them expiring. This morning was the closest she'd ever come to one of her terrifying visions becoming reality, so she shook out two pills, put them in her mouth, and swallowed.

The pills were in her purse now sitting between her feet. Like having them was a talisman to ward off the madness, even though the doctor had said they would take weeks to work. She didn't tell Ben about the prescription two years ago, and she wouldn't tell him now. How could she explain that she, the person who spent all her time with their daughter, could slip into The Blank and lose her. You have no idea how terrible a mother I am, she thought as she looked out the window at the sparkling lake. But what lay under that golden surface? Madness was knowing that death was right there, constant and waiting and inviting her in.

CHAPTER 8

JASON

2003

The lake had always just been there. As a kid, he could go for months never seeing it. His family wasn't the beachy type. The closer you got, the more expensive the homes and the groceries, so the Wards lived, worked, and shopped in the cheaper inland towns. The lake was the playground of "the summer people." That's what his dad called them. They were the reason the roads were clogged between June and September and the price of gas skyrocketed. When Jason made the mistake of asking if they could go to the beach for Memorial Day like the kids in his class, his father made it very clear that the lake wasn't for people like him. After his father was arrested, going anywhere besides school or the grocery store, the inexpensive one, was out of the question, and over the years, he almost forgot it was there.

But once he was old enough to get his own car, he found himself drawn to the lake's immensity and the more time he spent watching it, the more he realized that the lake was indifferent to the people who played on its surface. And anyway, Jason liked it best in the other seasons when the water lost its summer sparkle and turned gray with churning whitecaps. Then it would crash against the shore, begging for attention. Or maybe it was reminding everyone that it was the one with the power.

One scorching July morning, on his way to work, he saw a boat sitting in someone's front yard with a For Sale sign on it. He didn't know shit about boats—he couldn't even swim well—but suddenly the idea of being out in that endless expanse of water was all he could think about. All that space that he'd only ever seen from the shore; with a boat, it could be his. It took passing it three more times before he finally called the number on the sign. He was nervous, like the person who answered was going to tell him he had no right to buy their boat, but the man didn't even ask his name, just told him to come out on Saturday to take a look at it. It needed work, he said, but work wasn't a problem for Jason. He'd worked in garages for years and mechanical things made sense to him in a way that people never did. And the man was willing to knock off $50 if he paid cash. He borrowed a trailer from a guy at work in exchange for beer and set the boat up on blocks in his mother's front yard, which she bitched about but he paid more of the bills by that point than she did, so he ignored her. The engine was dirty and looked like it hadn't been taken care of, but besides a lot of buildup and some corrosion in the lines, it was in decent shape. He took the engine apart and cleaned every piece. He loved the logic of an engine, the way everything had its purpose and function. There weren't any surprises. All he had to do was put it back together and then he'd have a working boat and no one could take it from him.

The guy who sold him the boat told him there were cheaper marinas farther west. For more beer, he got the trailer again and drove the boat to one that was far enough away from the tourists to keep the slip cost reasonable. After signing some paperwork and handing over more money, he got his boat into the water. He piloted it straight out toward the blue horizon. When he was far enough out that the land was just a faint line, he cracked open a mickey of whiskey, poured a little on the side of the boat to christen it, and drank the rest. Sitting out there, feeling the boat gently rocking, the smell of the lake, the vastness of open water and sky and nothing else, he was at peace. Out there, no one knew who he was. Jason Ward, the son of the "Terror Trucker," disappeared and now he was just a young man in his boat. He could go anywhere he wanted—hell, he could weave his way through the Thousand Islands and follow the St. Lawrence all the way to the Atlantic Ocean. If he hadn't been so happy, he would have kicked himself for being so close to freedom for all those years and taking this long to find it.

After that, whenever he wasn't working, he was on his boat. He never planned where he'd go, just let the wind and the waves move him wherever they might. Jason never talked to the other boaters at the marina, but every once in a while, one of them would try to start a conversation with some comment about the weather or fishing. He didn't want to get friendly enough that the "who are you and where do you live" conversation would come up, as it inevitably would. And, after a couple of friendly people out on the water tried to "rescue" him, assuming he had engine problems because he was just floating aimlessly, he learned to carry a fishing pole. After that, people mostly left him alone.

It was hard to describe the feeling he got each time he drove to the marina and took out his boat. "His boat." That alone made him feel . . . different. Free. Maybe even normal, or what he imagined normal to be. Other guys his age played their music loud and catcalled girls and knew that no matter what anyone told them, they were like gods: young, strong, immortal. He'd never felt that until now. After he'd been in his boat, he'd drive home with his windows down and play his music loud—sometimes he'd even sing—trying to carry the freedom of the lake back into his regular life.

One night, after hours on the open water, he couldn't stand the thought of going back to his stuffy bedroom in the trailer he still shared with his mother. On the far end of the strip of St. Thomas, there was a bar he'd noticed before. It was called McGregor's and had a shamrock where the O was supposed to be, though he figured the guy who owned it was probably no more Irish than he was. He'd heard that the beer was cheap and it wasn't one of the places where the summer people would be caught dead, even if they were "slumming" in St. Thomas.

There weren't many people in the place, which was fine. It was pretty dark but he could hear the clack of pool balls coming from the back. He sat at the bar, keeping his head down. The bartender had one of those weedy mustaches and his sleeves were rolled up to show a tattooed snake wrapped around his biceps. He glanced at Jason when he sat down but seemed more interested in the conversation he was having with some guys at the other end of the bar.

"I'll have a beer," Jason said.

Mustache raised his eyebrows. "You'll have to be a little more specific." One of his buddies snickered. Was he laughing at him?

"A Bud," he said because it was the first thing that came to mind. His dad had drunk Bud so he did too, even though he didn't like it that much. Mustache turned around, grabbed a Bud from the row in the fridge, kept turning and in one fluid motion flipped the cap off and placed the bottle down in front of Jason. Was he supposed to be impressed?

"You want to run a tab?" he asked.

Jason shook his head and put a $5 on the bar. Mustache put his hand over it for a moment, then Jason said, "Keep the change," and he smiled. His canine teeth were long.

The interaction with the bartender had made him regret his choice to come in, but once paid, Mustache lost interest in him and went back to the other end of the bar with his friends. Rows of empty shot glasses were lined up in front of them. Their loud sloppy laughs told him they'd been at it for a while.

He finished his beer and ordered another, once again, paying with cash. He didn't know how much a beer actually cost, but he figured he must be giving Mustache a pretty good tip since he appeared as soon as Jason took the last sip.

Toward the end of the second bottle, he was starting to get more comfortable. Then he heard female voices and two young women came over to join the guys at the bar. Another round of shots was had and then Jason made the mistake of lifting his head right as one of the women looked at him. She smiled, and maybe it was the beer or the high of being on the lake, but he smiled back. It only lasted half a second before he realized what he was doing and put his head back down, squeezing the now warm bottle between his hands. He should have just gotten a six pack and sat in his car. Jason had cultivated his invisibility for so long now, he took it for granted. There was nothing about him that particularly stood out. He was average height; strong, yes, but he didn't accentuate it the way some guys did. His hair was in need of a cut but he almost always had his ball cap pulled low over his face, so it didn't matter. His clothes were old and usually had grease stains on them and he never, ever, made eye contact. He was a watcher, but now he'd been seen.

He lifted his head slightly and then put it down right away. She was still looking at him. This girl was the prettier of the two—that was immediately obvious. Her hair was dark and piled on top of her head but with loose strands hanging down to tickle her face. She had on one of those billowy blouses, a peasant blouse, he thought it was called, and jean shorts. Her friend was blond but even in this bad lighting he could see roots. She was wearing a tight tank top and it was obvious the friend thought her breasts were her best feature, the way she stuck them out like they were the welcoming party.

"What's your name?" the brunette called out. That got her friend's attention too.

He coughed. "Um, Jason," he said.

The blonde laughed and said, "Um-Jason. I've never heard that name."

Mustache was lining up shot glasses again and holding a whiskey bottle.

"You want to do a shot with us?" the brunette said. The two guys who'd been ignoring him so far were looking at him now.

"Uh, no, that's okay," Jason said.

"Ah," she said in mock disappointment. But she turned away and did the shot with her friends.

"You want to play pool, then?" she asked as soon as they'd put their shot glasses back on the bar.

"Fuck, Sam, let the man drink in peace," one of the guys said.

"I'm just being friendly. It's not nice to leave people out."

"It's not fucking second grade," the other guy said, which got a laugh from the blonde.

They continued bantering back and forth and Jason found it impossible to ignore them. The way they called attention to themselves, like they were performing for the rest of the bar but pretending not to. Jason could tell that the blonde and one of the guys were together the way he kept pawing at her. He wasn't sure about the brunette. He didn't realize how openly he'd been watching them until the other guy wrapped his arm around her waist and said, "You got a problem over there, *Jason*?"

Jason shook his head.

"Then stop staring," he said.

This time, he didn't look away. This was more familiar. Girls made him nervous but threats he could handle.

The brunette smiled at him again. "You can stare," she said. "Some girls think it's flattering."

"W-what?" Jason stammered, which immediately made them all laugh, the bartender included.

"Wh-wh-what?" the guy said and sneered at him, then turned away, clearly done with the conversation.

Jason left. But he stayed in the parking lot. He didn't like what had just happened. He hadn't done anything wrong, but that girl had baited him just so they could laugh at him. All the freedom and happiness of his boat ride had evaporated and now all he could feel was heat. Maybe that was better. If he needed to fight, heat was what he'd need.

He sat in his car for another thirty minutes until they came out. The guys were drunk but the girls didn't seem too bad. In the bar, Jason was out of his element, but out here in the open parking lot, out here he would do just fine.

He waited for them to get far enough away from the bar that they couldn't duck back in. The guy who had taunted him was having trouble finding his keys. Jason got out and closed the door loud enough for them to hear.

"Um-Jason, you're still here?" one of the girls said. He wasn't sure which but thought it might be the pretty one.

Jason stayed quiet and kept standing by his car. Let them come at him if they wanted to. Then the brunette left the group and walked over to him. This wasn't what he was expecting. She stopped about five feet in front of him.

"Hey," she said quietly. "I'm sorry if we were assholes. We're just having fun."

He'd been ready for a fight. He'd been ready to hurt, not ready for this.

"It's okay."

"Well, you're still here, so I'm guessing it's not okay," she said. One of the guys called out to her but she ignored him.

"Look, I don't want any trouble. Honest. I'm not like them, I promise."

"You don't seem like it. Like an asshole, I mean," he said. She was going to think he was an idiot.

He could just see enough of her face in the lights from the bar sign; she was smiling. "Well, thank you very much. I appreciate that you don't think I'm an asshole. I'm Samantha—Sam—by the way. Sam Curry."

"I'm Jason."

"I know," she said. "Jason what?"

"Jason, um, Ward." He waited for the reaction but it didn't come. Maybe she wasn't from around here.

"Well, I'll see you around, Jason Ward," she said. "And Bud's just two dollars. Don't let Ryland con you into a bigger tip. He already steals from the till."

With that she turned and walked back to the car. She jumped in the passenger seat and the car swerved out of the parking lot and down the almost abandoned strip. Jason waited until he couldn't see the taillights, then he got in his car and drove home. Without even knowing it, he was smiling.

CHAPTER 9

FIONA

Now

"So, you came," Carole Dunn says as soon as she opens the door. I can't tell if she's referring to the downpour, or if she thought I wouldn't show.

St. Thomas is the poor cousin to St. Rose. It's a few miles inland from the lake, so the houses are cheaper. Maybe in another era it was charming, but the old homes I drive past now have all been divided into apartments and are packed tightly together with collections of garbage cans between them. Lawns are small and overgrown. Chunks of broken sidewalk stick up like crooked teeth. This isn't the type of place where people are out strolling. Between the two towns is "the Strip," one long multilane road with all the big-box stores, fast food chains, and car dealerships. It's where the two towns meet, do their business, and then go back to their respective sides, with as little contact between them as possible. Carole lives in a trailer park on the far side. Her street has two lights with a large patch of darkness between them and I can just make out the house numbers through the rain.

She's tall but stooped forward, everything about her coiled inward. Her gray hair is thin and long, held back in a ponytail, and her skin has the sallow yellow look of a lifelong smoker, which she was by the sound of her low, ragged voice. She's holding two large dogs back with a hand command.

"Well, come in if you're coming. Make me lose all my heat."

The sour smell of old cigarettes is immediate as soon as I step inside. The dogs come forward to investigate and I hold my hand out for them to sniff. "They're well trained," I say.

Carole doesn't take the compliment. "They know who feeds them. That's Rocket and the smaller one is Sadie."

She glances at the little hallway that leads off on the right and I can see a closed door that I guess is the bedroom. "Kitchen's warmest. You can dry out in there," she says nodding at the pool of water my jacket is making on the floor. She shuffles off in that direction and I follow, squeezing past two overstuffed recliners with bright-colored homemade afghans over them. The television flickers silently on a game show. When we get into the kitchen, she points to a chair at the little table in the corner.

"Rocket, move," Carole snaps at the rottweiler who is blocking the chair, and as soon as I sit down, he reclaims his spot. I can feel his weight pushing against me. Sadie, who looks like she's part bulldog, part brick, wedges herself under the table with her haunches on my feet. I'm pinned by the dogs, but their warmth and solidness are strangely comforting.

Carole doesn't offer anything to drink. She doesn't strike me as the type to bother with the charade of playing hostess. Instead, she sits down, hands folded on the table in front her, like she's waiting for the interview to start. Her face has a practiced blankness, probably from years of questions she can't, or won't, answer. I open my mouth to speak but she holds up her hand.

"Look, I don't talk about this, and I'm not going to do it again. But I figure you got screwed by this whole situation too. So that's why I said yes. But I don't know much."

"Your message made it sound like you were expecting this."

"He's dead. I figured someone might call. Didn't expect it to be you, but . . ." She shrugs.

I'm guessing Carole isn't someone who does a lot of talking. She's spent half of her life with the stain of being the wife of a serial killer, so it's not surprising. She's changed her name—David told me she filed for divorce as soon as her husband was arrested—but that's not enough to remove the mark. Why stay in the same town? Why subject yourself to whatever these last thirty years have been?

The dog on my feet shifts and I reach down to scratch her head.

"She bothering you?" Carole asks.

"No," I say, and bring my hand up on the table where she can see it.

"Why now?" she asks. Seeing my confusion, she continues. "Just struck me as odd. He dies and here you are. How'd you even know?"

"I came back to talk to him. A friend knows one of the COs at the prison. That's why they told me, because the visit got canceled."

"They tell you he was sick? You thought you'd get him to confess to you when he was weak."

"No, I—"

I don't know if she knows what he said about my mother and I'm not going to tell her.

"He wouldn't have told you shit." There's no emotion in how she says it; it's just a statement of fact.

I open my mouth to answer, though I'm not sure what to say. She pulls a pack of cigarettes out of a pocket on her cardigan and starts turning it over in her hand. "My son went to see him. People get some dumb idea that when a person's dying, they change, but they don't. He was a sick piece of shit when he went into that prison and probably stayed that way until his last breath. The chaplain tried to tell me about some grief group. All I told him was, 'I hope he hurt, right up until the end.' Nobody's grieving that bastard, definitely not me." She tosses the pack of cigarettes back on the table and glares at it, then she looks at me again. "You got a picture of your mother?"

The change of topic is disarming, baiting, which I guess is the point. I squeeze my hand into a fist under the table. I don't want to give her the satisfaction of knowing she's getting to me. "That's not why I'm here."

"You want me to just tell you everything? To open up my life for you?"

"I am just trying other understand why—"

"Listen," she says. "You're young so you haven't figured this out yet. Sometimes, there is nothing to understand. Sometimes things just are what they are. There's no big secret for you to discover here. I know in movies they make guys like him complicated like they got their own messed-up code, but he didn't. He just thought he could take what he wanted. That was his code. Because he wanted to."

She grabs the cigarette pack again, takes one out and lights it. She inhales deeply. "My granddaughter's on me to quit," she mumbles. She blows the smoke out of the side of her mouth.

I lean down and fish through my bag, then pull out my wallet. In the billfold, I keep an old picture of my mom I tore out of a high school yearbook that I found packed away at my grandparents' house. I unfold it carefully and flatten it with my hands. It's black-and-white and the folds have worn deep grooves into the glossy paper but I can still see her clearly. The yearbook committee took the photo from the local paper. She's coming up out of the water, smiling. "Youngest Swimmer to Cross Lake" reads the headline. Grandpa Lukas stands in a boat in the distance. He was her swim coach and was with her through the whole crossing. I push the picture toward Carole. She reaches out to pick it up but changes her mind and leaves it on the table.

"That's a few years before," I say.

"I didn't know anything about her," she says after a moment. She lets out another long puff of smoke and ashes the cigarette into a chipped coffee mug. "Aside from what they said at the trial. It was easier to know less. About any of them. Not that it mattered. Didn't change anything." She leans forward again to look at the picture. "I remember the lawyers going on about her being a swimmer."

"She wanted to swim across all the Great Lakes."

"Why the hell would she do that?"

"Because she could. She would have done it too."

That gets another grunt. I take the page back and return it to my wallet.

She looks past me and I stay very still, not tense, but quiet, and let my gaze wander around the room. The kitchen is crowded but not messy. Dishes are stacked in the dish rack, the cloth folded neatly over the sink. A lone violet sits on the kitchen window. I wonder if it's real. In the top corner of the fridge are two school pictures, too small for me to see clearly from here. A boy and a girl.

Carole pushes her chair back from the table and the legs scrape over the floor. The sudden movement makes both dogs scramble to attention. She goes to the sink and drops the cigarette into it. The dogs' nails click on the linoleum floor as they walk over to her and push into her with their heads.

"Don't get excited, you damned fools," she says to them. "I got nothing for you."

She takes a glass out of the drying rack and fills it with water, then comes back to the table and sits down, placing it in front of her without drinking.

"You don't look like her."

"I look more like my dad's side."

"Your dad," Carole says. "I remember him. Big family. They live around here?"

"No. They have a cottage in St. Rose."

"You related to a Joey Green?"

"I don't know. There are a lot of second and third cousins. It's hard to keep track."

She grunts again and then says, "Joey Green complained to my boss. The trial was done, but he didn't think I should have the job. Cut my hours down to nothing."

If she decides to hold this against me, then this conversation is over. I guess I should get used to this—a series of dead ends. This was a shot in the dark anyway. I'm braced for her to tell me to go but instead, she starts talking.

"My husband kept himself to himself. Had expectations about the way things should be, about what was his right. Like a lot of men back then. He didn't go in for all that emotional crap you see nowadays. But he did his part. He'd already started driving when I met him. He'd seen the whole country, both coasts, top to bottom and everything in between. I'd never left home. The year Jason was born, he tried to switch to local routes but then he got bored." She takes a sip of water. "Eddie got bored real easy. That's why he went back on the road."

"The victims were from all over," I say to prod her on.

"That's what they told me."

"But he picked up my parents close to here. Why'd he change his routine?"

"Don't know."

"But did something happen? I've read the reports. You told the police that night he came home but then he left again right away."

"I didn't keep track of his comings and goings."

"But he either picked up my parents right before coming here, or right after. Was he acting different or—?"

"If you read the report, why are you asking questions you already know the answers to? He got home in the middle of the night and left just as quick. That's it."

"Is that when he'd usually get back?"

"He'd get back when he'd get back. I don't know. It depended on where he was coming from."

"But he came back and then left right away? Didn't that seem odd?"

She looks at me for a moment, deciding. "We had a fight."

"What did you fight about?"

She sighs and shakes her head. "How am I supposed to remember something that happened thirty years ago?"

"Because a few weeks later, he was arrested. And according to what I've read, he didn't come home again. I think you'd remember that. The last time you saw him, you had an argument."

"We had arguments all the time. He was angry we were here."

My eyes stray back to those two school pictures in the top corner of the fridge. The kids are young, but there's no way to tell how old the photos are from here. I can't imagine children being in this environment, calling this woman "Grandma" or "Mom."

"It was the end of August," she says. "That's when I'd usually take Jason to my sister's in Ohio, right before school started. Eddie never came with us. Couldn't stand my sister." She lets out a puff of air. "The feeling was mutual. So he knew we were going to be gone when he got back; we'd talked about it, 'cause he was supposed to be doing some work on the house."

"But you were here."

So, maybe he brought my mother to his house, to his graveyard, thinking it would be empty.

"My niece was sick so Annie had canceled. I was in bed when he came in but I heard the truck. I knew he was going to be pissed—Eddie hated surprises—but he was livid. Dragged me out of bed. He woke up Jason with his yelling. I tried to reason with him—told him we'd go stay in a motel if it meant that much to him, but he was . . ." She goes quiet.

"He was . . . ?"

She shakes her head. "He left. Stomped out. That was the last we saw him."

We sit in silence. Outside, the rain is turning to sleet, tapping against the window.

I get up and go to the school photos. This woman wants to claim innocence in her ignorance. I can't buy it. Complacency, maybe, but not innocence. But these children, they're collateral just like me. The boy looks like he's seven or eight, messy hair, no smile, just looking directly at the camera. He's wearing a green-and-blue striped shirt. He looks like a child with a world in his head.

"Who are these kids?"

"My son and my granddaughter. They got nothing to do with this."

"What was your son like as a boy?"

"He was a kid. He adored his father."

"Did he know who his father was?"

I'm still looking at the photos, and suddenly she's right behind me. I hear the low growl of the dogs before I hear her.

"Get out of my house."

I turn and look at her. I open my mouth to say something, but what can I say? She is doing what she has to do, what she's been doing for years. Protecting the tiny bit that's left. And I'm doing the same.

I grab my coat and walk out of the kitchen. I can't breathe in this place. I let the screen door slam behind me.

CHAPTER 10

FIONA

Now

I've just turned the car on when Carole's door opens again. At first, I wonder if it's her, but instead a teenaged girl comes out, trips down the steps, and runs straight at me waving her arm. With the other, she's lugging a huge backpack.

"Wait," she calls. "I want to talk to you—"

I roll down my window a couple of inches.

"Hi," she says, coming up to the car. She's out of breath. "Wow. I almost just wiped out there, did you see that? Those steps are super slippery. You were just talking to my grandma, right? I wanted to meet you but she said I had to stay out of the way. I'm Lily." She smiles and sticks out her hand to shake through the window, then laughs at herself and shoves it back in her pocket.

"Hi," I say. "Uh—"

"You're Fiona Green, right?" Off my surprised look she says, "My grandmother told me you were coming to ask her questions. That's why I had to stay in the bedroom. I was going to try to meet you inside, but you didn't stay that long."

She speaks as if she can't stop for breath, words tumbling out of her one on top of the other. It takes a beat for me to register what she's said.

"I guess we didn't have that much to talk about."

"Yeah, she's kind of prickly, especially about that stuff. Can I ask you a favor? Can you give me a ride? It's just to the bus depot in town. They don't run much in the evenings out here and I have to get home. I live in St. Rose. Wait, are you going to St. Rose? Can you drive me there if you're going?"

Before I have a chance to answer, she runs around to the passenger side of the car and opens the door. She's tall and gangly and now soaking wet. The coat she's wearing is too big for her and the sleeves hang down past her hands. Her backpack looks like it weighs as much as she does.

"You know you shouldn't get in a car with a stranger, right?" I say as she gets in, stuffing the dripping backpack at her feet. She slams the door and turns to me.

"You're not a stranger. You were just visiting my grandmother." She smiles at me as if challenging me to argue this logic and wipes the water from her eyes. "Besides, I really have to get home and she won't drive at night, especially in this. I stayed later than I was supposed to but I was trying to stay out of the way so I missed the bus and they only come once an hour out here. And plus, I really wanted to meet you."

"Why?"

Apparently, this is a stupid question. "Well, I mean, we're like, connected."

"Connected?"

"My grandpa. Your mom. Did my grandma answer your questions by the way?"

"Not really." I'm so used to the anonymity of Vancouver. I have to remind myself that in this area, everyone at one point knew about what happened to my mother. But still, it's jarring how casual her mention is.

Lily nods, like this is what she expected. "I don't think she knows much. I don't think she *wants* to know much. She's always been like that." She smiles and shrugs, as if to say, "What are you going to do?" and then settles back in her seat holding her hands in front of the Jeep's meager heaters.

"It's going to take a bit to warm up," I say. I pull out and start weaving slowly back through the trailer park to the main road.

"I was supposed to go to my friend Reilly's because we're working on this project," Lily says. "But it's got too late, so I should just go home. But honest, you can just drop me at the bus stop if you're not going that way. I take the bus all the time."

"It's fine," I say. As much as I don't want her in my car, it doesn't feel right to leave her at some middle-of-nowhere bus shelter.

We pull out onto the main strip. Lily keeps up a steady commentary about the restaurants and stores we're passing but I'm only half listening. I'm still trying to process everything. For my entire life, Eddie Ward has been more of a presence; an idea of evil more than a real person, but being in the home of his ex-wife and now meeting his granddaughter, there's also something ordinary and recognizable about him.

I realize that Lily has fallen silent and is just watching me. "So, what's the project you're working on?" I ask.

"It's pretty cool. We're creating a three-dimensional map of this part of the lake leading into the mouth of the St. Lawrence. We're supposed to be talking about early industry, but I want to do it about the shipwrecks. You know the bottom of the lake is covered in sunken ships, right?"

"I think I remember hearing that."

"There's all these ghost ships. Like, there are stories of people seeing ships that sank ages ago. And there were smugglers in this area too, during Prohibition. And gangs. It makes this place sound so much more exciting than it is now."

"I guess when you live in a place, you get used to it. I used to only come here in the summers, so it was always kind of magical for me."

She opens her mouth, then closes it again and turns back to look out the window.

"I can't wait to get out of here," she says after a moment. "The second I turn eighteen, I'm gone." The change is immediate. The bright, bubbly girl is suddenly replaced by someone who seems much older and more weighed down.

"Anyway," she says, her voice light again, "we're trying to narrow down which ships to show, but how do we make them look ghostly? I was thinking of painting them all white, but maybe that's lame, you know? Reilly says we should just pick one or two, but I think it would look so amazing if it was covered with shipwrecks, don't you think? Like an underwater graveyard."

"Sounds like a great project."

"Sorry, I'm talking a lot," Lily says. "I think I'm nervous."

"Oh?"

She shrugs. "Just, you know. Who you are. Who I am. You're the first person connected to my grandfather who I've met. It's one thing to read about what happened, but it's another to actually meet someone. Did you know he died?"

I nod.

"Is it weird to feel sad? I mean, I've never met him and obviously, he was a terrible person but . . ." She looks out the side window and chews her lip. "No, it's not sad, it's like it's a missed opportunity, you know? He's not really real to me. I mean, nobody in my family talks about him but he's always been *there*, you know? And now he's not.

KEEP THIS FOR ME

I guess, it just feels like it should mean something, but I don't know what that's supposed to be." She turns back to look at me.

"I'm trying to learn everything I can about what my grandfather did. I think it's important. I'm kind of the opposite of the rest of my family that way. They either don't want to know about it or won't talk about what they do know. It's pretty frustrating, but there's a lot of information online if you look hard enough."

"What's online?"

She cocks her head, like this is a trick question. Maybe it is. I've looked online, of course I have. Sub communities of sub communities. If you dig deep enough, you can find people who have all sorts of ideas and theories. Nothing I found felt real and the deeper I got into those rabbit holes, the more disconnected I felt from the few pieces of information that I do have. They were already as fine as a spider's thread, so I stopped those online searches. But I'm not going to tell this strange girl any of this. She may think we are connected, but that's not a connection I want anything to do with.

"It's just people speculating, you know? Like there might be a lot more people that he killed that were never found. Some people are obsessed with serial killers. I even had one person who offered to give me money if I could send them stuff of his."

"Like what?"

"Anything." She shrugs. "I guess if I'm ever really desperate for money . . ." She grins, waiting for a response, which I don't give her.

"I'm totally kidding. But for real though, I do want to learn about it. I think I have an obligation, you know? That's why I wanted to meet you. Most of the time, when I read about it, it feels like I'm reading a story, like some TV show, but then I remember no, that's *my* family. It's real. Why did he do that? Is it in me too? And you're real, and you're obviously looking for answers too."

"Yeah," I say, more to myself than Lily. "I'm not sure they exist though."

She thinks about that for a moment.

"So, do your grandparents still have that cottage in St. Rose?" she asks.

I'm glad the car is dark and she can't see my face clearly. I know I shouldn't be surprised that she knows this. As she said, everything's online, but I feel myself wanting to curl around these facts about my family and hide them from her.

"The cottage is still there, yeah."

"Sorry, is it weird that I asked that? I'm just, I'm always looking for information, you know? The kids at my school know about my family, obvi. Most of them just ignore me, but every once in a while, someone says something and—it's like the only way I can get ahead of anything they're going to spring on me is if I get all the information first. Then they can't surprise me. Some of them are like, why don't you change your name if you don't want people to know you're related to a murderer? Like officially, my last name is Curry. That's my mom's maiden name because she and my dad weren't married when they had me. But all the teachers know, I'll only answer to "Lily Ward." Even in elementary I did that. My grandma changed her name the first second she could, but my dad didn't, so it's like my one connection to him. It's not about my grandfather, it's my dad. Like, even though you didn't know your mother, you still want a connection to her, right?"

I keep my focus forward.

"And some people just don't get that," she says turning back to face front. "Like there's other people in my family besides my grandfather and I don't think it's fair that the rest of us are like *tainted* because of what he did." She swallows and there's a catch in her voice when she speaks again. "Sorry. I've never met anyone who actually understands."

She's fiddling with a loose thread on the hem of the coat, her damp hair hanging in her face. She seems like someone who learned from a young age that she is alone in the world. My whole life, I've felt like I had "victim" stamped across my forehead. I wonder if it's been the same for her. I squeeze the steering wheel and focus into the rain. I am not going to empathize with her.

"Anyway, so this project we're doing," Lily says after another moment of silence, "Reilly did some snorkeling last summer. Her family's really into all that outdoorsy stuff. She actually saw one of the ships, so that's where the idea came from. She said it just looked like a bunch of broken wood covered in barnacles, but still. There's probably like *bodies* down there. Wouldn't that be amazing to see?"

"Maybe she'll take you next summer."

"Yeah, maybe." She shifts in her seat. "I can't swim. It's embarrassing. I mean, who can't swim?"

"Lots of people."

"Not around here. Can you?"

"Yeah, but—"

"Oh, of course. Your mom was a big swimmer, right? I remember reading that."

I'm not falling for it. She wants information—she's said as much. "Do you go to the high school in town?" I ask instead. "There's a pool there, right?"

"That's just for the swim team."

"No, the public can use it too. That's where I'm going to swim while I'm here. I just have to go really early before practices start. Maybe one of the kids on the swim team could teach you."

"The jocks at my school are dicks. It's like all anyone cares about is sports." She slumps down into her huge coat.

"Well, I used to teach swimming. The mechanics aren't hard. Most of it comes down to learning to trust that you're safe in the water. I'm sure you'll find someone." We've come into the outskirts of St. Rose and I slow the car. "Where am I taking you?"

"My house is on Barnhart Way. Turn left at the next light past the church; it's down a ways. Number fifty-six."

As we turn onto her street, it suddenly occurs to me that I could be taking her to Jason Ward's house. David thinks he's on the West Coast, but what if he's right here, on this quiet street with basketball hoops in the driveways and Thanksgiving decorations on the front steps?

"Do you live with your dad?"

"No," she says. "My parents split before I was born. I wish I could live with my dad, but he's not around much."

We pull up in front of her house. It's dark, the curtains drawn. I wonder if anyone is even home. She starts to open the car door and then turns to me.

"Can you teach me?"

"Teach you what?"

"How to swim." She smiles at me. "I can get up early. I like doing that."

"I'm not going to be here very long. Probably just a few days. I'm sure you can find someone though."

"Okay," she says, looking disappointed, then she shrugs again. "It was worth a try. Thanks for the drive." She leans over and gives me a quick hug and says quietly, "You're so nice. I thought you'd hate me." Then she pushes the door open and jumps out before I can respond.

CHAPTER 11

ANA

August 28, 1993

9 P.M.

When they opened the door, the party was a solid mass of bodies, music, voices. This is going to be awful, Ana thought. And as much as she'd yearned to be back to normal, to be with people her own age, what if she had forgotten how? In the kitchen, Ben grabbed a beer out of a bucket of ice—much fancier beer than the usual college party fare—and handed it to her.

"No thanks," she said.

"It'll help you relax."

"I am relaxed." She had taken two of the pills a few hours ago. The doctor had told her not to mix them with alcohol.

Ben put the beer down and took her hands. "Hey," he said, pulling her close. "You deserve this. We both do." He wrapped his arms around her and said in her ear, "Whenever you want to go, we can."

"But we just got here."

"I know. But if it gets to be too much."

She wanted to make a joke, the way she would have before, but that part of her brain was too rusty for quick use. He put his nose to hers and smiled and then he kissed her. His lips were warm and soft and she closed her eyes and focused on the feel of them, that familiar knowing. *Ben and Ana. The two of us.*

"Against the world," she mumbled. Their old phrase. Had they said it since Fiona was born?

Before Ben could respond, someone called out, "It's Green, in the flesh." A guy clapped Ben on the back and the moment ended. "Back from the dead. Holy shit, it's Benana."

Ben and Ana, "Benana" as Ben's friends had called them. They'd started dating only a month into her freshman year. She barely knew anyone, while Ben, who was a year ahead of her, seemed to know everyone. At the time, she hadn't minded being known as half of "Benana," but now it struck her as odd. At her high school in St. Rose, she was just Ana Lukas, the swimmer. When she set the record for youngest swimmer to cross Lake Ontario, the athletic department had even given her an award for "Superior Accomplishment in Sport." She'd been embarrassed by the attention but had taken for granted that this was her identity. At college, she was shy and was happy to be shepherded into social groups through her old friend, Tia, and then by Ben. She still swam and believed that would be how she'd find her place. But then they got pregnant. She looked around at the mass of people. Is that how they saw her, as the girl who got knocked up and dropped out?

Ben was grinning at the group of guys now gathered around them. She recognized their faces but was blanking on names. What was wrong with her brain? One of them was Carlos. He was the one Ben was closest to. Ana had always liked him the best. But the other two?

"We didn't know if you were going to make it."

"I said I would."

"Yeah, but, you know. Daddy bondage."

Ben laughed. "That's why they invented babysitters."

"Hey, Ana," Carlos said. "How's the kiddo?"

"You had a boy, right?" asked one of the guys whose name she couldn't remember.

"A girl you twat," another guy (Rip, maybe?) said and elbowed him in the ribs. Ben laughed then looked at Ana and rolled his eyes. "What's her name again?" the guy asked.

"Fiona," she said.

"I dated a Fiona in high school," Rick—right, that was his name, Rick and Rip, she never could tell who was who—said. "She was crazy. In all the right ways."

"Shut the fuck up, Hopper," Carlos said, then he turned back to Ana. "Ignore him. He's an ass." That got a roar of laughter out of the rest of them.

"Holy shit, Green. It's so good to see you, man!" another guy who'd just walked up said and grabbed Ben, pretending to wrestle him to the ground.

Rip started in on something that swerved the conversation elsewhere and Ana drifted away.

She moved through the crowd, letting her body be jostled left and right. Like moving in water with currents running in every direction. Music was loud and people had to lean in to each other to speak. Some people smiled at her vaguely but she didn't recognize them and let herself keep moving until she reached a huge window that took up almost the entire wall. The house was modern and bright, sitting high up over the water. Fat purple clouds were rolling in from the west, pushing out the pink of the evening sky. The water held the sunlight in its ripples but further out she could see waves forming. There's an energy to a summer storm; violence created by all that contained heat, she could feel it. Behind her, the party throbbed.

Before, she would have been comfortable inside that noise but now she was craving the huge expanse of the lake.

Her life had shrunk down in these past two and a half years to the immediate needs of her daughter, their crowded apartment, and the small park across the street with its wooden swing set and the messages carved into its posts that she had memorized. It was all so small and precarious in a way it never was before becoming a parent. She felt unbalanced from the strangeness of being here, being dropped back into her old life, or what would have been her life, except now she was just an imposter trying to remember how to play her old self.

She'd drifted in and out of conversations for a while, and then someone tapped her on the shoulder and she turned around. Her friend, Tia, grinned at her and gave her a big hug. "Hey stranger," she said. "I'm so glad you came. I told Ben he had to bring you."

Tia was wearing her hair loose and it fell in soft ringlets all around her. Ana breathed in the coconut smell of her shampoo and was immediately brought back to their messy shared bathroom at college. Four girls with enough hair products, lotions, and makeup to stock a pharmacy. Ana's were all for dry skin and hair since she was perpetually chlorinated from so much time spent in a pool. Tia's were for Black hair and everything was scented as papaya, coconut, or mango. Becks switched hair dyes monthly and the sink would regularly be stained purple or green, and Pia refused to use anything that wasn't organic and all of her beauty products smelled like patchouli or lavender. Ben had joked about needing to take allergy pills just to use the bathroom at their suite, but Ana had loved that heady mix of smells. For that year they'd lived together, it was like having sisters. They shared clothes, books, CDs—everything. Tia and Ana had grown up together, but they hadn't grown close until college. Tia skipped a year of school, which meant she'd gone to college first so she was the one who introduced Ana to Becks and Pia, and to Ben. The girls had welcomed her and she had slid right in.

And when she left school, she slid right out just as easily. No, that wasn't quite true. She thought of the phone messages Tia left in those first few months, their growing urgency. "How *are* you?" "I want to meet your baby. I want to help." How desperately she wanted to talk to her, but what would she say? If she told her she was drowning it would become real and then everyone would realize how unfit she was to be a mother.

The bus she took to the pediatrician went right past the campus. Once, about three months after Fiona was born, Ana had seen Becks and Pia on the sidewalk in front of the chemistry building. She was suddenly terrified that they were going to get on and they'd see her with her unwashed hair pulled into a messy ponytail, her baggy sweatpants, the giant diaper bag that had replaced her college backpack. She remembered seeing women like her looking worn and trapped with kids attached to them. She'd glance at them and feel pity, and then she'd immediately forget them. Is that how people saw her now?

"How's Fiona? How old is she now?" Tia asked, breaking her out of her thoughts.

"Two and a half."

"Come on, show me a picture," she said, grinning.

Ana opened her purse and pulled a photo out of her wallet. It was from Fiona's second birthday. Her face was covered in cake. "She's bigger than this now," she said giving her the picture.

"Oh my God," Tia squinted at it. "She's so adorable. She's a perfect mix of you two."

"Do you think?" Ben's family was always talking about how much Fiona looked like him. It was nice to have someone see her in their daughter as well.

"She has your eyes," Tia said. "I love the little pigtails. I used to wear my hair like that."

Another girl who was standing nearby noticed the picture and leaned over to look. "Ah cute," she said. "Is that your little sister?"

"My daughter," Ana said.

The girl looked up in surprise but covered her reaction quickly. She reached to hug Tia, and said, "Give me a call so we can figure out tomorrow, okay?" Then she turned back to the conversation she'd been in.

"How are Becks and Pia?" Ana asked, putting the picture back in her wallet. This wasn't the place for kid talk. She wanted to ask something about Tia's life but she had no idea what that was anymore. All she ever talked about now was kids, whether it was with Ben, or his parents, or other mothers. How had she become so boring? "Do you guys still live together?" she asked, then immediately felt dumb. Tia was in grad school now. She wouldn't be in the dorms.

"No," Tia said. "Pia and her girlfriend, LeeAnn, moved in together, and now they've gone to Colorado for grad school. Becks and me and this other girl, Gina—you'd love her—we're in a place off campus but it's close to the lab, which is where I practically live now. Gina's premed. We hardly ever see each other. It's not like before."

"Are you still going to apply to Stanford for the PhD?"

She nodded and started telling her something about a research advisor and a conference, but her voice was lost in the tunnel of noise around them. Ana was watching Tia's lips moving and could understand the words, but she couldn't make them make sense. Tia pointed to an elegant-looking woman standing nearby who might be one of her professors, but she couldn't tell so she just nodded. It was starting to get hard to breathe.

Tia must have sensed it because she said, "Do you want to go outside and check out the balcony? I need a break from all of this."

As soon as they stepped outside and closed the heavy glass door behind them, Ana felt the tight band that had been wrapped around her chest begin to loosen. The air smelled of seaweed and pine and its warm dampness was a relief after the air-conditioning of the house. They walked across the concrete deck to the wood steps built into the rock that led down the cliffside to a little private beach.

They had it to themselves. Ana held her shoes in her hand and stood in the wet sand, her feet slowly sinking as the water spread over her toes and then receded again.

"I've missed you," Tia said, perching on a large piece of driftwood. "I miss our nighttime talks."

Early into living together, they had discovered they both suffered from insomnia. They would make Tia's mom's special recipe for sleepy-time tea and snuggle into either end of the giant couch with their blankets bundled around them until they got tired. Something about those loose, rambling conversations in the dark brought them closer than Ana had ever felt with anyone.

"I'm still up at all hours," Ana said. "Fiona's up at least once a night."

"Call me next time. I'll be up."

No, I won't call you, she wanted to say. As much as I'd like to. I will never let anyone hear the thoughts that come into my head in the middle of the night. She thought again about what had happened that morning. The Blank was always just there. How do you explain something as irrational, as illogical as these dark chasms in her brain to someone like Tia who is so confident, so smart, who makes everything she does look so effortless?

"So, you said you ran into Ben?" she said instead. "Do you see him in town a lot?"

"Not a lot, no. He's usually running around getting ready for the dinner rush when I'm in there getting our lunch order. I've been doing this research assistantship all summer. Dr. Cullen forgets about lunch all the time." She put air quotes around "forgets." "Seriously, I've taught myself to eat a humungous breakfast because I know we're not going to stop until three or whatever. It's fine. But yeah, I've seen him a few times. Does he also work at the college?"

Ana came over and settled on the driftwood next to her. "He's on the landscaping crew, yeah. Then he waits tables at Swintons. It's a crazy schedule. We barely see him. We're staying at his parents' cottage this summer, so he has to commute back to Syracuse each day. It was his idea. There's no AC in our apartment. It's been nice for us but it just made it harder on him. He works two jobs, and now he's going back to school."

"What about you?"

"Me? I have Fiona. I know it doesn't sound like much but—"

"Are you kidding? Don't you remember, I used to babysit my cousins all through high school. *Every* Sunday. That was way more exhausting than what I'm doing now."

"Tell Ben that."

"Is everything okay with you guys?" Tia asked.

"Yeah. I mean. It's different now."

"Just, call me next time. I don't know shit about kids—" Tia laughed. "But if you need someone to listen." She picked up a smooth stone and tried to make it skip over the top of the water but it just sank. "I can never get them to bounce."

The water looked like glass. How far would those ripples travel, she wondered. They'd touch parts of the lake that knew nothing of the stone that caused them.

"How are things with your parents?" Tia asked. Ana kept watching the ripples, not wanting her voice to give her away. Tia had been the one who'd found her curled up in her bed after the visit home when she'd told her parents she was dropping out of school and having a baby. Her mother's anger was awful, but expected. In some ways, it would have been a relief if her dad had just got mad at her too. But he was disappointed, and that was so much worse.

It's not that her parents had disowned her. They had just removed themselves to the periphery. When she called them, they would ask about Fiona and update her on their lives, but it felt perfunctory. They'd started traveling over the winter holidays, though they always sent a gift for Fiona. As soon as Ana had told them she would be spending the summer in St. Rose at the Greens' cottage—a mere ten-minute drive from their house—her mother told her they were leaving the country for a research trip.

"They're in Eastern Europe somewhere."

"Huh," Tia said. "All summer?"

"All summer."

Up at the party the door must have opened because music wafted down to them. Something with a strong bass beat, and under that the hum of voices.

"It's like my mother thinks if she just doesn't engage with the reality of my life, it'll change. The last time we saw them, Ben told them he was thinking of going back to school. Holy shit, you should have seen her. It's such an irony that she's a supposed expert in women and gender studies when hello, I'm her daughter struggling with motherhood, trying to raise a little girl but that's not worth anything. She gets so excited about these young mothers in rural Belarus and their literacy programs, but her own granddaughter is right in front of her and she won't read her a bedtime story."

Tia reached out and put her hand on Ana's shoulder. "She'll come around at some point. She'll have to. If she wants a relationship with you."

"She only wants a relationship with one version of me. And my dad just—" She shook her head. "Sorry. I'm just dumping all this on you. I don't mean to be such a downer."

Ana hadn't expected any of it to come out, but how long had it been since she'd had someone to talk to? Ben didn't count because he was just as buried in it as she was. It's not like she could tell Ben's mom. The only other woman she talked to on a regular basis was Barbara Connor, her neighbor at the cottage, but her life looked nothing like Ana's. She'd done it in the order you were supposed to: school, marriage, kid.

"There's just so many ways you can hurt a child." She'd said it before she even realized it. Her hand almost went up to her mouth to stuff the words back in.

"What?"

"Sorry. I just—"

Why had she said that?

"But what do you mean 'hurt'?" Tia was looking at her differently now. "Do you mean like what your parents are doing to you?"

"It's nothing."

She stood up. She'd been holding herself together all day with Ben's family, acting like everything was normal and now Tia was going to think—was going to *know*—

"You're looking at me weird. You think I'm some kind of monster—"

"No, I don't—"

"Forget I said it."

She turned and started walking quickly toward the stairs. Tia came after her. "Wait, I wasn't looking at you weird, I promise. I'm just trying to understand. Did something happen?"

"No. But it's like, what if she falls when I'm pushing her on the swing? Or what if she chokes because I haven't cut her food small enough, or—?"

"But it's not like any of that stuff has actually happened. You're just afraid it will, right?"

"It's more than that. I see it happening. The second it's in my head, I *see* it. And it's so real, then I don't know what's real and what's just my imagination. Like what kind of a mother even thinks about that sort of thing? I know how it sounds. This is why I can't tell anyone, not even Ben."

"He doesn't know?"

"You *can't* tell him. Tia, I know he's your friend—"

"You're my friend too," she said. "I won't tell, I promise." She smiled and traced an X over her heart. "Cross my heart and hope to die. Did you tell your doctor?"

"He said it was normal to have some baby blues and they'd pass. He gave me pills. But that was like two years ago. I don't think it's depression."

"Well, just be careful what you say to a doctor. Did you tell him about being afraid of hurting the baby?"

Ana shook her head.

"Good. Don't," Tia said. "My cousin, Janice, got the baby blues when her son was born. Like bad. And she told her doctor and she put her in the psych ward. She was in there for two months and she couldn't even see her son. She almost lost custody of him. And she lost her job."

"Holy shit."

"It was seriously messed up. My mom and my aunt went to war to get her out."

"How could they do that?"

Tia shrugged. "I don't know. I guess if they think you're a danger to your child they can legally take your child from you. So just be careful what you say. But you should tell Ben."

"No." It came out more forcefully than she meant. "And you can't either."

"So, you're just going to handle this on your own? That doesn't sound like it's working too well."

"Be honest, do you think Ben and me are a good couple?"

"Sure."

"But if we didn't have a child?"

"Don't do that. 'If this' and 'if that.' Deal with what's real."

"Sometimes . . ."

"What?"

Ana shrugged again. "Sometimes, I just think about leaving. Like, just getting in the car and driving away and never coming back."

Tia laughed.

"What?"

"You and every other woman I know. My mom used to threaten us with that all the time. She'd tell my sister and me, 'One day, you all are going to come home and I'm going to be in Tahiti.' Or sometimes it would be Vegas. She always said she'd send a postcard so we'd know how much fun she was having without us. And then I found out that all my aunts were saying the same thing to my cousins. It's normal. Doesn't mean it's going to happen."

High above them, voices rose in laughter on the patio. She could just catch the smell of cigarette smoke drifting down to them.

Tia grabbed both of Ana's arms and looked at her. "Listen. There are people who love you. We want to hear from you. I guess I believed you when you said you were fine. You seemed so natural at it when I visited you that one time that I assumed—and we got all caught up in school or whatever. But now I know. And now Becks and I are going to be there. We can take turns when you guys come back to town. We can give you a break, or just come and hang out."

KEEP THIS FOR ME

"You don't have any time."

"We'll *make* time. School's just—*pffft*. This is real."

It was so hard to accept this, but how desperately she wanted it.

"Don't you guys think I'm so stupid, throwing my life away?"

Tia shook her head vehemently. "That's your mom talking. Not us. And hey, if my mom finds out that you're struggling, well watch out. You'll be drowning in casseroles. Seriously though. People aren't meant to be alone. Ben may complain about working so much, but he gets a break. You don't."

"What do I complain about?"

Ana and Tia both spun around. Ben was standing just a few steps above them. He was smiling but there was an edge to his voice. Tia may not have heard it, but Ana did. How long had he been standing there?

Tia smiled up at him. "I said, you may be complaining about working two jobs—"

"I don't complain."

"Okay, but you get to have a break. And this woman doesn't. So, Becks and me are going to come and take her out sometime and you're going to have to find a sitter or stay home with the kid."

"Sounds good to me," he said, then he said to Ana, "We should get going."

Tia hugged her. "Call me." She squeezed her hard. "Seriously. Any time. No judgment, I promise." Then she climbed up the stairs and disappeared around the bend.

Ben stayed where he was. "What was that all about?"

Ana shrugged. She knew that would drive him nuts but what could she tell him? "What time is it?" she asked.

"A little past eleven."

She looked back out toward the lake. The clouds had moved

closer, and far out on the water, she could see whitecaps. "Maybe we can beat the storm."

She started back up the stairs and went to move past him but he reached out and pulled her to him.

"Hey," he said softly.

She could smell the beer on his breath. It reminded her of before, of parties and college and everything being as simple as getting to class the next morning.

"I had this crazy idea," he said. He was smiling now. "What if we didn't go home tonight?"

"What?"

He ran his hands down her arms and grabbed her hands. He pulled her tight against him.

"How much have you drunk?" she asked.

"I'm fine to drive," he said, kissing her neck. "I was just thinking, we passed a motel. It's just a couple miles from here. We can get up early and be back home."

"But you have to work."

"It's the end of the summer. I'll call in sick. We haven't had any time as just the two of us. I miss you." His hand moved over her waist. How long had it been since they'd been together? They were always so exhausted. Whoever got into bed first would be asleep before the other even finished brushing their teeth. She could feel herself responding to him. Could they do this? Could they have a night together like they'd had before?

"Get a room, you two," someone called from the stairs above them.

"I'm trying, man," he called out then turned back to her and smiled. "So? What do you say?"

"Did you call your mom to check in?" she asked.

"Was I supposed to?"

"You said you would. I would have called if I'd known you hadn't."

"I gave Mom the number here if there was an emergency. She's raised four kids. I think she can handle one night."

"Maybe we should call now. Then we can tell them we'll be back in the morning so they don't worry."

"I'm not waking them up for nothing."

"It's not nothing—"

She moved away from him. He thought they could just put their lives down and reenter what they'd had before, but it didn't work that way. Why couldn't he get that?

"Let's just go," she said. "It doesn't feel right being away this long." She started walking back up the stairs and after a moment, he followed.

The party had become louder and looser. There was no sign of Tia. She'd expected to feel embarrassed by what she'd told her, but it felt like a bit of relief to have somebody know. Ben had been right; it was good she came.

She looked for a phone but didn't see one, and then they were through the crowd and walking to the car. The wind was picking up and plucked at her dress. Exhaustion was coming for her. She just wanted to be home, to check on Fiona, to brush the hair off her warm little forehead, to know she was safe.

Ben started the car and she watched the lights of the beautiful house get smaller behind them as they drove away.

CHAPTER 12

JASON

2003

Jason waited a week, then went back to McGregor's. This time, it was an old man working the bar and when he ordered a Bud and laid down $2.50, the guy didn't blink. The music was turned down a few notches and he could afford to drink a third beer, but there was no sign of Sam.

The week after, he decided to try one more time. As soon as he approached the door, he could tell that Mustache was working since the music was heavy metal again, and loud. This time there were four guys clustered together at the far end, rows of empty shot glasses in front of them. So, he went back to his car and got his switchblade out of the glove box. He wasn't going to start anything, but he wasn't going to shy away either. He'd probably just need to show them the blade, but if they were as drunk as last time, there was no telling what they could do. It didn't matter. He could do worse.

Jason had been fighting since he was eleven, and winning since he was thirteen. The school would call and complain but his mom never gave him shit about it. She'd give him some Band-Aids and aspirin and as long as he wasn't suspended, she'd send him back the next day. She was fighting her own battles those first few years. Hers weren't fought with fists, but he knew how the phone never rang any-more, not even her sister who she used to complain about calling all the time. He once caught her outside at three in the morning scrub-bing spray paint off the side of their trailer. After that, she got a dog and kept it outside at night. His mother's fights continued in those unseen ways, in the grocery store, in having her hours cut or being moved to night shifts, in the way people turned away from her. He never heard her cry, not once, and so he didn't either.

The switchblade in his back pocket, Jason went into the bar. Sure enough, Mustache smiled at him and came right over, seeing a walk-ing cash machine.

The guys at the end of the bar ignored him at first but they were giving him little looks. He started a tab. He didn't want Mustache to know that he wasn't going to get such a hot tip until he was done drinking. It seemed like the guys were without their dates but on his third bottle, the door opened and Sam and the blonde walked in. When Sam saw him, her face lit up.

"Hey, Jason," she said. "I was hoping I'd see you again." She was speaking loudly so she could be heard over the music, which meant the guys heard her too.

The douchebag he guessed was the boyfriend called out, "Yo, Ward," emphasis on the last name, "we know who you are."

Jason swallowed but didn't move. They weren't going to get a re-action from him that easily.

"Chris, don't," Sam said.

"No, people should know who they're drinking with. Don't you want to know who's in your bar, Ry?" he said to Mustache.

Mustache shrugged. "Don't care as long as he pays."

"Is it true?" the blonde asked. "Are you really the son of that murderer?"

"Serial killer," the one called Chris said. "Sick fuck who killed chicks and buried them in his backyard. Local legend. Finally, something for this shithole town to brag about."

"Not just chicks," one of the other guys said. "He killed some fag too. Probably thought he was a girl and then, oh shit." The other guys laughed.

"You done?" Jason asked, then he turned to the blond girl. "Yeah. I'm the son."

The girl's eyes went wide. But Sam cocked her head; she didn't look horrified, just curious. "It must be hard," she said. "I mean, if this is what happens."

"What, you want him to cry on your shoulder, Sammy?"

One of the other guys who was new spoke up. He was the biggest of the four, and the one Jason had already noted as being of concern if things got bad. He had his full sleeve of tattoos on display, and unlike the others, he seemed sober. "You work at George's Garage in Carling Falls, right?"

Jason swallowed and hoped the guys hadn't seen it. He needed this conversation to end, now.

"I got a buddy who works there." The guy turned to his friends. "Says half the guys there have done time."

"Yeah, well I haven't," Jason said.

"Not yet," the guy said.

The blonde turned to Sam but made sure to speak loud enough that Jason could hear. "I remember when he was caught. My cousin knows someone who almost got in his truck."

"Bullshit," one of the guys shot out.

"No, I'm serious." She'd turned to him but then she turned back to face Jason, her voice was rising higher, or was the music getting quieter? There were a few other people in the bar and they'd stopped their conversations to listen. "Her car broke down and this truck pulled over and she almost got in but she had a real bad feeling. She said when she saw him on the news, she knew it was the same guy who'd almost got her. She recognized him right away."

The guys mumbled to themselves. Jason pulled a twenty out of his pocket and laid it on the bar. Mustache ambled over, his hand already out.

"I need some change," Jason said. He was focused on the sneer of the bartender's face, and the guys, so he didn't notice the man behind him until he grabbed Jason's arm and wrenched it up and back. The man leaned in, the smell of beer on his breath, and said in his ear, "We don't want scum in our bar. Leave the money and get out."

Jason nodded. The tendons in his shoulder were screaming. Another inch and something would snap. The guy let him go but then he must have seen the switchblade because in the next second, Jason could feel it being pulled out of his back pocket and then there was a lot of yelling.

"He's got a blade—"

Someone screamed. He heard the click of it opening at the same moment a hand grabbed his hair and jerked his head back, exposing his neck.

Now the guys were up and the big one, the one he'd been worried about, was striding over to him.

"Bringing a fucking blade in here—"

"You know what he's going to do with that—"

Someone else from behind said, "I had a chance to hurt his daddy once. I let him go. Look what happened."

"Like father, like son. Someone needs to take care—"

It all happened so fast. Jason's head was still held, but his good arm was free. He slammed his elbow into the gut of the faceless man behind him. He was solid but it was enough to surprise him so that he let go of Jason's hair. He whipped around as the guy slashed toward him with the knife. There was no way he was going to get his knife back; all he could do was try to get to the door, but people were swarming him. The heat came on full inside his chest now and the pain in his shoulder disappeared. He grabbed his half-drunk beer bottle off the bar and smashed it on the head of the guy with the blade. The knife dropped and Jason kicked it skittering across the bar. He felt the big guy reach out for him and he swung around and punched him, but it didn't land right and just as fast, the man used that tattooed arm to hit him in the side of his head.

Jason had been hit in the head a lot. It always hurt, but he knew how to keep his balance, how to keep moving. He staggered away, turned toward the door, and ran. He'd parked on the far end of the parking lot where it was darkest. He lurched toward his car, digging for his keys as he ran. He felt dizzy and nauseated. The hit had been much harder than any he'd gotten in high school. The guy must have weighed over 250 and he was solid. He managed to get the car door opened, but he didn't think he could drive because there was too much swimming in front of his eyes. What were the chances they were going to come after him? He wasn't sure. They probably wouldn't bother, but if they did . . .

He pulled the gun out of his glove box. Having it was still new to him, but each time he handled it, he felt more comfortable. He'd got it as soon as he turned twenty-one, and he'd been teaching himself how to use it ever since. Usually holding it calmed him down, but his heart was still hammering and his head felt like it was going to explode. He tightened his hands around it and squeezed, trying to focus on the cold metal instead of his pounding head.

He closed his eyes and leaned back in his seat to stop the swimming feeling but his eyes snapped open when he heard footsteps on gravel. Someone was coming from behind the bar. Then he saw Sam moving toward him. She was holding something in her hand. She came up to the passenger side and gave a little wave, then she opened the door. As soon as she saw the gun, she stepped back.

"Whoa—" she said.

"Oh shit, sorry," he said, and he put it down between his legs. "Sorry. I didn't know if you were—"

"I get it," she said. She slid into the passenger seat and closed the door. Now he could see she was holding a wet cloth that was dripping in her hand.

"Are they going to—?" he started, nodding toward the bar. If they came out and found her in his car, he'd have to show them the gun. Four of them, maybe more, and they had his knife. Not that the police would care. It would get bad, fast.

She shook her head. "I went out the back, but I grabbed this from the kitchen. Don't worry, it's clean," she said. She held the rag up. "May I?"

Jason nodded. Very gently, she pressed the cold rag against the side of his head where he'd been punched. The cool water felt like instant relief and he closed his eyes and breathed out involuntarily. When he opened them again, she was smiling.

"I'm in nursing school. Doesn't look like you're bleeding too bad, but I bet you're going to have a terrible headache tomorrow. How's your shoulder?"

"It's okay," he said, trying to sound like it didn't hurt.

"Those guys are assholes. Honestly, Chris used to be okay, but he's been hanging with those other guys and he's always trying to impress them. We're not even together anymore. I just came because Carly is with Scott and she always wants me to come along."

"You told them my name."

She winced. "I'm so sorry. I knew it sounded familiar, but I had no idea why. Seriously, I never would have if I'd known."

"But aren't you . . . ?" He didn't know what to say. Afraid of me, or disgusted by me, or don't you think I'm guilty by association?

"You don't seem like the killer type. Even with that gun. Am I wrong?"

She smiled again. Her smile was amazing, he thought. It started small, kind of playful, but then it spread across her whole face.

"Look," she said, "my dad's a dentist, totally conservative. He stands for everything I hate and I am *nothing* like him. So, no, just because your dad was like that, it doesn't automatically mean you are."

She took the rag away and he touched the growing bruise gingerly.

"Are you okay to drive?"

"Yeah. I'm fine." He wasn't sure about that, but he certainly wouldn't admit it. "I don't have far to go."

"You live around here?" she asked. He nodded. He wouldn't bother mentioning that he lived with his mother. "Me too," she said. "For the summer. I go back to school next week."

"Oh," Jason said. He hadn't meant to sound so disappointed but being around this woman he felt how easily he could become un-guarded. He had to be careful. "Where's that?"

"University of Rochester. I'm in the pediatric NP program."

"NP?"

"Nurse Practitioner."

"That's like a doctor, right?" he said.

"Well, sort of. Like, I'll be able to do more than an RN, but not as much as a doctor."

"You must be smart," he said. Now he really did sound like an idiot. She laughed though, which was a relief.

"I don't know if I'm smart. I'm just stubborn." She turned to face him full on and smiled. "I work hard when I want something."

She kept looking at him but didn't say anything else. He opened his mouth to reply but then closed it again. Part of him wanted to hide. He'd never felt as seen as he did now, sitting here with her looking right at him—right into him. But instead of turning away, the way he normally would have, he wanted to stay here. To let her see him. Because she wasn't treating him like some kind of freak the way girls, the rare times he'd talked to them, usually did.

She reached out and put her hand lightly on his. "I'm curious about you, Jason Ward."

"Oh?"

"Is that strange?"

"Uh, I don't know," he said. He thought about the guys he worked with, what they'd do. Most of them talked a big game when it came to women, though none of them had girlfriends and he guessed most of them weren't quite as sure of themselves when they were actually face-to-face with one. But they'd at least be able to hold a conversation.

"Well, I am—interested, that is," she said. She didn't seem bothered by his inarticulate response. "So maybe sometime we could hang out. Would that be okay?"

He nodded dumbly.

"Great," she said and opened the door, then turned back to him. "Remember, take some aspirin and a big glass of water when you get home." And with that, she slid out of the car, and was gone again.

He sat there for another few moments, too dumbfounded to move, and then he drove home. His mind was spinning in too many directions to know what to think. He had been seen, and for once it hadn't hurt.

CHAPTER 13

FIONA

Now

The pool glows turquoise from the underwater lights. High above, fluorescents buzz, their light barely reaching the deck, leaving it a dim middle ground. I shed my boots and layers of clothing on the side, pad barefoot across the cold tiles, slip into the water, and drop to the bottom, ten feet below the surface. The dreams of long black fingers of lake water reaching up from the shore, that feeling of being so close to *him* in Carole's trailer, all of it is pushed down by the shock and the weight of the water. I count. 31 . . . 32 . . . 33 . . . When the squeezing in my lungs reaches its peak, I push up off the bottom, break the surface, take a huge breath, and begin swimming. This is what being strong is. To go up to the edge of panic and make myself stay there for a moment. To be able to swim long and hard when all I want to do is stop and gasp for more air. Recover *in* the stroke. Slow my heart. The first few laps always hold that taste of animal panic. The control gets stronger each time I'm able to push it by another second underwater. By the third lap, I'm in rhythm. It's the best way I know to turn off my head. At my YMCA pool at home, there are usually other swimmers but here, I have the pool to myself.

That's why it takes me a moment to realize that there's someone standing in the hallway next to the bleachers. My goggles are foggy so I pull them off. Lily steps out from the shadows.

"Hi," she calls out and steps further into the light. She looks nervous. "You're a good swimmer."

"What are you doing here?" I ask. I'm breathing hard. I swim to the side and she comes over to meet me. "How did you get here?"

"I walked," she says.

"At six in the morning?"

"I walk to school most days. I know you said you're only here for a few days, but I thought I'd try, you know? 'Cause, like you said, it's just feeling comfortable in the water. So, I thought maybe I could just watch you? And then, maybe—if you have time—you could give me a few pointers? I didn't know how else to find you."

"And your parents know you're here?"

"They're fine," she says and shrugs off the oversized coat, letting it drop beside her, oblivious to the pool water on the deck.

I could kick myself for telling her I'd be here, but it never occurred to me that she'd come find me.

"I can go," she says, pausing midway into pulling off her sweatshirt. "If it's a problem."

"It's fine," I say. I hate myself for feeling guilty, but I immediately do.

"Really? You're sure?"

"You're here now."

She adds her boots and sweatpants to the pile of clothes. Her bathing suit sags in places her body can't fill. She looks at the water and chews her lip. "I couldn't find goggles," she says. "This is my mom's suit."

"You need something for your hair."

She pulls an elastic off her wrist and tucks her hair into a low ponytail, then sits down on the side. When her feet touch the water, she immediately pulls them back out.

"It's freezing."

"It's a competition pool. Once you start swimming, it'll feel fine."
I pull off my goggles and hand them to her.

"Don't you need them?"

"You're going to have your head in the water, I'm not."

She grins. "Thank you, Fiona." She sounds strangely formal.
Maybe it's her way of showing that she's serious about this lesson.

Lily adjusts the goggles over her eyes, makes a show of taking
a big breath, and slides into the pool, but instead of holding on to
the side she pushes off the wall, then claws at the water and drops
straight down. It's so fast, it takes me a second to realize what has
just happened. She isn't thrashing around, she's just sinking, but
some people do that. Some people get so scared their bodies freeze.
I angle my body down and swim after her, grabbing her around the
waist and kicking hard to pull us back up. She's a dead weight in
my arms. When we break the surface, I'm the one who is gasping. I
reach out for the side of the pool, my other arm still wrapped tight
around her.

"What the hell? What happened? Why didn't you grab the side?"

"I wanted to see." She's grinning.

"Wanted to see what?"

"What it felt like. If fear's the biggest problem with learning how
to swim, I figured I'd face that right away and then I could learn faster.
Plus, I knew you'd save me."

"Well, don't do it again."

"Okay. But I was right, wasn't I?"

"About me saving you?"

"And the fear part."

We move to the shallow end and I show her how to coordinate
her breathing and arms for front crawl. After a few minutes of

that, she's using a flutter board and kicking back and forth across the width of the pool with her face in the water. It seems strange to admit, but it's actually nice to spend time with a kid again. It makes me miss my daughter. Despite the age difference between them, there's something very young about Lily. Plus, she isn't very coordinated and keeps swallowing water and coming up sputtering, whereas Zoe is already like a little frog, as comfortable in the water as out. The ache is automatic when I think of her. I repeat the same refrain: *She's safe, she's happy, she's secure. She's better with them than with me.*

Lily's stopped swimming and is looking at me, her head cocked to the side. "Are you okay?"

I shake my head to snap out of it. "Sorry. Still getting used to the time change."

"Oh?"

"Okay, let's do one more thing," I say, taking the flutter board and throwing it to the side. "Lie back. I'll keep my hand close, but I want you to just float."

"I'll sink. You saw me."

"You can float. And I'll be right here, I promise."

Lily lies back in the water and lets her feet float up so her middle sinks, pulling her down. I put my hand under her low back. "Make yourself into a starfish." I realize I'm using the same language I used when I taught Zoe. "Arch your hips up a bit, and just relax. You can move your arms a little. Just gently wave them back and forth."

She does the movement but she's tense, her eyes wide.

"Breathe."

I feel the breath going into her and her body loosens a bit, but all of her earlier playfulness has been lost.

"Close your eyes." Her body slackens a little more. "You have to trust the water. If you relax and don't fight it, you'll float. If you're swimming and you can't touch, you can always do this if you get tired."

Lily breathes out, keeping her eyes closed, but then her hips drop and she starts to sink again. Her eyes shoot open and she wraps her arms around me, clinging to me desperately.

"It's okay." Her grip on me is surprisingly strong. I manage to get her arms untangled. "You can touch here."

"Sorry," Lily says. Her lip starts to quiver like she is about to cry. "It was just this feeling, like the water was pulling me down." She yanks the goggles off and wipes at her eyes. "I'm like the only person in this school who can't swim. Mom said she'd put me in lessons, but I'd have to be with the little kids."

"You did great. It's a process." I look at the clock. "The swim team will be here soon. We should go."

Lily wades to the side and pulls herself out in one easy motion, lithe and strong. There it is again, this disconnect. I spent years being a lifeguard and pulled my fair share of people out of water they shouldn't be in. There's an energy you can feel in a body when it thinks it's going to drown, that fight for survival. I felt it in her in that moment, but not before when she dropped into the deep end. But I don't think it's something you can turn on and off.

"That was so much fun. Thank you!" She's beaming down at me. "That's like the first time ever that I've had fun trying to swim. Maybe, by the summer, I'll actually be able to go to the beach like everyone else."

"Sure you will." She seems so genuinely happy over such a little thing. She's like a shapeshifter. In one moment, she's a kid but then I get these glimpses of someone who is older, not by years but by experience.

I tell her I'm going to swim a couple of quick laps to finish my workout and direct her to a spare towel in my swim bag; of course, she hasn't brought one, but after two laps it feels strange to be swimming with her watching me.

"You make it look so easy," she says when I get to the bench where she's toweling off.

"Well, I've been doing it a long time."

"And your mother was a swimmer, so it's in your genes," she says. I wonder if she notices how my shoulders automatically tense.

"I don't know if that sort of thing can be genetic," I say. "I think it's just practice."

"Did she teach you how to swim? Like before she . . . ?"

"I don't remember." I focus on pulling my clothes out of my swim bag to throw them over my suit.

"That's a cool necklace."

I should have put it in my pants pocket when I took it off, but I didn't know I was going to be swimming with anyone and just tossed it into my bag. She picks it up, and I resist the urge to yank it out of her hands. "Oh, it's two broken hearts. Sad."

"Not broken. Just halved."

"So, who has the other half? Boyfriend?"

"My daughter and my mother."

"Oh." She squints at it. "Oh right, there's writing on here. Your names. Is your daughter's name Zoe?"

I take it out of her hand and slip it over my head, then pull my sweatshirt over it so it's out of sight.

"That's a beautiful name. How old is she?"

"She's almost two," I say. I don't want to talk about Zoe with this girl. She can be fascinated with my mother, but she doesn't get that other part of me.

We finish getting dressed in silence. Lily wraps her hair into a loose knot and stuffs it under her hat. Mine freezes into straws as soon as we get outside. Once again, I am giving her a ride. I can hear myself rationalizing to David already. It's 6:30 in the morning. Am I going to risk her getting pneumonia by walking home?

"You got a bunch of texts," she says as we get into the car. "Sorry, I wouldn't have looked but the phone kept buzzing while you were in the pool."

I slip it out of my pocket and look. There are three texts, all from David.

> Checking in. U ok?

The next two texts are about the missing woman.

> Still nothing on Ramirez.
> State may get involved.

I toss the phone back in my bag without responding and turn on the car.

"I'm sorry," she says as we pull out of the parking lot. "I honestly didn't mean to look. But I didn't know if they were urgent."

"They weren't."

"My mom texts me like that when she *really* needs me to respond. She types three words, hits send, types two more words, hits send. Ugh. So annoying."

She fiddles with the heat but only cool air blasts out.

I turn it back to a reasonable level. "The engine's cold. Give it a minute."

"I saw stuff on the news about that woman. That's who your friend is talking about, right? The woman who disappeared?" she asks after another moment of silence.

"Yeah."

She blows on her hands then stuffs them into her coat. "Is your friend a cop?"

"Yeah."

"Are you?"

"God, no. I could never be a cop."

She turns to look at me. "I always thought that people who went through something like you did, became cops. You know, like to right the wrongs of the world," she says in a fake movie announcer voice.

"Maybe on TV. I don't know if it's that straightforward in real life." She's still looking at me like she wants a better answer. "There's too much to lose. Like, if something goes wrong."

Lily nods, looking thoughtful. "Yeah, that's true. The only cops I know are on TV." She cocks her head. "Is David your boyfriend?"

She must have seen his name on the phone.

"You ask a lot of questions."

"My mom says I'm nosy. But it's the only way to learn stuff. So . . . ?"

"No, he's not."

I'm bracing for more questions but Lily seems done with the conversation. She reaches forward and turns on the radio, fiddling around until she finds a station she likes. I resist the impulse to say something about boundaries.

When we pull up in front of her house, it's dark, though other houses on the street have interior lights on and some people are already out, coffee cups in hand, heading to work.

"Thanks for the lesson. I know I just landed on you but I didn't know how else to find you."

"Your parents did know where you were, right? I can come in and introduce myself to them." She looks at me, confused. "Because I'm an adult who they don't know and I just gave you a swimming lesson and a ride."

Lily rolls her eyes. "They won't care. I told them you were grandma's friend."

"But I'm not."

"Oh my God, it's fine. Besides, my mom won't be back from her shift until eight. My stepfather usually sleeps till seven-thirty. My little sister, Maisy, wakes up like a million times a night, so they sleep late. Next time, okay?"

It's a relief not to have to go in and have a conversation about how I came to meet Lily's grandmother. I'm waiting for her to open the door and get out, but instead, she digs around in her coat pocket and says, "I made you something." She holds out a woven bracelet in her palm. "It's a friendship bracelet." When I don't pick it up, she says, "It's probably dumb," and goes to stuff it back in her pocket.

"No, let me see," I say, a beat late. She holds it out again, more tentative this time, and I take it. "Wow." It's made from different strands of blue and white thread woven into a chevron pattern. "This is really intricate."

"The pattern is meant to symbolize multiple points of connection. I don't know if that's officially what it means, but it's what it means to me. Like you teaching me how to swim, but also the other. We're connected by that. The blue is a symbol of trust, and it's my favorite color. Plus, your eyes are blue, so I thought it would look good. And white is for honesty."

"Wow, you've given this a lot of thought." It comes out sounding snide, which I don't mean it to, but she doesn't seem to notice. "Lily, can I ask, how old are you?"

She rolls her eyes. "Seventeen. I know. Friendship bracelets are for kids."

"I didn't mean that."

"But I like stuff like this. See, I have one too." She pushes her coat sleeve up. I'd noticed the ones she had on each wrist during the lesson, but now she pulls one apart from the others and I can see that it matches mine.

"When did you make these?"

"Last night." She shrugs. "I couldn't sleep. Doing stuff like this helps me chill out."

I run my thumb over the threads. "We used to make these but ours were plastic. This is so much more complex."

"I just thought, I don't know, I thought maybe you'd like it. You don't have to wear it. I know it's more of a kid thing. Probably I should have just made you cookies."

"No. I really like it," I say. I'm about to put it in my pocket but the way she's looking at me, so expectant, makes me slide it onto my wrist. I hold my arm out looking at it. "No one has ever made me a bracelet before." She brightens at this.

"It will tighten a bit when you get it wet. It's not meant to come off. Obviously, you can cut it off whenever, but that's the symbolism." She throws open the door like she's suddenly embarrassed. "Okay. Well, thank you for the lesson. I hope I can see you again, Fiona."

I'm about to ask her why she wants to see me again but I stop myself. Is it just curiosity? A lot of people throughout my life have wanted to get close to me to find out more about what happened to my mother. It's titillating from a distance. Sometimes I'd let them just because it was nice to pretend for a bit that they were genuinely interested in me, but it usually didn't last. It feels different with Lily. She's so open about her interest, but, as she has pointed out, she is also connected to what happened. We are each tethered to a random, violent event that happened years ago, but does that mean we are connected to each other, the way she seems to want us to be? Yesterday, my answer would have been unequivocally no. Now? I look down at the bracelet. This is a gesture of friendship from a strange and probably lonely girl, no more.

At the house she turns and gives a little wave, then lets herself in. As soon as the door closes behind her, I take out my phone and text David back.

You didn't tell me Jason Ward had a kid.

David's answer is immediate, as is my regret in telling him. I can already feel his annoyance if he thinks I'm sniffing around Jason Ward.

??????

The message is followed by the blinking ellipsis but then it disappears. It is too early and too cold to wait around for David's texting indecision. I put the car in drive and am about to pull out when the phone rings.

"Why do you know about Lily Ward?" he asks in lieu of "hello."

"I met her, that's all."

"How?"

I look at the dark house and the bracelet on my wrist, and think about that disconnect feeling, wanting to keep myself separate but also being pulled toward Lily. She didn't ask to be born into this family, and it seems, from the little she's said, that she's punished for it.

"Is it a big deal?"

David sighs. "No. Yes. I don't know yet." His voice has changed. There's an edge that wasn't there before.

I know how he's going to react but there's no avoiding it. I'm not going to hide things from him. "I met Carole Dunn, yesterday, which was your idea. Her granddaughter was there. I gave her a swimming lesson this morning—"

"Why?!"

"Long story. Doesn't matter."

David doesn't say anything. I can hear the police station behind him, then it gets quieter. He's stepped into the corridor now. "So, you're hanging around with Lily Ward?"

"I'm not— Do you know her or something?"

"She's a Ward. Of course I know her."

I wonder what it would be like to be that young and be known by the police, even if you hadn't done anything.

"Is this actually a big deal, or is it just because of her dad?" I'm getting defensive and I don't know why. I don't owe this girl anything.

"I don't think you should be spending time with—"

"David, she's a kid."

"Not just any kid."

"It happened. It's done, so don't lecture me. I gave her a ride home last night and then she showed up at the pool this morning."

"So you send her away. I mean, Jesus, Fi—"

"I'm not going to see her again."

"You sure about that?" he asks and I don't answer. "I'm just pointing out the obvious. You're the one who's spending time—"

"Her grandmother didn't know anything. Lily probably knows even less. No one knows anything except the guy who's dead."

"Well, her father's still a suspect in our current investigation, so I'd appreciate if you weren't hanging out with the family. This doesn't need to get any more complicated."

The wall. The wall is roaring up in front of me.

"I gotta go," I say, and hang up before he can respond. I throw the phone on the floor of the Jeep. A movement outside catches my attention. I look at the house in time to see a curtain in the upstairs window drop back into place from where it was being held back. The phone begins to vibrate into the floor mat but I turn the radio up so I don't have to hear the insistent buzzing of David's need to fix something that can't be fixed.

CHAPTER 14

JASON

2003

Late August brought out the college kids. Maybe it was knowing the end of summer was near, or it was the buildup of all those long days of heat, the lack of boundaries, sun on skin for hours and hours. The St. Rose Festival only compounded the energy, bringing even more people to the tiny town with their enormous RVs. The lake was filled with roaring powerboats, always being driven by some bare-chested bro. Music blared and their shouts to each other carried across the water like the lake was their private playground.

What had happened at McGregor's had made it clear: no matter how invisible he thought he was, Jason was still marked. Who was that man in the bar who'd grabbed him from behind? He'd never properly seen his face. He was one of many in that town who were just waiting for the moment to get their shot in. It wasn't just them—teachers, cops, social workers, even the priest of his mother's church, not that she ever went. None of these people ever gave a damn about him before his dad was arrested, but after, they watched and waited for him to act out, to get violent. To become his father.

It had been a few days since the fight and he hadn't been able to stop thinking about Sam. She'd suggested they hang out. She'd made the opening and like a fucking idiot, he'd walked right past it. Now she was going back to college. Or maybe she'd changed her mind. If her friends knew, they'd try to talk her out of it. Each day, he swung between these thoughts, moving between hope, despair, and anger.

Today, even though he knew he should point his boat in the opposite direction, he was pulled toward the crowds and the noise of the festival. He wasn't allowed to be a part of this, that was what he'd grown up believing. But why not? He had as much right to be there as the summer people—more even—so instead of heading west, he went east toward St. Rose. Plus, maybe Sam would be there. He'd wait until it got a bit later, and then he'd go in and see if he could find her.

He was far out on the lake so the noises coming from the midway and the beer tent were muted. He had his prop fishing rod set up as usual and was slipping into late afternoon drowsiness when he looked up and saw one of the powerboats heading straight for him. The kid at the wheel was turned backward talking to two girls in bikinis who were lounging behind him. He must have been mid-story, gesturing wildly with the hand holding the beer while his other hand barely rested on the steering wheel. They were approaching too fast for Jason to get his boat started and move out of the way. He stood up and braced himself to jump into the water. In the back of the powerboat were two other guys, also bare-chested and holding beers, and it was one of them who saw him and yelled. The boat was four hundred feet away and closing the gap quickly. The driver swerved into a sharp turn with the roar of the boat's engine mixing with the screams of the passengers. The wave sent Jason's boat rocking dangerously and he instinctively dropped down, keeping his weight low to prevent it from flipping.

The boat sped away and then he heard the shouts of a girl thrown into the water. She was yelling something at him and pointing and that's when he saw the second person. It was one of the guys from the back. He was flailing in the water and kept going under. The girl swam toward the guy, but as soon as she got close, he grabbed her and started to pull her down with him. Instinctively, Jason started his boat and moved toward them, but then he stopped. They were less than ten feet away now. It was hard to make out whose arm was whose but then the girl's head surfaced and she looked right at him. Her eyes were huge. She knew she was going to die. Right in that second when her eyes met his, he saw her understand what was about to happen. And he was going to watch.

Then, he heard the powerboat coming back. He turned around and sped away in the opposite direction, letting the kids' cries get drowned out by his engine and the *smack, smack, smack* of his little boat's nose lifting out of the water and slamming back into it.

Every decision Jason had ever made was to cultivate invisibility, but there was a price to that too. He could disappear like a stone into water and no one would miss him. But what if he didn't? Sam had seen him because he'd let her. That girl in the water saw him too, and she begged for his help. This was a new feeling. It was terrifying, exhilarating, having that kind of power. It was a high like nothing he'd ever felt. He wanted to feel it again.

Jason went farther out into the lake than he had gone before, so far out that he couldn't see the land. It gave him a giddy unmoored feeling how infinitely small he was in the vastness of this water and sky. What he did, what he didn't do, who he was, who he wasn't, maybe none of it mattered. It certainly didn't to the lake. It was a new kind of freedom.

His gas gauge was dangerously low so he turned around and headed straight for St. Rose. The marina was teeming with boats, and the old habits kicked in. Instinctively, he pulled his baseball cap lower and ducked his head as he got close, but then he thought about those kids in the water. That power. Fuck these people, he thought. They didn't get to decide what he did anymore.

He had twenty bucks in his wallet, which was just enough to get him a half tank of gas and a couple of cheap beers from the marina store. Refueled, he took the boat back out into the water. After he'd gone far enough that the shore was a blur, he killed the engine and cracked open the first beer. It was as good as expected. By the time he moved on to the second beer, his boat had drifted past the town and he could see the peninsula that was the state park.

He had just dozed off when he heard voices. Drowsily, he opened his eyes and saw a canoe coming toward him. Two men sat on each end with three young kids in puffy life vests between them. The man in the front nodded as they moved past him, but when Jason made eye contact with the man in the back, he froze. It was Ben Green, the survivor—the one who had identified his father and put him in jail. The shock was like a jolt of electricity in his gut. He immediately looked away but the man hadn't reacted. He hadn't recognized him. Of course—Jason had been only thirteen when they were in a courtroom together, so Ben Green didn't know what he looked like now.

The canoe passed him, heading for the shore. Jason watched it go and when it was a little way away, Ben turned around and looked at him again. From this angle, the sun wouldn't be blinding him as much. Their eyes met again and this time . . . something passed between them. Jason saw it in the way Ben suddenly went still.

No. There's no way he could recognize him. Eight years had passed since he'd sat in that courtroom. And yet . . .

All the drowsiness of a moment ago was gone. When the canoe was far enough past him, he lowered his anchor into the water and set up his fishing rod. The sun was almost below the horizon. To the people on the shore, he'd just be the silhouette of a man doing a little evening fishing. The shoreline was dotted with cottages, some of which looked like they'd been there for decades. He watched as the canoe made its way to the largest one. It was too far to see faces, but he could tell there were a lot of people. Indistinct voices rang out over the water. Somewhere, a dog barked.

Jason thought back to what he knew about the case. Ben Green and Ana Lukas had been staying at Ben's family cottage—that cottage straight ahead of him, he assumed—on the night his father picked them up. If anyone had ever asked, and no one did, Jason would have denied that he was looking for the Greens, but like all the people from his father's case, their presence so close to his home was a gnawing awareness. It was one of the reasons, though certainly not the only one, that he avoided St. Rose and had never gone to the state park. He never drove on the road where his father picked them up or on the one where he had tried to kill Ben Green. These places had taken too much from him already. But now? *I've found you,* he thought. He'd found the family cottage and there they all were, oblivious to the lone man out on the water watching them.

His mother's response to any of his complaints growing up was to blame his father. Why they lived in a trailer. Why she had to keep driving the same piece of shit car. Why she couldn't keep a job and they had to live on her disability checks and handouts. But they hadn't lived in a trailer when his dad had been around. He'd had a bike and video games and cable. He'd had a normal life. When his father was arrested and charged, he and his mother had lost all of that. And they hadn't done a damned thing to deserve it.

Jason was about to pull up the anchor and head back, when Ben Green came and stood at the end of the dock. Jason's hand hovered over the throttle. The two men faced each other across the expanse of water. Neither wanted the other in his life, but it didn't matter. It would never change. They were locked together forever.

CHAPTER 15

FIONA

2003

Later, after her father had moved them away, first to Toronto and then to Vancouver, putting more and more distance between them and St. Rose, Fiona would lie in her new bed remembering this night the summer she was twelve and wondering if Jason Ward had found them because she agreed to watch the fireworks from Mikey Lonergan's boat.

The St. Rose Festival was a three-day event that marked the end of the summer season and the town was packed. On one end of Lake Street was the town hall with the farmers market in front. On the other end was the large stage with the sprawling beer tent beside it. Between these, restaurants expanded their outdoor seating; there were food trucks, an art market, carnival rides, and games where you could win giant stuffed bears or Pokémon characters. For three magical days, the quaint town transformed into something wonderfully unrecognizable.

At least it would have been wonderful, except she and David hadn't been able to escape her gaggle of younger cousins. Her aunts and uncles seemed to think because they were now legally old enough to babysit, that they actually wanted to. It's not that she disliked her cousins, but there were seven of them, and they were all loud and constantly arguing and definitely not who she wanted to spend her precious final days of the summer with. They ranged in age from four to eight, with the exception of Jaimie who was ten. She was the worst of them because she thought she should be included in everything Fiona and David did, which meant they had to do a lot of sneaking around to avoid her.

Tonight, her aunts, uncles, cousins, and grandparents had all gone into town for the closing night's fireworks, and for some reason—he refused to say why and the tone of his voice when she begged made it clear it wasn't up for discussion—her dad had given strict instructions that she stay at the cottage with Aunt Charlotte and the baby. It was totally unfair since he knew how much she loved the fireworks and everyone else was going. Why he had suddenly decided this, he would not say. He had gone back to their apartment because he had to work the next day. He always got edgy around the anniversary of her mom's death, which was in a few days, so she put it down to that. David stayed with her out of sympathy. They were lying on the floating dock when Mikey Lonergan paddled up to them in a beat-up canoe.

"Where'd you get that thing?" David asked.

"Found it. Someone was throwing it out," Mikey said, sounding incredulous. "Those rich assholes in Bonasera Bay don't know how to patch a simple hole."

"Looks like it needed more than just a patch," David said.

"Who cares," Mikey said. "It's mine now. It got me here, didn't it?"

David always said the Lonergans weren't to be trusted. He'd heard that from his dad who'd pulled over Mikey's older brothers and maybe even his father for drunk driving on more than one occasion. But that wasn't Mikey's fault, Fiona thought. He seemed okay.

"What's up, Fiona?" Mikey asked. He smiled at her. He was wiry and shorter than she was, even though he was fourteen, and he was sporting the meager beginnings of a mustache, which he'd reach up and touch with his finger every few minutes, as if checking to see that it was still there. Aside from that, he was actually kind of sweet-looking and he'd always been nice to her. "You guys want to go for a ride?"

David spoke first. "Nothing personal, but that thing doesn't look like it'll float with three people in it. Besides, we've got canoes here." He indicated the rack of canoes and kayaks sitting beside the boathouse.

Mikey shrugged. Maybe he hadn't expected them to say yes. "I'm going to watch the fireworks from the lake. I'll be right underneath them."

"Is that safe?" Fiona asked and then immediately regretted it. That probably sounded lame.

He grinned. "Safe enough. It'll be worth it."

She looked at David but couldn't tell what he was thinking. "We can get back before they do," she said. "There's always so much traffic."

"What about your aunt?" David asked.

Fiona shrugged. "She's with the baby. She won't even notice." She stood up unsteadily as the dock moved below her.

"Come on, Connor," Mikey said. "Stop being such a pussy."

"I'm not—" But David bit back the rest of his reply and stood too. They threw the empty soda bottles and the chip wrappers into the canoe and carefully got in. As soon as they did, more water started leaking through the patches. There was only one paddle so Mikey sat in the back with Fiona in the middle and David in front. He tossed the bucket to David and said, "Make yourself useful."

Mikey paddled them west. By land, it was three miles from their cottages to St. Rose but that was because of the windy road. On the water, it was just over one mile so it didn't take long for them to start hearing the noise from the festival. A band was playing; it sounded like one of the eighties tribute bands that festivals like this attracted. Under the music there was the hum of voices, the grinding of the rides, and screams of excitement.

Mikey reached into his backpack and pulled out a plastic bottle. He held it out to Fiona. "My own concoction," he said. She reached for the bottle and sniffed it. It smelled like orange. She put her lips to the bottle and took a little sip, then immediately coughed and spat it out.

"Hey, don't waste it," Mikey said, but he was smiling at her. He grabbed the bottle, tilted his head back, and took a big gulp. "Connor, you want?"

She could see the moment of indecision on David's face, then he reached for the bottle and took a slug. He coughed a bit but covered it pretty well. "What is that, gasoline?"

"Antifreeze," Mikey said.

"Fuck off." David sounded different around Mikey, like he was trying to be tough.

"Is it actually antifreeze?" Fiona asked. "Isn't that poisonous?"

"Relax," Mikey said, taking another sip. "It's just whiskey and vodka. I put a shot of some kind of orange-flavored shit in there too to try to make it taste better. I had to improvise." He grinned again and waved the bottle in front of Fiona but it was obvious that he didn't think she was going to drink it.

She grabbed it, tilted her head back like the guys had, and took a sip. It made her eyes water, but she managed not to spit it out this time. It burned in her throat all the way down, but once she'd swallowed the burning changed to a warming feeling.

They passed the bottle back and forth drinking with determination. Mikey had the most. She was trying to keep her sips small and hoped it wasn't obvious. She had a feeling David might be doing the same. When they finished it, Mikey tossed it overboard.

"Hey—" David said.

"Your dad going to arrest me for littering?" Mikey said.

Fiona thought about trying to reach for the bottle but she might rock the canoe and tip it over. Soon the bottle filled and disappeared under the surface. "All gone," Mikey said, then he looked at her. "I can't be caught with that or my dad'll beat the shit out of me." He sounded kind of sheepish saying it. She figured he was telling the truth. She'd seen him before with a black eye. David said he was always getting into fights at school, usually with people who were bigger than him, but he'd also told her that the police had gone to the Lonergans' place more than once for fights and parties that had gotten out of control. She couldn't imagine living in that kind of chaos. No wonder Mikey wanted to have his own boat and spend time out here on the lake.

The last traces of light were leaving the sky and soon it would be dark enough for the fireworks to start. Would her grandparents smell the alcohol on her breath? She couldn't tell if she was drunk. She didn't feel dizzy or sick, but when she turned her head quickly, there was a delayed feeling like the picture wasn't quite lining up with the sound.

"You haven't actually seen that though," David was saying.

She'd tuned out of their conversation. "Seen what?" she asked.

"Ghost ships," Mikey said. "There's a whole exhibit about them in the town hall. Didn't you see it?"

The historical society always put on a display in the town hall but Fiona figured it was just boring pictures of old buildings. She was surprised Mikey had gone in.

"I think all that history stuff is cool," he said. "You know the bottom of the lake is covered with shipwrecks, right?" Fiona looked down.

In the distance, the lights of the town reflected off the surface, but the water around them was black. They were pretty far out from the shore. She'd been out in the deep parts of the lake lots of times in the boat with her grandpa and her dad, and she and David had done some canoeing, but she'd never been out at night, or in such a rickety canoe.

"Do you think they're below us?" she asked. She imagined the hands of long-drowned sailors reaching up from below them and pulled her hand out of the water quickly.

"Any ship that sank would've been way out in the shipping channel," David said. "And they definitely didn't leave behind ghosts."

"They're real," Mikey said. "There's proof."

"What proof?"

"Just because you never seen anything doesn't mean it isn't true," Mikey said. "They had pictures."

"Since when can you take a picture of a ghost?" David's voice was rising a bit like he was a little less sure of himself.

Mikey was quiet for a moment and it seemed he was going to let it go, but then he said, "I saw something once. I didn't know what it was when I seen it. But now, I think it was the burning boat of Jenny Glick."

"Who's Jenny Glick?" Fiona asked.

"You know those islands off the end of the park? You can see them from the beach."

Fiona nodded. They didn't ever go to the big beach in the state park, but she'd noticed a cluster of islands about half a mile off the tip of the peninsula. Most of them looked pretty small, but maybe she'd just been too far away, having only seen them from a canoe.

"The largest one is Smuggler's Point," Mikey said. "It's where rum runners used to hide their booze if they thought they were going to get caught by the cops or the gangs."

She knew dimly about Prohibition and people crossing from Canada to sell illegal alcohol, but she'd never been very interested in it.

"Jenny Glick's husband was a rum runner, but he disappeared."

"Disappeared?" she asked.

"Yeah, he got killed probably. They were real poor. Had a few kids. One night, she must have been real desperate, so she borrows a boat and takes the booze he'd made and crosses over to here. She took her kid with her too."

"Why?"

Mikey shrugged. "It was a baby. She left the others behind. So, when she gets close one of the gangs must have spotted her and so she goes and hides on Smuggler's Point."

"How would she even get to it?" David asked. He sounded doubtful but also like he was getting caught up in the story. "People who try to boat around those islands destroy their hulls because of all the underwater rocks. There's signs about it on the beach."

"Well, I guess she didn't exactly have a lot of choice," Mikey said. "It was either hide there or get shot by the gangs."

"How do you know all this?" Fiona asked.

Mikey shrugged again. "Everyone knows this story. Plus, it was in the exhibit. So, she goes to Smuggler's Point. There's this big cave on it—that's probably where she and her baby woulda hid. But, they followed her."

"They killed her?" she asked.

"Worse. They got her boat. Lit it on fire and set it adrift."

"What happened to her and the baby?"

"No one knows. She was left on that island and never seen again, but people have said that if you go there, you can hear a baby crying inside the cave. And, some nights, people have seen her burning boat."

"Bullshit," David said. "Those're just stories."

"It's real. I saw it," Mikey said. For a second, he sounded like a little kid, all attempts at machismo gone. "That's what I'm telling you. I saw something once. I didn't understand it at the time but now I know. It was Jenny Glick's burning boat."

There was a hissing sound and a firework exploded right over their heads. Fiona let out a shriek and instinctively ducked, which rocked the canoe. Mikey laughed. "Holy shit, don't sink us."

"Sorry." Cautiously, she turned back to face him. "What did you see?"

"I was out one night with my dad in his boat. Before he sold it. It was late, like October or something, and there was all this fog. We'd got disoriented and ended up close to those islands. I was looking into the fog trying to see where the hell we were. My dad was pissed because he'd already promised the boat to someone and didn't want to get it damaged on the rocks. Anyway, so I was looking into the fog and all of a sudden, I saw this movement. Like flickering."

"Fire," Fiona said.

"Yeah. But not orange or red or whatever. It was gray, like almost the same color as the fog."

"Then how'd you see it?" David asked.

"'Cause it was moving." Mikey reached his hand out into the darkness and Fiona followed his gaze, trying to imagine what it looked like. "It was just for a second, but I saw it. The tip of a boat and that flickering, and then I blinked and it was just regular fog again. That was the ghost of Jenny Glick's boat."

BOOM. Another firework exploded over their heads. Fiona felt her heart leap but she managed to keep herself from ducking again. She tilted her head back and watched the sparks fly outward and then disappear. Another firework exploded into purple sparks that turned orange and then yellow as they expanded. From the shore, she could hear people cheering. Could they see their small boat out on the water?

They'd drifted farther out than she'd realized. She thought again about those drowned sailors far below, but then another firework went off and she tilted her head back up to watch. Better to focus on that. Her body felt heavy but she also knew that all her senses were vividly alive in a way they hadn't ever been before. She could still taste the alcohol. She could smell the burned chemicals of the fireworks and under that, the briny smell of the lake. And Mikey had a smell too—the sharpness of body odor and floral laundry soap, different from David's smell. She felt like all of her skin was a giant sensor. The smell of these boys in the canoe with her, the heat from their bodies. The distant sounds from the festival. Thousands of conversations, of exclamations of wonder. And beyond that, the endless lapping of the lake on the shore.

David turned around and touched her arm. "You okay?" She nodded. He was speaking quietly, like he didn't want Mikey to hear.

"How long would it take to cross the lake to Canada?" she asked.

"Why?" Mikey asked. "You want to go?"

"No," she said. "I was thinking about Jenny Glick. Heading out all alone with just her baby. I wonder how long it took her?"

"Wouldn't take that long in a motorboat," David said. "A few hours, maybe?"

Fiona glanced back at Mikey. He was looking out toward the dark part of the lake, like he was considering whether his canoe could make it.

"I was thinking I'd like to find some of those shipwrecks," he said. "I bet there's treasure."

"They weren't pirates," David said.

She didn't understand why he was being pissy with Mikey. He was nice enough to take them out on his boat after all. "My mom swam across the lake when she was fifteen. She's the youngest person ever to do it."

"No shit," Mikey said. "How long'd it take her?"

"Twenty-three hours and fourteen minutes," Fiona said. "My grandpa stayed in a boat beside her, but she swam the whole way without stopping. She wasn't even allowed to touch the boat. Like, she could eat and drink, but he had to pass the food to her. There's all these rules."

"That's awesome." Mikey sounded genuinely impressed. It was nice to be able to tell somebody something about her mom and not have it be about her death. Maybe it was being out here. Anytime she went far out into the lake, she thought about her mother and what that swim must have been like, trying to imagine how it felt to be so far out that you couldn't see land. To know you just had to keep swimming and trust that the other shore would appear.

"She got these really bad leg cramps and it was the middle of the night and she started getting disoriented. So, Grandpa got in and swam with her for a couple of hours until she started to feel better. One of his friends drove the boat."

"Could you do it?" Mikey asked. Before she could answer, he said, "I bet you could." He sounded like he really believed it too. She'd never thought about it before, but maybe she could.

"You could get your grandpa to help you," Mikey said.

"No, he doesn't swim anymore."

"Why not?"

"He . . ."

How to explain Grandpa Lukas to these boys. Even David, who knew her dad's half of the family like his own, had never met her other grandparents. They'd moved to Connecticut a year after her mother died. True her grandpa had suffered a stroke, but it was more than that. It was that he'd gone inside himself and not come back out. It made Fiona think of a snail that had sucked itself back into its shell. She envied her grandpa that hiding place; a way to isolate yourself in a tiny invisible room even while surrounded by people. Grandma Lukas, on the other hand, was harder to pinpoint. She did the things she was supposed to do with her granddaughter; she would take her for ice cream and buy her books, always books, and ask about school, but Fiona couldn't help feeling that the moment she wasn't standing in front of her, her grandma wasn't aware she existed. Maybe it was the way she'd always say, "Oh, Fiona," like she'd just remembered her again whenever she and her dad would arrive for their annual visit.

She realized that she'd stopped talking but neither boy had said anything.

"Uh, my grandpa just doesn't want to swim anymore. They moved to New Haven. But they're coming back this week."

They were coming back for the ten-year anniversary of her mother's death, which was going to be marked with a memorial. That was probably another reason why her dad was on edge. Her grandmother was a professor at Yale, and they were going to announce a scholarship. This memorial, and more importantly for Grandma Green, the details of the dinner she was hosting before the ceremony, had been the topic of much conversation for the past month.

The fireworks had stopped, though the show couldn't be over yet. Far away, the band started playing their cover of an Aerosmith song she couldn't remember the name of. She closed her eyes. Songs like this made her think of her dad. He always had the car radio on the classic rock station, which she usually complained about to no avail. He probably would have liked this band.

"So, I wanted to tell you," Mikey was speaking quietly so both she and David turned back to him. "My brother works at this bar." Mikey had a collection of older brothers, she was never sure how many. In his stories it was always, "my brother this" and "my brother that," and most of it sounded pretty unlikely. "And the guy who killed your mom—"

She took a breath in. "What the fuck, Lonergan?" David said. Mikey had always been fascinated by the story and would press for morbid details, which was another reason why David didn't like him.

"He's in prison," she said.

"No, not him. His son. He's like twenty or something."

Fiona thought about what she knew about *him.* He'd had a son, she had been told that. But of course, that boy wouldn't stay a child forever.

"My brother saw him in his bar—"

"What bar?" David asked.

"The one he works at. I don't know what it's called. It's in St. Thomas."

"Well, how'd he know it was him?"

"'Cause he asked him, and he said he was."

"It could be someone else just messing around."

"It was HIM. Fuck, Connor. I'm telling her because she should know."

"Did he do something?" she asked Mikey. She wanted David to stop interrupting.

"He started a huge fight. He had a knife— What if it was the one his dad had—?"

"That'd be in evidence—" David said.

"But my brothers stopped him. And they got his knife. Chris showed me."

"You should turn it in," David said.

"No way. We're keeping it. We got it fair and square—"

A series of fireworks went off—*BANG-BANG-BANG*—behind them now instead of above. She looked at the shore, so far away now.

David snorted. "The police are watching him. He can't do anything."

"They are?" Fiona asked.

David turned all the way around in his seat to face her, causing the canoe to rock. "Well, I just figure. Yeah. Probably."

"But you don't know that," Mikey said. "Just 'cause your dad's a cop. Like he'd even tell you."

"I know stuff," David growled. "A lot more than you do."

"The police can't do anything unless he actually does something, and by then it'll be too late." Mikey looked at Fiona. "That's why I wanted to warn you," then, to David, "My dad says the cops here are f-ing useless."

"What's he know?"

"Come on, you guys." But they were back to ignoring her.

"They couldn't even find her mom. That's a pretty major fuckup if you ask me," Mikey said.

"Well, we didn't ask you. You don't know anything about that case. The FBI couldn't find her either—"

"The FBI had to come in because the police here can't do shit—"

"It was a national case, dickhead. There was a whole task force —"

"STOP!" The canoe was swaying side to side as both boys were half off their seats. If they kept up, the canoe would tip and they'd have to swim back. *BANG*. Another firework. They must be heading into the grand finale she thought, which meant her grandparents would be back soon.

"We have to go back," she said. "Now."

"Fi—" David reached out to her but she yanked her arm back, which made the canoe sway even more. She would not cry. She clenched her teeth together, hard.

David turned to face forward, moving gingerly this time. He took the bucket and started scooping while Mikey began to turn them in the direction of home.

This huge lake and here they were, three kids in a beat-up canoe floating in utter darkness. She was breathing hard. They all were. She closed her eyes and listened to the dipping of the paddle in and out of the water. Mikey was trying to paddle quickly and he kept hitting the sides of the canoe, but they were moving now, the music and the *pop-pop-pop* of fireworks getting farther away.

The son of *him* was here and had been this whole time? She had assumed the wife and child had moved away. Why would they stay? Were they still living in that house? Did Mikey know? She wanted to ask him more but she didn't want to do it with David around. Mikey was right; David didn't really know any more than the rest of them, he just got possessive about it whenever it came up around other kids. It had happened before. Was he trying to protect her, or was he protecting his dad?

It was a relief when she saw the light from their cottage, but then Mikey stopped paddling. Fiona turned back to him to ask but he held his finger to his lips. He nodded to the left, toward the open part of the lake. There, not a hundred feet from them, was a motorboat. It had no lights on and was just floating, silent and dark, straight out from their cottage. She squinted into the darkness. Someone was in the boat. All she could make out was a silhouette—a man in a baseball cap sitting very still. Tentatively, Mikey put the paddle back in the water and tried to steer them farther away but they were moving and it was hard to change their course.

They floated right past the boat. The man watched them glide past, but he didn't say anything. He had to have seen them. Did he hear them arguing too? They'd been much farther away but the boy's voices had been raised and sound traveled differently over water.

When they were past him, Mikey started paddling again and she risked a look back. The person in the boat was standing now. He could catch up to them in seconds, if he wanted to, but whoever it was didn't move. At last, Mikey brought them to the dock. He was breathing heavily and she could see the sweat on his face glistening in the outdoor lights.

David got out first and then held the canoe so she could climb out.

"Where are you going to go now?" she asked Mikey when he didn't get out of the canoe. As far as she knew, his family didn't have a cottage and lived outside town.

"I want to see who that was."

"Probably just some guy watching the fireworks," David said.

"Out here? No way. And he was facing your cottages."

"You don't know that—"

"It's fucking weird," Mikey said, ignoring David. "Dude just sitting there like that. Creeping up on us."

"He wasn't creeping," David said. "We floated near him."

"I'm telling you, Connor, I got a sense for these things. That dude is off."

"Oh, you've got a sense? What does that even mean? You're going to go challenge him in your beat-up canoe—"

"Come on you guys," she said again, "I need to get inside before my aunt realizes we snuck out."

Mikey pushed off the dock and started floating away.

"Hey," she called after him, "what's the son's name?"

"You don't know?"

"My family doesn't tell me anything."

She'd been trying to remember ever since Mikey had told her about the fight in the bar but realized she didn't know.

"It's Jason," Mikey said. "Jason Ward."

CHAPTER 16

JASON

2003

On Monday morning when Jason arrived at work, the St. Rose police car was already there. Police Chief Connor himself, what an honor, he thought. He watched as the man hauled his bulky frame up out of his cruiser, the effort showing on his face. When he'd testified in court eight years ago, he'd been broad-shouldered and towered over those around him—a man who was used to controlling a room. Now that muscle had gone soft and sagged over his belt, which he hitched up as he stood, gun and handcuffs barely visible. Two of the guys in the shop were watching him but trying to make it look like they weren't. Jason saw them step farther in so they were hidden by the car on the lift.

"Your car need some work, Chief?" he asked when he got close enough that no one else would hear the conversation. "I thought you guys had people who did that."

"Morning, Jason," the chief said. "Just thought I'd see how you were doing."

"Doing fine," Jason said.

"Heard you had a little altercation at a bar last week. Some of the guys giving you trouble?"

"I didn't think St. Thomas was in your jurisdiction."

"Our departments talk. Professional courtesy. Don't want the trouble from one town to spread into the other."

"Right."

"So, you've taken up fishing."

"That's allowed, far as I know."

"You got a license for that boat?"

"I figure you already know the answer to that."

The chief looked off toward the silent shop and ran his tongue over his teeth. "Come on, kid," he said. "Don't make trouble for you and your mom."

Jason felt the muscles in his back and shoulders contract. He took a breath and held himself still. Chief Connor looked back at him. His eyes were bloodshot. That was another change.

"Just a little tip," he said. "The fishing's better further west from where you've been doing it."

He got in his car and drove away. Jason stayed where he was until the car disappeared around the corner. He spat onto the parking lot to get the acid out of his mouth. Inside the shop, the music turned back on.

Just a reminder that we will always be watching you.

But unlike other times when a cop or some drunk asshole decided to remind him who he was, Jason didn't feel himself shrinking back into his invisibility. Ever since those kids in the water, he'd changed. How far would the change go? There was only one way to know. So, he went back to St. Rose.

He had to wait a few days, then toward the end of the week, the shop was quiet and he took the afternoon when it was offered. He was in his boat within an hour. He decided to have his lunch in St. Rose.

Conveniently, he found a bench in a shady spot right across from the police station. He watched the officers coming and going. He knew most of them, not personally, but he knew their names. Just like they knew his. It was the same with the St. Thomas department. It was good to keep track. Information like that might come in handy.

After he got tired of sitting, he bought a chocolate bar and a couple cans of beer, went back out onto the water and headed east. He stayed far enough out so he wouldn't attract attention. When he got near the Greens' cottage, he killed the motor, set up his fishing pole, and cracked open the beer. It was hard to see from this distance but he didn't want to go closer, not yet. And what was he looking for exactly? He didn't know yet. Maybe it was just to know they couldn't hide from him. He had spent his life hiding because of them, being ashamed of who he was: *son of.* To be defined by your father's actions, what a cliché.

When Jason was younger, he filled his hours with books. They only had one television that got three channels, and he couldn't even watch those if his mother was home. She always had to fill the trailer with the noise from her shows. So, Jason would lock himself in his room and get lost in a story and for that time, he could escape being *son of.* Detective stories, Westerns, classics set in Medieval Europe or Victorian England or Colonial Africa—he read them all. Fathers and sons, fathers and sons. The son must impress the father. The son must avenge the father. And of course, the son must surpass the father. But how does he do this? Could he do what his father did? Was it inside him too, needing only to be nurtured into rising? He thought about how it felt to watch those two kids struggle in the water. In that moment, he had a say in whether they lived or died. He'd like to feel that power again, but what if it was more than he could handle?

Am I here watching this family for my father, or for me, he wondered.

He didn't know. That bothered him.

The sun was making him drowsy and he'd drifted past the Greens' cottage. He scooped up some water to splash on his face. He was thirsty too. The chocolate and beer were long gone. He'd just decided to head back when he saw a canoe leaving their little dock and going toward the state park. He couldn't be sure, but it looked like two kids were in it. A boy and a girl. They looked like young teenagers. Were they the same ones he'd seen the night of the fireworks? Could the girl be Ben Green's kid?

He let them get well ahead then started to follow. When he saw them again, they were following the shoreline of the park, then they started heading for a little group of islands about a half mile off the shore. Buoys bobbed in the water warning boaters about underwater rocks. He watched as the canoe passed the warnings and went into the cluster of islands. He couldn't follow them in a motorboat, but he could get to the other side and catch up to them when they came out. He started navigating his boat around the outside perimeter. Looking between two small islands into the center area he saw the canoe. The girl was pointing at the largest island on the far side but they didn't go closer. Then, after a few moments, they turned the canoe around and started paddling back the way they'd come.

He was low on gas, his stomach was growling, and home was a long way away. As he sped away from the islands, he turned and looked at the large one on the end that they'd been pointing at. Maybe it was the angle, or maybe it was the hours of sun playing tricks on his mind, but it hit him: this was his first snow globe, in real life. It felt like a sign. He would gas up and get some food, and then he would come back and learn for himself why that island was so special.

CHAPTER 17

FIONA

Now

David texts me later. Sorry if I overstepped about Ward girl. Drink tonight?

I wait until it's late and then text back an apology and say I fell asleep. I don't want to fight with him, I really don't. I need him, but I was wrong to think that he could help me with this. David's world is black and white, right and wrong. There's something too narrow about that thinking. I don't even know precisely what I'm looking for, but being back here, immersing myself in this place, I feel like the answer is here if I can figure out where to look. The only concrete thing I can think to do is talk to Jason Ward to find out what his father told him, but David's already made it clear he won't help with that.

The next morning, when I finish swimming, there is a paper bag sitting on top of my gym bag. I do a quick scan of the bleachers and the deck but there's no one else in the pool except for a man swimming in the far lane. I open it and pull out a stack of papers held together with an elastic. They're folded so I can't see what's on them, but tucked into the top of the stack is a note:

*Fiona, I know you wanted to know him. I did too. Maybe these will help.
xo Lily*

Her writing is looping, girlish. It reminds me of notes I used to pass in middle school. I know I should wait until I'm in my car to open this but I can't resist. I remove the elastic and unfold the papers.

Samantha,

You say your friends call you Sam, but that's a man's name and I just can't bring myself to address a young woman—

I flip over the page and scan to the bottom.

Most sincerely yours, Edward J. Ward

I almost drop them all. Handwritten letters from Eddie Ward. Who is Samantha? Where did Lily get these? Even just reading a few lines my response is physical. A rush of heat. Acid in the stomach. I don't want to read more, to ingest more of his words, but I can't resist.

I scramble to gather my stuff, throw my clothes on over my bathing suit, and rush out to the freezing car. I'm expecting Lily to be waiting for me, wanting to see my reaction to her package, but there's no sign of her. As soon as I'm in the driver's seat, I unfold the letters and start reading.

Samantha,

You say your friends call you Sam, but that's a man's name and I just can't bring myself to address a young woman that way. I don't get many opportunities to talk to women in this place and I take a real pleasure in knowing that a beautiful woman like you is taking an interest in me. How do I know you are beautiful, Samantha? I can feel it in your writing. I am talking about inner beauty—the beauty of the soul. That is something that lifts off the pages you sent and goes right inside me.

My eyes are moving quickly over the pages, as I jump from one letter to the next. They're dated and seem to start in 2006 and go for about nine years, but they aren't in order. On my first quick glance through, I can't tell who Samantha is. Some young woman who was writing to Eddie Ward in prison, but why? Then I find it:

Samantha,

You have made me a grandfather. You have given me a gift in this child. Lily. A flower. Her name means innocence and beauty. In the Bible, lilies are meant to represent Mary's purity. You must save these letters so someday she will know me. My son may have abandoned her—it does not surprise me, he has abandoned me, too—but I will not. I can be this child's grandfather <u>and</u> her father if you will let me.

Lily's mother wrote letters for nine years to Eddie Ward. Nothing I read answers why. Some people are drawn to prisoners, especially violent ones. Lily said her parents separated before she was born, but did her mother want a relationship with Eddie Ward for her daughter's sake, or for her own? I don't know what she wrote to him, the letters are all his responses, and scanning them, he seems to talk mainly about himself. Each is multiple pages, single-spaced. The writing is compact, the pen ground into the paper.

Samantha,

So much time passed between your last letter and the one before that I began to think you had forgotten me, but then this evening when mail call came, there it was. You did not address the delay, though I wish you had. No matter. I forgive you. Time for you is not what it is for me in here. You have a child to keep your days filled, while I have only the numbing routine, the slight changes of light outside my small window are the only way I have to track the passage of days.

Sometimes, to pass the time, I trace the routes I used to drive. I remember them all. The roads of this country are etched in my memory, but the people I met along the way? They are lost; not worth remembering. My first love was always the land. This morning, I took myself on a drive down into the southwest. Have you ever been to New Mexico, Samantha? You must go, and when you do, drive in the night and give yourself the gift of a sunrise over the Bandelier National Monument . . .

As time passes, the dates of the letters get further apart. The last one is from a little over ten years ago and it's the shortest by far. Ward's indignation howls off the page.

Samantha

Why do you keep Lily from me? I only asked for a picture. You cannot even begin to imagine what the blankness of this place will do to a mind like mine. I do not understand your refusal to let me meet her. Is it this new husband of yours? <u>I am in her blood</u>—he is not. She is more mine than his.

Maybe it should give me satisfaction to see his impotent rage, but it leaves me cold. This monster, bellowing from his cage, his weapons reduced to a pen and a sheet of lined paper ripped from a notebook.

My phone buzzes and makes me jump. I throw the letters into the passenger seat, as if the person calling me will be able to tell what I'm reading. I'm expecting it to be David, but it's a FaceTime call from Aaron. It's four in the morning in Vancouver. Panic immediately clenches my stomach. He'd only be calling if something had happened. I answer but the screen is dark.

"Aaron? Aaron, are you there?"

There's a muffled sound of hands on the mic and then the blurry image of my daughter's face comes up on the screen.

"Mama? Mama phone?"

"Zoe? Sweetheart what's—"

"Mama."

She's mashing the phone against her cheek. Hands take the phone from her and a sleepy-looking Aaron comes onto the screen with Zoe climbing on top of him.

"Hey," he says. "Did you call us? Is everything okay?"

"You called me," I say. It's dark in the room where they are, but from what I can see, it looks like they're on the couch.

"Mama home?" Zoe asks.

"Someone misses you," he says. He shifts, so he's sitting up properly with Zoe on his lap. She tries to reach for the phone, but he holds it away from her. "Just look at the screen sweetheart. Mama can see you better like that."

Zoe looks at me, cocking her head to the side. She's wearing the pink Christmas pajamas that I got for her. They're covered in dancing reindeer and, according to her father, she's refused to wear any other pj's since. I love that she wants to wear something I gave her, though it probably has more to do with the reindeer.

"Where are you?" Aaron asks. I hold the phone back from me so he can see I'm in the car. "Why's your hair wet?"

"I just got out of the pool. I'm in New York." I told him I was leaving town, but not where I was going.

"New York? Is something going on with your grandparents?"

"No." I swallow. I can't not tell him. "I can explain some other time, but I'm in St. Rose—"

"Oh. Wow."

I know I should have told him where I was going, but it was all so fast and he's got enough to worry about with his wife eight months pregnant, and Zoe, and our court date. I can feel the excuses piling up in my mouth.

Zoe squirms off his lap, obviously distracted by something on the other end of the couch.

"Is everything okay?" he asks. "You just suddenly decide that November is a good time to go back there?"

"I'm sorry. I thought there was a good reason, but I was wrong. I'll get a flight back."

"Two days before American Thanksgiving?" he says. "Good luck."

Shit. I hadn't even been thinking about the calendar. "Is Zoe okay?" I ask. "I'm guessing she's the one who called."

"Yeah. Not even two yet and she's already fascinated with my phone. I guess of all the people she could have accidentally called, it's good she got you and not my boss. Good thing you're my only FaceTime contact."

"How is she?"

"She's great. It's four in the morning, so of course she's full of energy. I'm on the couch—"

"I see that."

"Yeah, well, Jenna can't sleep these days, so it's just better for everyone if I stay out here. This little rabbit can hop right out of her bed now—" He reaches off camera and I can hear her giggle as he tickles her. "So, here we are. I'm going to have to break the rules and put on a show or something. It's the only way I'm going to get any sleep."

The distance I've put between us suddenly hits me and I can feel a lump growing in my throat. "Okay, well, I'll let you go," I say.

He turns to Zoe. "Hey, sweetie, say bye-bye to Mama."

"No," I hear her say. "Mama go. Mama bad."

He looks at me, worried for a second, then turns back to her. "Honey, Mama had to go on a trip but she's coming back. Just say bye-bye to her for now."

"Aaron—don't," I say.

He turns back to me. "She just doesn't understand the concept of distance. It's not because of—"

"I gotta go," I say. "I'll be back as soon as I can."

I disconnect before he can say anything else. I lean back in my seat, breathing hard. Zoe's voice in my head. "Mama go. Mama bad."

Yes, sweetheart. Mama bad.

It's all there rushing into my head, all the times I have been a horrible mother. Not being able to get her to stop crying. Standing in the middle of my apartment, soaked with sweat and breastmilk, holding a screaming infant, both of us hysterical. My love for her is terrifying in its ferocity. The thousand ways this little person could be hurt by me. And then that time on the beach, the baby carrier on my chest, walking into those waves . . .

"But she wasn't with you." I can hear the counselor's voice at the day program. "You have to keep telling yourself this. You didn't take her with you. She was safe. You weren't, but she was." But no matter how many times she told me that and made me repeat it to myself, it doesn't change what I know. I was in a state of psychosis. I strapped that baby carrier onto my chest because I *thought* she was in it. And I walked into the pounding waves of the Pacific. A man who was on the beach with his dogs was the reason I came out. Him calling out to me, his dogs' insistent barking. I walked out of those waves and drove myself to the hospital and checked in. Aaron and Jenna had already been taking Zoe for longer and longer periods by then. And after two months in the hospital, and another three-month day program, I came to the conclusion that even though I was "well enough" I couldn't guarantee it wouldn't come back. So, I told them we should file for a stepparent adoption. I will give up my legal right to be Zoe's mother. And in two weeks, a judge is going to sign a paper making that happen. Without even realizing it, I've reached for my necklace. Maybe Lily was right: maybe those are two broken hearts.

CHAPTER 18

FIONA

Now

I park outside Lily's house and try to pull my wet hair into a ponytail, though it's tangled from the pool water and my swim cap. My bathing suit is clammy but I don't want to take the time to go home and change. Arriving at Lily's house early gives me the best chance of catching one of her parents, or Lily herself, and I don't want to lose my nerve. The only child I need to be concerning myself with is my own. I'll return the letters—I feel I owe her that much—and I will sever the connection to this girl who thinks she's my friend.

It's a little past seven in the morning. The house is dark again, though as with last time, other houses on the street have their lights on and people are heading off to work. I ring the doorbell and can hear it in the house, but there are no sounds of people coming to the door. I step back to see if Lily's watching me again from upstairs. Nothing. I give it one more try, and this time I hear someone calling out. After another moment, a woman in purple scrubs opens the door. This must be Samantha. On first glance, she doesn't look like the type of person who would be pen pals with a serial killer. She's wiping her hands on a towel and I can hear a child upstairs calling out for her.

"Yes?" She says sounding annoyed and probably confused about why someone is on her doorstep at this hour.

"I'm so sorry to bother you," I say. "My name is Fiona Green. I know Lily."

"Oh?" She's got dark hair the same color as her daughter and it's pulled back into a clip though pieces have fallen out all around her face. Embroidered across the chest pocket of her scrubs is a little giraffe with the words "Lancaster Children's Hospital."

She calls out to the child upstairs. "Just hold on, there's someone at the door," then turns back to me. "How do you know my daughter?"

I haven't thought this far ahead about how to do this. "I wanted to try to catch you—" The girl upstairs calls out again. "It can wait until you're done."

The woman yells up to her then turns back to me. "What can wait?" She sounds impatient.

"I wanted to talk to you about Lily."

"Do you work at the school?"

"No."

"Then how do you—?"

"That's what I wanted to talk to you about."

"Did she do something?"

"No—no, it's nothing like that. I don't know if she mentioned me. I'm the one who drove her home the other night when she was at her grandmother's. I was there too."

"My mother lives in Florida."

"No, uh, Carole Dunn. It was, uh, a couple nights ago? It was raining quite heavily and I was worried about her waiting at a bus stop by herself. I'm sorry, I should have introduced myself then."

She looks at me strangely for a moment, probably deciding

whether or not she wants to go further with this, then says, "Just a minute. Let me get my husband to finish the bath."

I step back because I assume she's going to close the door and want me to wait outside, but she opens it wider. "Come in. It's cold out there."

Inside, the house is cozy, it just looked dark because of heavy curtains pulled across the living room windows. There's a large sectional with a spattering of Barbies and their clothes across one side, stacks of magazines and books on the other, a closed laptop balancing on top of them. Family photos line the wall leading upstairs. An old piano that reminds me of my grandmother's sits in the far corner with beginner sheet music spread out across its music shelf.

I can hear Lily's mother talking to someone and then a minute later a door upstairs opens and she steps into the hall, followed by a man I assume is Lily's stepfather. "I know it's on Zoom but I still need to prep," he says.

"You just have to finish the bath. I'll take her in."

She comes down the stairs shaking her head. "It's like I'm asking him to upend his entire morning."

"I can come back," I say. "I really don't mean to interrupt."

"No, no, you're here now. And if there's something going on with Lily, I need to know. Come back to the kitchen and we can talk there. I'm Sam, by the way."

The kitchen is much brighter than the front of the house. The window over the sink looks out to a small backyard dominated by a children's play structure. There's an open lunchbox on the counter with a half-finished sandwich beside it. Sam picks up a mug of coffee and then turns to me. "Coffee?"

"No, thanks. I don't want to take much of your time. I know it's a school morning."

"It's fine," she says. "I'm on nights this month. I probably shouldn't be drinking coffee if I want to sleep, but it's the only way to get through the morning. Please." She sits and indicates that I should do the same, though the only chair that isn't covered in papers is at a place set with a cereal bowl and glass of apple juice. "Sorry," she says and moves the food out of the way. Next to the juice is a blue oval pill. She sees me noticing it. "My younger daughter is an epileptic. One of the perks of being a pediatric nurse. Her seizures still freak me out but at least I understand the medication." She sounds exhausted. "So, you gave Lily a ride home from her grandmother's?"

"And from the pool yesterday."

Now she looks completely confused. "The pool? Who are you again?"

There's no avoiding the connection we have. It's the only way to make sense of how Lily and I came to know each other. I take a breath. "My name is Fiona Green. My mother was Ana Lukas—" When I say my mother's name she looks away, like she's trying to place it. I continue. "She was killed—abducted—by Eddie Ward."

She puts her cup down heavily on the table. "Oh, God." She closes her eyes then opens them. "Sorry. Yes, of course. I know who— That's horrible. About your mom, I mean. I was just a kid, but I remember it."

"I was really little when it happened. We used to come here every summer. This is the first time I've come back. I'm trying to learn more about what happened, but he, uh, died before I could talk to him."

"Right, yeah. Lily told me," she says. "I think her grandma must have told her?"

"That's why I went to see Carole, and that's where I met Lily. She asked me to drive her home—"

"Why didn't her grandmother drive her?" I start to respond but she cuts me off. "Never mind. I learned a long time ago not to ask questions. I do not know what my daughter gets out of her visits with that woman."

"I assumed she'd told you that I drove her."

She snorts. "Lily doesn't tell us much. I'm not even sure I knew she went out there. I was at work."

"And then yesterday morning, she surprised me at the pool and I gave her a swimming lesson."

"A lesson?"

"We'd been talking about swimming and she asked me to teach her. I didn't think she would actually—" I can see how easily this could look predatory. "I said no, but she showed up and threw herself in the deep end."

"Why would she do that?"

"It definitely got my attention. I brought her back here after. I just wanted you to know. I don't mean to get her in trouble."

"Lily's more than capable of doing that herself. I understand her being at her grandmother's, but this lesson?"

"I assumed you knew what she was doing, but I wanted to make sure."

She sighs. "As if we don't have enough going on. I'm picking up extra shifts because my husband is between jobs, and with our other daughter's health stuff, and now Lily just goes off and starts swimming with strangers—no offence. I am so sorry. I'll talk to her. It won't happen again."

She gets up and resumes making the sandwich.

"One last thing." I pull the letters out of my bag and put them on the table. "She gave me these."

Sam wipes her hands on her scrubs and picks them up. She folds back one of the papers, and then immediately drops them back on the table.

She opens her mouth to say something, then closes it again.

"I knew I should have burned those. But I just couldn't. I don't know why. Did you read them?"

I nod.

"I'm sorry," she says. "My God, what you must think."

Now it's my turn not to know what to say. It was easy to be angry with a person I didn't know. But this woman standing in front of me with her kid's school lunch and her frazzled morning routine seems so normal, so like the mom I would have wanted to have, I can't connect those two people.

She takes a breath. "I guess, what he said about being a part of her family, I didn't know if I had the right to take that connection away from her, even if I didn't want her to have it. I hadn't decided if I was going to show her those. I should have known she'd find them anyway."

"Did she ever meet him?"

"No," she says adamantly. "No. Absolutely not. She's always had this morbid fascination with her father and his family. I suppose it's to be expected. The kids at her school have been pretty nasty about it. I mean, when people find out you have any connection to someone like that . . ."

"She seems to . . ." I'm not sure how to say this. I should have thought this through before I rang the doorbell. "She seems to want to be my friend. But I'm not sure that's—"

"It's not appropriate, no," her mother agrees.

"I don't mean anything against her. Lily's a very nice girl, but . . . Anyway, she left that for me at the pool this morning."

"This morning? She's asleep upstairs. Hold on." She leaves the kitchen and I can hear her stomp up the stairs. A minute later she's back down, followed by the stepfather and a young girl with wet hair wearing a plaid school jumper.

"Is Lily in trouble again?" the girl asks as they all enter the kitchen. The man is buttoning up his shirt, the sleeves are rolled up and the tie around his neck is undone. He looks as harried as his wife.

"But didn't you hear her leave?" Sam's asking him.

"How would I hear her if I was asleep?" he says. "She must have left at five in the morning. Maisy was up at six." He turns to look at me, and holds out his hand. "I'm Brent. You're Lily's friend?"

"No, I—"

The kitchen feels crowded with all of us in it. The little girl looks at me and says, "That's my seat."

"Maisy, that isn't how you talk to a guest," her mother says to her.

"But—"

"I was just leaving," I say, standing up and moving to the door.

"Are these yours?" Brent is holding the pile of letters out to me.

"No," I say.

He pulls the elastic off and starts flipping through them. "What the—?" He turns to his wife. "She leaves this crap on the kitchen table? What if Maisy sees this?"

"No, sorry, I put it—" I try to say.

"Sees what?" Maisy asks.

"You gotta talk to her, Samantha. And no more going to that woman's house. She doesn't need to have anything to do with—"

"Can we talk about this later?" Sam asks him, then she turns to me. "I'll walk you out."

At the front door, she says, "She's not in her room. I have no idea when she snuck out because I just got home. Brent's been threatening to put a lock on her door."

"Does she sneak out a lot?" I ask.

"It's been happening more the past while." She glances back to the kitchen then leans toward me. "I don't like her being at her grandmother's either, but how can I stop her? She's got a right to see her family. Carole's not the nicest person, but she's harmless."

"She's probably at the school," I say. "That's where she left me the letters."

"Honestly, that would be a good thing. She's missed so much school already this semester. Let me give you my number. If she asks for a ride again, or anything, just call me."

She gives me her number and then I text her mine. It's clear she wants to get back to whatever is happening in the kitchen, but I have to ask. "Is Lily's birth father in town?"

"I doubt it. I haven't spoken to Jason in over three years. Once Lily got old enough to contact him herself, I've let her handle those negotiations, but I don't think she's seen him in months."

"Is he . . . ?"

"Dangerous?" She sighs again. "I don't think so. He was pretty rough when he was younger. Got himself into some trouble, but none of it was that surprising when you think about the house he grew up in. That's what I told myself when we got involved. He's never shown much interest in his daughter, which is fine by me." She pinches and rubs a spot between her eyes. "Lily's looking for something. I don't think he's going to be able to give it to her and I certainly can't. I'll be glad when we're through this phase."

The voices rise from the kitchen again as Maisy protests the amount of milk poured on her cereal. I hear a cupboard door slam.

"I gotta go," she says, opening the door for me. "Thanks for letting me know. Really."

I want to ask her why she wrote the letters in the first place, but I don't. In the daylight, I can see the dark circles under her eyes. Would I want to be questioned for my actions twenty years ago? As I'm getting in the car, I'm struck by two things. How wonderfully ordinary Lily's family is, and how clear it is she's searching for something more.

CHAPTER 19

ANA

August 28, 1993

11:40 P.M.

They hit the detour about half an hour into the drive. Ben cursed under his breath as the headlights caught the neon orange sign directing them onto the smaller side road. The wind was behind them and pushing them along and Ana could feel it pick up as they got off the interstate and closer to the lake.

"This would be a pretty route if it was daytime," she said. The road followed the bends and curves of the lakeshore.

"This is the old highway," Ben said. "My father always says he likes this route better. It's slower though."

They went through a little town and he slowed, but no one was out on the road. A few fat drops of rain hit the windshield. She looked at the clock. 11:47 p.m.

"Do you want me to try to get a weather report?" She turned on the radio. Static.

"We already know the weather. It's raining."

She turned it off. What she meant was, do you want the radio on to fill the silence?

That catch, the rough edges between them. He was probably pissed that they weren't staying in the motel now that the driving was bad. She could see how tightly he was gripping the wheel. He'd always hated driving in storms. She could have offered to drive—storms had never bothered her—but she was so tired. The effort it would take to make that offer. And then there was the risk of The Blanks.

She clenched her hands into fists. What had happened this morning? How could she prevent it from happening again if she couldn't figure out what it was?

"What is it?" Ben asked.

"Nothing."

"You seem—"

"I just want to get home. It's weird being away from her."

"It's not that big a detour. It's probably going to kick us back onto the highway at the next exit. We'll be home in an hour."

"Do you think she's slept all right?"

"I'm sure she's fine. She sleeps better at the cottage, have you noticed?"

Does she? Ana hadn't noticed, but maybe Ben was right.

"I always did when I was a kid. She's outside for lots of the day. And it's quieter."

"The lake is like a giant white noise machine. I could never hear it growing up because my parents' house was too far back. I love being right beside it. I wish I could hear that sound all the time."

"My mom told me they're going to winterize the cottage. Dad's going to be retiring in about five years and then she'll retire soon after. They want to spend more time there."

Out on the lake, lightning arched down and touched the water followed by the low growl of thunder. She rolled the window down and the rain hit her face and neck. The air and the wetness would wake her up—

"Can you not?"

She rolled her window back up.

"It's just if your window is down then my window has to be down or my ears do that thing and—"

"I just wanted some fresh air."

They crossed out of the town and were back on the road. There hadn't been any signs saying when the detour was ending.

"Do you think we missed the turn back onto the highway?" she asked.

"I'm sure it's coming up. You didn't answer my question before. What was it like being there?"

She was caught off guard by the change in subject. "I recognized some people, but I couldn't remember their names. It was nice to see Tia."

"So, do you think you could go back? Even part-time?"

"And do it without funding? It's full-time or nothing." Ever since he had decided to go back to school, he had started talking about her doing it too. But there was no way that was possible.

"We can figure it out," he said. "There's that child care place. I just haven't had a chance to go by it."

"That's for faculty kids."

"But I talked to Professor Peterson tonight. He's willing to talk to them. He had all three of his kids there. He says it's a good place."

"Maybe when she's a bit older."

"You've got to rejoin the world at some point."

She clenched her jaw. Not tonight. Please not tonight, she thought. "I can't right now. I'm not you."

"You think this is going to be easy for me? I don't know how I'm going to manage working full-time *and* going to school but it doesn't seem like an option to give up either. We need the money and we're never going to get anywhere if we can't get real jobs—"

"I'm sorry that Fiona and I are such a huge burden to you." She was picking a fight and she knew it.

He banged his fist on the wheel. "Don't. All I'm saying is if you're going to enroll, you need to do it this week."

"I'm not enrolling. I'm sick of talking about it."

"Have you even looked at the course catalog?"

"Fiona needs at least one of her parents to be around."

That sick feeling was in her stomach. Ben was silent. A car passed them and in the moment of the lights hitting him, she could see the set of his jaw.

"I'm sorry," she said. "I didn't mean—"

"I am around as much as I can be," he said. "I can't be two places at once."

"I know. I said I'm sorry—"

"—And we agreed that I would take that second job for the summer. I am doing the best I can."

"I know." She reached over and touched his arm, leaving her hand there. "Can we please not—"

There was a clunking sound from the car. Three orange engine lights blinked on at once. Ben tapped the brakes and geared down. The car shook as he put in the clutch.

"What the—?"

"Did we hit something?"

"No, it's the—"

He dropped down another gear, which just led to more shaking. The clunking sound was getting louder. It sounded like there was a loose piece of the engine being knocked around under the hood. He put on the blinker and pulled over. Gravel crunched under the tires as they rolled to a stop.

Ben flicked on the hazard lights and popped the hood, then got out. Ana sat in the car for a moment looking at the lifted hood in front of the window and feeling useless. She got out. The air was thick and she could smell the electricity of the storm. Crickets must have been all around them. Thunder rumbled, behind them now but coming soon. She walked over to stand beside Ben. The gravel was sharp on her feet through the thin soles of her flats.

"What do you think it is?"

"Could be anything. This car's such a piece of shit. I just haven't had time to take it anywhere because how am I supposed to get to work without it?" He was leaning over the engine and she could feel the heat radiating off it. He reached his hand in, then yelped and pulled it out.

"Fuck!"

"Are you okay?"

"No, Jesus. I need a light."

She went and checked in the glove box and the trunk, but there was nothing. He was standing in front of the car, holding his hand close to his chest. She went back to him.

"I have one of Fi's blankets in the back. I can give it to you if you need to touch anything."

"What I need is a fucking light."

He didn't mean to snap at her. She knew this. It didn't matter. She couldn't do anything to help. She couldn't provide him with a light. She couldn't stop his hand from being burned, and most of all, she couldn't fix the car.

She looked in both directions at the dark road. It had to be almost midnight. At some point, another car would come along. There would be more cars redirected off the highway. That was the solution. She would wave down a car—they'd see the hazards, yes—she'd wave down a car and ask if they could take them to a pay phone.

There would be another little town coming up. Where were they? They couldn't be far from home now. Thirty miles? Forty? Ben's dad would come out and get them and tomorrow they would get a tow truck for the car. She turned around to tell him this but he was leaning over the engine again, keeping his hands away but looking at it. Neither of them knew anything about cars, but this was going to be his solution, to stare at it until he could figure it out.

She walked down the road. She was awake now, and it felt good to be out of the car and away from Ben. Away from all of it; from his frustration and hers, from feeling so useless. She heard an engine coming from the same direction they had come from. It came over a small rise and she saw the headlights. A transport truck. A truck would have a radio. They could call for help on the radio.

She watched the truck come closer and made a decision.

She stepped out onto the road and raised her arms.

She heard the engine gear down. He'd seen her. She imagined what she looked like silhouetted against the flashing orange of the hazard lights, the wind picking at her dress like Marilyn Monroe.

The engine dropped down another gear. He flashed his lights at her.

Another. The hiss of air brakes.

And then the huge truck rolled to a stop on the shoulder. The engine rumbled low, like a giant animal breathing.

Waiting.

She heard Ben call out, but she was solving this now. She would find a way to get them home.

Ana ran toward the truck.

CHAPTER 20

FIONA

2003

The anniversary of her mom's death was always there, waiting at the end of the summer like a rotten spot you discover in the last bite of a perfect apple. And this year was the tenth anniversary, so everyone was making an especially huge deal about it. There was the dinner with both sets of grandparents and then the memorial in town. It was going to be a whole big thing, a whole big thing that Fiona didn't want anything to do with.

"It's to remember your mom," her aunt Charlotte had said. "To show she's still in our hearts."

Show who? Fiona wanted to ask. It's not like she or her dad needed to be shown. They lived it. Besides, that was bullshit coming from Aunt Charlotte who hadn't even met her mom because Uncle Mike, Charlotte's husband, was her dad's youngest brother and he'd been fifteen when she died. Aunt Charlotte was "just so shocked that something so *awful* could happen to such a nice family." Her words. Fiona had a feeling it was the first thing she told anyone, that *she* was that close to the "Terror Trucker's" last victim. Barf.

If anyone had asked Fiona what she'd like to do on the anniversary she would have said to join her dad for his drive. Every year he drove the night through. They wouldn't have to talk. No one understood better than Fiona and her dad that you don't have to fill silence with words. It would be enough to just sit in the car with him. There was no fixing. There was no talking it through because there was no "through," no resolution. It just was.

But no one asked her, and her dad never invited her to join him. Instead, she'd had to listen to her aunt Charlotte going on about how "meaningful" it was all going to be. And Grandma Green was planning a big dinner to host her other grandparents and everyone was stressed because it had to be perfect. It had been a relief to get away with David in the canoe to prepare for their night's adventure to Smuggler's Point—they were going to go check it out for themselves after hearing Mikey's stories. But Grandma and Grandpa Lukas had already arrived when they returned and that sick edgy feeling came right back into her stomach.

Grandpa Green was down on the beach with most of the cousins trying to get them to help him set up the bonfire. Jaimie called out to ask where they'd been but her grandpa told her to stay with him. That was the one good thing about all of this. In the past few days, her aunts and uncles had been a little quicker to tell the cousins to "leave Fiona alone" and no one had asked her to babysit.

Grandpa Lukas was sitting in front of the cottage. She knew that he was staying up there because ever since his stroke he couldn't navigate the steep stairs to the beach, but still it seemed weird when everyone else was down below.

"Hi, Grandpa," she said, leaning down to give him a kiss on the cheek. "This is David."

David stepped forward and mumbled, "Nice to meet you."

"I remember you," her grandpa said. It was a bit hard to understand him because his voice was quiet and a little slurred. David instinctively leaned closer so that he towered over him. "But you were only about this tall. You've grown a bit." He smiled and the lines around his eyes crinkled.

"That's my family's cottage," David said, pointing at the one next door. "We've been here as long as the Greens."

"Have you seen my dad?" she asked her grandpa.

"I think he went to town for supplies," he said. "You've grown some more too, Fiona."

She wanted to say, yeah, that's what kids do, but knew it would sound meaner than she meant it so instead she said, "We're going in to get some iced tea."

Her grandpa glanced back at the cottage then said quietly, "Why don't you stay out here for now?"

"I'll just be a minute," she said, but as soon as she swung open the porch door, she realized why he'd wanted her to stay out. Her grandmothers were in the kitchen and it didn't sound like it was going well.

"Adele, I'm sorry," Grandma Green was saying. "With all the children here, it's hard for us to do something more formal. That's why I thought if we did the dinner here—"

"It's just too much for Bill," Grandma Lukas said. "If he gets a headache—"

Her grandma always used her grandpa as an excuse, Fiona thought bitterly. He'd seemed okay to her. David went to say something but she held her hand up. She wanted to hear this.

"The kids know they're to stay down on the beach," Grandma Green said. "That's why we're doing the cookout for them."

"And Bill and I have our own traditions for this day."

"But I have all this food."

"Well if you'd asked us first, I would have told you not to bother," Grandma Lukas said.

It was quiet for a moment. She could hear the sound of cupboards being opened and shut.

"I think it would be better," Grandma Lukas continued, "if we just met you at the memorial."

"But you haven't even seen Fiona yet. I know she'll want to see you both."

"We aren't in the right frame of mind—" What kind of frame of mind did her grandmother have to be in to see her?

The kitchen faucet went on, then off. *Chop, chop, chop.*

"I'm sure coming back here must stir things up. This is a hard day for all of us," Grandma Green said. She sounded like she was trying not to cry.

"For some more than others."

"I don't think there is any value in comparing."

"I wasn't comparing, Sharon. I was pointing out a fact."

Their voices got quiet again and Fiona moved farther onto the porch, walking carefully to avoid the creaking boards. She looked back at David but he shook his head and pointed to his own cottage, unwilling to eavesdrop with her. "See you later," she mouthed and sank onto the couch, hugging her knees into her to make herself small.

"And you well know why we moved away," her Grandma Lukas was saying. "If her father wants her to have a relationship with us, he can bring her out to New Haven. She could spend part of her summer out there. I have made that clear. He is the one who chooses not to come."

"Ben goes as much as he can. He's still struggling. Surely you can understand—"

"What exactly am I supposed to understand?" Grandma Lukas's voice was rising now.

"Adele, please—"

Her grandmother swept onto the porch. Fiona slid further down into the couch so she wouldn't see her, but her grandma must have sensed her because she spun around.

"Ah, Fiona."

"Hi, Grandma."

"I didn't realize you were here," she said.

"I just got back."

"You are coming to the memorial?"

Fiona nodded dumbly.

"Good. Well." She looked outside then back to Fiona. "We need to go. This—" she motioned vaguely at the cottage, the cacophony of cousins down on the beach. "Is too much right now. You understand. We'll see you there, then."

"Okay," Fiona said. She should say something else. Maybe she should get up and hug her, or walk them back up to their car, or, or, *something*. But the distance between her on the couch and her mother's mother at the door felt like so much more than ten feet. They looked at each other for a moment across that space, then her grandmother turned and walked out. The screen door banged shut behind her.

Fiona didn't move. Maybe the ancient couch would suck her into it and not spit her out until tomorrow when this stupid day was over.

A moment later her dad walked in with his arms full of groceries. His face looked strange. He'd probably just seen her grandparents leaving and knew things were going badly.

"Hi, sweetheart," he said. "Did you guys have a good canoe ride?"

"Grandma and Grandpa Lukas just left," she said. "They said they'll see us at the memorial."

He sighed. "Yeah. They told me." He glanced into the cottage. "I'm going to go see if Grandma needs some help. You doing okay?"

She could feel tears welling in her eyes, but she didn't want her dad to see.

"Do your best, okay?" He started to move toward her but then he stopped. "I've got to get this stuff into the fridge," he said, and then went into the cottage.

The memorial was in the small park that overlooked the water. The bandstand was decorated with white string lights and a picture of her mom from college that was blown up and glued to a poster board. It was leaning on a rickety A-frame that looked like it might topple at any moment because of the wind coming off the lake. There was a full moon rising, but she could see thin wisps of clouds starting to cross in front of it. Even though it was August, the hint of fall was in the air.

People were standing around in little groups near the bandstand with more coming in. There were dogs and kids running between the adults. Fiona had thought it was going to be sad but no one seemed too somber. Had all these people known her mom? She caught little snippets of conversation as she moved through the crowd looking for David, but people were talking about their summer vacation or their kids. She saw Grandma and Grandpa Lukas standing off to the side of the bandstand talking to a woman. She was Black, which automatically made her stand out in a place like St. Rose. She was taller than them with her hair in braids piled onto her head. But it wasn't the woman who caught her off guard, it was her grandpa's face. He looked so animated. The woman leaned over and hugged Grandma Lukas who remarkably hugged her back. It was like they were different people from the grandparents she'd just seen a few hours earlier.

"Fiona."

She turned to see David moving through the crowd toward her with his mom in tow. He ran over and she was about to say, "Let's just go down to the beach and skip the speeches," when Mrs. Connor caught up with her son and gave Fiona a big hug.

"Oh, sweetie. I have such good memories of your mom. We spent hours on the beach together with you two." She pulled Fiona in for another hug.

"Mom, come on," David said. "You can't force hugs on people."

"Oh hush, you," his mother said, batting him away.

Mrs. Connor had started selling lakeside real estate in the past few years and become more glamorous as a result, always in makeup and pantsuits even at the cottage. She came and went at odd hours, much like David's dad, so Fiona rarely saw either of them. David was basically part of the Green family and usually only went back to his cottage to sleep.

"Thanks, Mrs. Connor," Fiona mumbled, then David told her they were going to try to get closer and she said, "Yes, yes, of course. Go be with your family."

After they'd stepped out of her view, they both rolled their eyes, which almost made Fiona burst out laughing. The whole day had been like this with these sudden swings of emotion.

"Do you know who that is with my grandparents?" she asked, but David shook his head. "I want to get closer to hear what they're talking about."

Her aunt and uncle were setting up to play their Coldplay cover and the crowd started moving closer. A few people had lit candles. As Fiona and David moved up front, the mystery woman turned, saw them, and she smiled.

"Hi. You're Fiona, right?" she said, stepping toward them.

Fiona nodded dumbly. How did this woman know who she was?

"I'm Tia." She stuck out her hand and Fiona shook it. "I was a friend of your parents.' "

On cue, her dad came through the crowd. As soon as he saw Tia, his face lit up.

"Hey, stranger," he said smiling. Again, not something Fiona had seen him do in a while. "Someone just told me you were here. I didn't know you were back in town."

"Ben," Tia said, and folded him into a hug. They looked so comfortable together. Maybe she just had that effect on people. "How're you doing?"

"Oh, you know," he said. "Thanks for coming to this. It means a lot."

"Of course. My mom sends love and prayers. She and my dad are on a cruise or they'd be here. I've just met your daughter." She turned back to Fiona. "You're how old now, thirteen?"

"Twelve," Fiona said, trying to stand a little taller. "But I'll be thirteen soon." Duh, a voice in her head said. I'm sure this lady can do math.

"Tia and your mom roomed together at college," her dad told her. "But they knew each other before then."

"We met when we were seven? Eight? In figure skating class."

Fiona's stomach did that jump thing that happened when she got another little snippet of information about her mom.

"And I introduced your parents," Tia said.

"The Red Lion," her dad said, grinning.

"The Red Lion indeed." Tia winked at Fiona. She had no idea what they were talking about.

"My mother's trying to flag me down," her dad said. "There's apparently a whole schedule to this thing. Are you in town for a bit?"

"I'll catch up with you after," she said, and her dad moved away. When he was gone, David stepped in.

"Hi," he said, sticking out his hand, which once again almost made Fiona laugh. So awkward and overly formal. "I'm David Connor, Fiona's best friend."

"Hello, David Connor," Tia said. Fiona was about to ask her more about sharing a room with her mom, or doing skating lessons, or any of the hundred questions that were crowding into her head, but Tia said, "I'm glad I ran into you. I brought you something."

"Me?"

"I didn't know if you were going to be at this, so I was going to just give it to your dad. I've had it for a long time, but I thought you'd like it." She dug around in her handbag and pulled out a small square package. It was beautifully wrapped in soft white paper with a yellow ribbon around it.

"What is it?" Fiona asked.

Tia smiled. "Open it and you'll see."

Fiona pulled off the soft paper. She gasped. It was a little framed picture of her mom holding her on her lap as a baby.

"When was this?" she asked, staring at the picture.

"Hmm, let me see," Tia said. She took the picture and turned it over. Written on the back it said,

Eliot Park, June 1991.

"You were born in the winter, right?"

"February."

"So, you're just a few months old in this. That was the first time I met you. I visited your mom and we went to this little park across from their apartment. It took me forever to get this developed and by the time I did . . ." She gave a little smile. "Anyway, I've had it for a while and thought you might like it."

Fiona couldn't stop looking at it. She knew she should probably say something to this woman but she bit her lip instead. The picture was a little blurry but her mom's face was in sharp focus. She was sitting on the ground and her body was curved around Fiona so she was partially hidden. Her mom was looking up at the camera. She wasn't smiling, it was a different kind of look, like she'd been caught off guard, but it was protective too.

"I don't—" Fiona tried to say but there was a catch in her throat. "I don't remember her."

Tia reached out and put her hand on Fiona's shoulder. "Oh honey. Your mom and I had lots of adventures. I'll tell you all about them whenever you want."

"Really?"

Tia smelled like vanilla and something spicy. She tapped her finger on the picture. "This day, we had a picnic. We were just finishing up when something scared you."

"What was it?" How desperately she wanted to remember this, impossible as that was.

"Oh, I don't know. A siren or a dog barking or something. You'd been such a quiet baby up until then, but when you cried, man, I'm still amazed at how much sound can come out of such a tiny body. But your mom started singing you this little song and you just stopped. Like she'd found the off switch. I told her she was magic. She was a great mom," Tia said. "Even if she didn't think she was."

Later, Fiona would wish she'd asked about what she meant by that, but in the moment, it was too overwhelming for her to get the words out right.

"Oh, look," Tia said, pointing toward the stage. "Your grandpa's going to speak."

Fiona turned around. Her grandpa never spoke in public. He

barely spoke in private. Grandma Lukas was walking up to the microphone with him. He had his cane in one hand and was clearly leaning on her.

"He looks like he's going to fall."

"Nah, he can do this," Tia said. "He's stronger than he looks. Your grandpa taught me how to swim. Your mom was like a fish—that's what he used to call her. *Little Fish*. But I was terrified of the water. So, one summer when we were like ten or something, your grandpa taught me. He coached the swim team at the high school too. He could have been coaching at a much higher level but he wanted to be here, working with your mom."

Fiona couldn't imagine her grandfather like this man Tia was describing.

"And your grandmother helped me get into college."

"How?"

"I had to write an essay as part of the application, but I wasn't good at writing. Science is more my thing. But she worked with me on it. She made me revise it so many times, but I got in. Mrs. Lukas is still one of the best writing teachers I ever had."

Fiona was transfixed but also confused. Neither of the people Tia was describing were like the grandparents she saw on the bandstand now.

"M-m-my name is B-B-Bill Lukas," her grandpa said. Someone called out, "Coach B," and Tia let out a whoop. More people had come into the park. It was dark now and there were candles flickering in the wind all through the crowd. "My daughter, Ana, and I used to spend hours down there"—he pointed vaguely toward the lakeshore—"D-d-dreaming about how she would cross it. And one day, she did."

Fiona looked back down at the picture and pressed it close to her chest. This was unlike any other picture she had. Anything she ever got about her mom—information, pictures—was carefully doled out, in small pieces. Her family was always trying to protect her instead of just letting her know things. But this was all hers.

Her grandmother started talking about the scholarship they were starting in her mother's name. People clapped but Fiona had stopped listening and was watching her dad. He was standing off to the side, apart from the clump of his family. A young woman had just come up to him and was pointing at a group of people farther off. They didn't look like they were really part of the memorial. More like onlookers. There was another girl and three tough-looking guys. One of them had his arms covered in tattoos. Someone held the glowing tip of a cigarette and they were all drinking.

David saw where she was looking. "What are they doing here?" he said quietly.

"Who are they?"

He squinted into the dimness. "Two of them are Mikey's brothers, Chris and Ryland Lonergan. I don't know the other guy, or the girls."

"Is that who Mikey was talking about?" Fiona asked. "The one who works in the bar and saw—"

"Shhhh." David said, surprising her. "Don't say his name here."

The girl had gone back to her group and the program continued with a few other people making little speeches, but now Fiona was too distracted to pay attention. When people started moving down to the lake, her dad turned and went to talk to them.

"Come on," Fiona said. "I want to hear what they're going to say."

They had to go the long way around so her dad wouldn't see them, so they missed the first part of the conversation. This part of the park wasn't lit and they squatted behind some bushy plants.

"He had a fucking blade, man," one of the guys was saying. "You should have seen it."

"He's trying to stir shit up," another guy said. "He's like a walking time bomb."

"He works at a garage with a bunch of ex-cons. Why's he working with them if he's not up to some shit?"

"But did he actually hurt anyone?" her dad asked. Who were they talking about?

"No man, we handled it," another guy said. She thought it was the big one with the tattoos but couldn't tell for sure.

"And then he ran away," the first guy said. "He's not going to be coming back any time soon." Someone laughed at that and there were some mumbled threats Fiona couldn't make out.

"But this was in St. Thomas," her dad said. "I thought you said he was near our cottage." Fiona's eyes grew wide.

"My kid brother thought he saw him in a boat. He was watching your cottage."

"Boat was probably stolen too."

"This was during the fireworks show last weekend?" her dad asked.

"He wasn't there for the fireworks, man. He was probably trying to see if your cottage was empty or something. Mikey said he was just sitting there. Didn't have lights on or anything."

She looked at David. He had a funny look on his face. Her dad said something about police but she couldn't catch it.

"They're fucking useless," one of the guys said. "Why's he even allowed to live here? He and the wife should'a been run out of town when their old man went to jail."

"You can't make people move because of what someone in their family did," one of the girls argued.

"I'm telling you, like father, like son. Jason Ward's not right in the head. And if he's checking out where you live? Shit, man, I wouldn't mess around with that."

"Yeah," another guy agreed. "That's why we wanted to warn you."

Someone from the memorial called out to her dad. "I gotta go," he said. "Thanks for letting me know."

When they were gone, Fiona and David came out of hiding and started walking toward the beach.

"Do you really think it was Jason Ward in that boat?" she asked David.

"I don't know how Mikey would have got close enough to be able to know," David said. "Does he even know what he looks like? I think he just told his brothers that to try to impress them." But he didn't sound very sure.

"Fiona?" her dad called into the crowd. He sounded worried. She stepped out from behind a group of people and he strode up to her. "There you are," he said. "I told you to stay with your cousins."

"Who were those people?" she asked as he moved her closer to the water. Her aunt Tanya and Grandpa Green were handing out paper boats with little tea lights in them.

"What people?" he asked.

"The people you were just talking to."

"Don't worry about that," he said, then he stopped and took her arm. "Look, you can't be wandering off. I'm going to have to talk to a lot of people and I can't keep an eye on you."

"I'll be with her, Mr. Green," David said. She almost burst out laughing again at how formal he sounded. "What?" he said to her, looking confused. But it seemed to be enough to reassure her dad.

When her aunt had described the candle ceremony, it sounded lame. She probably got it out of some cheesy romance book, she'd grumbled to David, but when they got down to the beach, her breath caught. There must have been a hundred candles floating on the lake.

The chatter that had been around them stopped and everyone stood quietly, watching the candles flicker in the darkness. How much she wished her mom could see this, to know there were still so many people sending out lights for her.

People were fading back up to the park, back to their lives. She didn't want to go. David was beside her and their hands brushed. It had happened a few times that summer and had always been awkward and unspoken. But this time—she didn't even know which of them had done it—their hands stayed together and squeezed tight.

CHAPTER 21

ANA

August 29, 1993

12:00 A.M.

The driver rolled down the window and looked at her. She couldn't see his face. He was wearing a baseball cap and was only lit by the glow of the dashboard.

"Our car's broke down," she said. "We need to get to a phone, or can you radio someone?"

"No one around here to call," he said. His voice was rough, like it hadn't been used much.

"We need to get to a pay phone, then."

He was quiet for a moment as he looked at her, maybe deciding if it was worth the bother. Then he said, "Sure. Get in."

Ben was still standing by the car. He didn't want to leave it, but there was no other choice. She ran back to him. "He's going to give us a ride."

"Where?"

"I don't know. To a phone. We can call your dad."

"Ana—"

She turned back to him. "We need help and he's going to help us. Come on."

She started walking back to the truck. If they took too long, the guy might not wait for them and this was their way home. Ben had to see that. She heard the sound of their car door slamming and then he caught up and handed over her purse. He put the car keys in his pocket and they walked to the passenger side of the truck cab. She reached up and opened the door. The two of them stood looking up at the driver. She still couldn't see his face. The radio played low, something country, a man singing about home.

"I've only got room for one," he said nodding to the other bucket seat. Ana turned to Ben but he said, "We'll make it work. It won't be for long."

Ben hauled himself up, then reached out with his good hand and helped Ana pull herself in. He sat as far over on the seat as he could to make room for her, but there was a large gear shift sticking up the middle and he couldn't go far. She perched half on his lap, half on the seat, and pulled the door closed. As soon as it slammed shut, the driver put the truck into gear and they pulled back onto the road. Everything looked different from this height. They passed their car and she watched the hazards get smaller in the sideview mirror until they disappeared completely.

"Thanks," Ben said to the driver. "That detour screwed us up so I'm not sure where we are. There must be another little town somewhere up here."

The driver nodded slightly but didn't say anything. He probably wasn't used to having people in his truck, she thought. But he had stopped. And it's not like they were taking him out of his way.

Ben had one arm wrapped around Ana's waist. She braced herself against the door with one hand, but with the other, she put her hand on his leg and squeezed it. How had everything changed so quickly? Just a few moments earlier they were in the car arguing about—what were they arguing about? It didn't matter. It was always this way; it took a moment for her mind to catch up with reality. This would become one of those stories. She'd tell Tia when they spoke next: "You won't believe it. Our car broke down and it was the middle of nowhere. We flagged down a transport truck. *I* flagged down a transport truck." She and Ben would each remember it slightly different as it moved into their shared mythology. She could see the phone booth where they would wait for Mr. Green to come and get them. They'd get home at two or three in the morning. Ben's mom would be up, waiting for them on the porch. And while Ben told the story, she'd go into the cottage and lean over Fiona. Breathe her in. The car repair would probably cost more than they had, but it was fine. They'd figure it out. This, more than the night out, more than the party, this was what made her feel close to Ben. She leaned her head on his shoulder. Benana, together against the world.

Her hand had drifted up to the necklace she always wore. A cheap little thing, half a heart, with the other half tucked away in her drawer to give to Fiona someday. The movement must have caught the driver's attention. He glanced at her, then turned back to the road. He didn't speak. He had one hand resting on the large steering wheel, the other sitting in his lap. She wondered if she should try to make conversation but he hadn't said anything. He hadn't asked them where they were coming from, or what happened to their car, or where they were going.

Minutes passed. She was getting drowsy again. Then the truck slowed and turned onto another small road. Maybe they were going back to the highway now, or maybe this was a way into a little town where there would be a phone.

"Thanks again, man," Ben said. "I hope we're not taking you out of your way."

"It's fine," the driver said.

"This is quite the detour. I thought they would have rerouted us back onto the interstate by now but I haven't seen any signs."

"We passed that a ways back," the driver said.

"Well, we don't want to take you out of your way," Ben said again.

"It's not far now," he said.

There's something about his voice, she thought. It's like he talks without wanting to move his mouth. And he didn't move his head, but probably when you're driving a truck this big, you need to keep your focus forward all the time. Should they offer him money? She tried to think about what she had in her purse. Maybe a five-dollar bill and some change? Hopefully Ben had some.

The driver grabbed the shift and began to gear down.

Out the window was only darkness. She hadn't seen any signs for a town but there must be something close by.

Now the driver kept his hand on the shift and they both instinctively moved away to give him room. Ben was craning his head too, looking for the lights of a gas station. Any sign of people. The driver maneuvered the truck onto the shoulder and stopped. He opened his door then, like an afterthought, said, "Gotta shift something in the back. I could use your help." He pulled a pair of gloves out of his back pocket and put them on.

"Oh, sure. Right," Ben said.

Ana opened the door and jumped down so Ben could get out. It felt good to move her legs. She could hear the driver walking to the back of the truck on the other side. Then the sound of him pulling a chain. She started to walk to the back too.

"You should stay in the cab," Ben said.

"But your hand."

"It's fine," he said, then more quietly he added, "I'd feel better if you were up here." He kissed her cheek and started to step away. She grabbed his arm.

"Ben?"

"What is it?"

"Nothing. We'll get home soon, right?"

He smiled and walked to the back of the truck. She could see his silhouette in the red lights, then he turned and was gone.

A chill ran down her back and she shivered. The storm was bringing in cooler air; autumn was just around the corner. She climbed back up into the truck cab to wait, but left the door open. She listened for their voices but couldn't hear anything over the sound of the idling engine. Then—

A thump.

Something falling to the ground.

Any moment now, Ben would walk back to the cab.

She should go back. Maybe she could help—?

He said to stay up here.

She put her hand on the door to climb down and—

The driver swung his door open suddenly and got back into his seat. He slammed it shut.

"Close your door," he said.

"But—"

Click.

A knife.

There was a knife in his hand. Not a kitchen knife. It looked like a hunter's knife. That was the click she just heard. He turned to her fully and the tip of the knife hovered over her chest. He was breathing hard. It was making the knife move. She looked down and saw that the knife was touching her right next to the half heart of the necklace. He was still wearing gloves. Why was he wearing gloves?

"I said, close your door."

She was both in this cab and out of it. This wasn't real. It couldn't be. He pushed so the blade indented her skin. It hadn't broken through but it would—

"Please—"

The word came out like a breath. Her arm reached out and she grabbed the door handle. The knife poked deeper. She felt the instant when it broke through. It would hurt if she was here but she wasn't here she wasn't here she wasn't here—

She closed the door.

She heard the deep *clunk* of the door lock. The knife was lifted off her.

He put it between his legs leaving the blade out and grabbed the gear shift. The engine roared in response, and they lurched forward onto the road. She looked into the mirror without turning her head but there was only darkness outside.

Ben?

It began to rain.

We will sit by the phone booth. Her mind was still stuck in the old story. *We will watch for headlights. Something so ordinary. I will put my hand on Fiona's back and feel it rising and falling—*

A car passed them going in the other direction.

I'll tell Ben about this vision I had of a truck and a knife. In the morning, I will look for shells on the beach with my daughter—

The driver shifted gears. They turned onto another road. The truck was moving much faster now than it had before.

Did Ben run away and leave me here? No. Did he get away? Yes. Yes—he ran to get help. He ran to a house and called the police. At any moment, there will be flashing lights in the mirror—

The driver turned off the radio. The cab was silent now.

I'll keep teaching Fiona how to swim but I'll ask one of Ben's brothers to come into the water with us. Philip. He's good with her—

Lightning pierced the sky and revealed small buildings. A garage. A car dealership. They were in the outskirts of a town. How much time had passed? Had she had another one of her blanks?

Dad in the boat and me in the water. Darkness all around. He always knew which way to go. I just had to look back and—

It was pouring now. The truck's wipers made a rhythmic *swish-swish, swish-swish.*

They passed a Wendy's. They passed a Western Union. No one will know I was here, she thought. It's like I am a ghost.

I am not really here. I am dreaming. I am imagining this. I am sitting next to the phone booth with Ben waiting for his dad to come and get us and I've drifted into this vision because I'm tired and it's late and a truck passed us and I imagined all of this but I'm not actually here because this isn't real this can't be real I'm

I'm

I'm lost in The Blank.

CHAPTER 22

FIONA

Now

I get as far as the end of Lily's street when I see her. She's slumped down on a bus stop bench almost disappearing into her brown sack of a coat, but she stands up as soon as she sees me. I roll up and she opens the door, looking pointedly at the empty bag on the passenger seat that once held the letters. She pushes it onto the floor and gets in, immediately returning to her slumped position.

"Where are they?"

"I gave them to your parents."

"Which means I'll never see them again." She crosses her arms, pouting.

I pull into an empty parking lot and turn the car off.

"What are you doing?" she says.

"I don't want to just drive around town. I can take you back to the school."

She blows air out of her lips as a response.

"Were you waiting for me?"

"I saw your Jeep in front of my house. Why'd you give those letters to them? They don't understand us."

I turn to her and try to keep my voice very calm. "There is no 'us.' I know you think you're helping me but—"

"Don't talk to me like I'm a child, okay? Just . . . don't."

It doesn't seem necessary to point out that this is how she is be-having.

"You have no idea what it's like to live with this mark on me. That's how people treat it, like it's some kind of deformity. Like it's my fault. I didn't ask my mother to go fuck around with my dad but she did. *She* sought out that family— I mean, you read them, right? What a hypocrite to say that *I* can't have a relationship with him when she— And now she thinks she can just erase that part of her life but she can't because she has me. So instead I'm supposed to just live with half a family. Half of who I am. And it's not like it's my dad's fault either. He didn't do any of that stuff. You're lucky. Your parents were victims; that's like a free pass."

"It's not—"

"Has anyone ever hung a noose in your locker? When you were in school did kids pour blood all over your clothes and post it to TikTok like you're some kind of fucking psycho killer?"

I don't answer her.

"Yeah. I thought so."

"Lily," I start to say and reach my hand to her arm, but she shrinks from me and huddles inside the oversized coat.

"Just leave me alone." She starts to cry and puts her face in her hands. I'm expecting her to open the door and bolt but she stays in the car. When the worst of it seems to be over she wipes her nose on her sleeve.

"There's tissues in the glove box."

She opens it, grabs a wad of them, and swipes at her face.

"You're right," I say after a few minutes of calm. "No one's done those things to me. People knew, but in some ways, it made me special. Sometimes . . . I kind of leaned on that. My friend David was the only one who truly got how much it sucked. And then my dad moved us away and I decided not to tell the kids at my new school. When they asked where my mom was, I told them she died in a car accident." I feel the usual hit of guilt when I say this out loud. I've tried to argue to myself that it was a form of self-preservation, but that logic never holds. "I'm not proud of that but sometimes I just desperately wanted to be—"

"Normal," she finishes.

I nod. "Like I was trying to erase what happened. Or maybe, disconnect it from myself."

"Did it work?" she asks quietly.

"No. I just lost her even more. I was really young when she died, so I don't have memories."

"Nothing?" she asks.

I won't talk about the dream with the shells, my mother rising out of the water. The smallest thing could burst the membrane and then it would be gone.

"But I had a feeling of her. For a few years after we moved, I was really angry and I wouldn't let myself look at pictures. My dad and I didn't talk about her. We were both trying to heal I guess, in our own ways, but it just pushed the pain deeper."

She turns to me and then puts both of her hands on her heart. "I'm so sorry my grandfather did that to you."

She's trying to be sincere. "This isn't yours to apologize for. It happened years before you were even born."

"But he's not around to take responsibility and someone needs to. So, that's me."

I want to tell her that's wrong, but I stop myself. Is that why I wanted to talk to her grandmother? Is that what I wanted her to offer me, some kind of acknowledgment of her role in what happened? When I was young, I was sent to a therapist, of course. I was sent to a string of therapists over the years, until we moved away and I refused to do any more therapy and my father, who was also sick of therapy, finally agreed. The one I saw the longest, *Monica*, talked a lot about closure. Whenever she said that word, I just pictured a scab; ugly, hard lumps of dried blood closing over a wound. And just like my fingers would do with scabs on my knees, my mind would find it and pick, pick, pick. There is no closure for something like this; there is just the wound and living with the wound.

A few school buses go rumbling down the road, which pulls me back into the present. Lily's calmed down. She leans her head against the window and closes her eyes. She looks so young. I'm about pull out of the parking lot to take her to school when she starts to speak.

"I'm probably the only kid in my school who actually liked COVID. I mean, not the virus or the masks, but not having to be at school. I did remote as long as I could. I wanted to switch to homeschooling but my mom said she doesn't have the 'bandwidth.'

"People have always known about my grandfather, but it kind of fades, you know? Like after a while, I think they get bored of making it a thing so they just ignore me, which honestly, is fine. But then these two brothers, Caleb and Logan, started at our school last year. They think they're so special. Their mom was on TV like a thousand years ago and their dad's in tech. They came from LA and their parents bought one of those huge houses on Bonasera Bay. They're jocks of course—that's all anyone at this school cares about—but Caleb also writes for the school paper.

"Someone told them that the 'Terror Trucker's' granddaughter goes to the school, which is also the same school his last victim went to. Caleb wanted to interview me. He told me it would be like a chance to tell my side of the story, which is just fucking stupid because, hello, I don't *have* a side of the story because I wasn't *born*. I told him no, which pissed him off because I guess no one tells Caleb Schaefer 'no.' And he decided to write about it anyway. He did all these supposed interviews with people at the school—his friends, obviously—who said how unsafe they feel because 'the family' still lives in the area and I go to the school. He bragged about how he was going to get police records and talk to your family. My mom complained but the school did nothing because 'freedom of the press' and he didn't name me directly. People started doing the usual shit. Even my little sister has had kids messing with her and she's only in second grade. And my stepdad's blaming me, of course."

"Why?"

"Because I won't change my name. Like it would even matter now. Everyone knows." She opens the car door then turns to me. "Look, I get that we can't be friends. But I meant what I said about needing to do something to make reparations or whatever. It's something I want to do for all the families, if I can find them."

"How can you possibly do that, Lily? You can't undo the past."

"I tried reaching out to one family but they told me essentially to f-off." She bites her lip. "They probably thought I was pranking them. But it's how I can own who I am, you know? So, there's one more thing I want to show you and then I will leave you alone. Will you let me do this?"

"What is it?"

She smiles, then takes a notebook out of her book bag. She tears out a page, scribbles something on it and folds it but doesn't pass it to me.

"Why can't you just tell me?"

She sighs dramatically. "Because, it's more fun this way. Just trust me. Come to this address at four. There's something there that you'll want to see."

"Lily, I'm not in the mood for a scavenger hunt."

"Fine." She rolls her eyes. "Spoil the surprise. I think I've found something that has to do with your mother, okay?"

I stare at her. What could it be? A thousand possibilities, most of them awful, flood my mind.

"You said you can't remember her, right?" she asks. "Helping you helps me."

I can hear David's voice in my head but I nod anyway.

"Great," she says and drops the paper on the seat. Before I can pick it up, she's thrown her backpack over her shoulder and started skipping away from the car across the parking lot. I open the paper.

3324 Beekman. Xo Lily.

CHAPTER 23

JASON

2003

Jason gassed up and got some food, and then he went back to the island the Green kids had been pointing at. If he stayed on the open water side, he would be able to get right next to it, though finding a spot to tie the boat and get onto it took a few tries since it was all sheer rock.

By the time he was on dry land, the sun had gone down. He wore out the batteries on his flashlight searching the island and all he found was a small cave about halfway up. There was nothing in it, but maybe there had been once. The ceiling had fallen in, so no way to know. Maybe that was why the kids were interested in the place.

After he explored the cave, he climbed to the top. From there, he could see beyond the islands to the park, and he sat there for a long time, watching the campfires begin to dot the shoreline. Facing the other direction, it was just open water, blacker than the sky. He liked the island; it felt untouched. Other people must have explored it, but there was no sign of anyone, no litter or graffiti. The island was its own, wild and separate. It would be the perfect place to build a little cabin, fill it with his books, and never have to deal with people again. If he couldn't do that, he could at least camp. He didn't have a tent but the night was warm and he was tired. He went back to the cave and sat down in the entrance. Leaning against the mossy rock, he closed his eyes.

He didn't know how long he'd been sleeping when he heard voices. His eyes shot open. The kids were back. He couldn't tell where they were, but they sounded close.

He scrambled out of the cave and the wind hit him. He heard thunder rumbling and the air had that electric smell of a storm about to crack open. He ran into the trees in the direction he guessed was up, assuming they would be coming from below. The rain started and just as it did, the boy and girl shot out of the trees, laughing and yelling, not fifteen feet from where he was standing, and ran into the cave.

The rain came down hard and fast, plastering his clothes to him. That was *his* cave. They had the whole fucking lake to play in. They had their cottages and their boats and their toys. And now, once again, he was being forced to hide.

He crouched down, feeling along the ground until he found a rock. It was the size of a baseball. He squeezed it in his hand and its unwillingness to yield felt . . . good. It felt right. He could go into that cave and take them both. The girl would be easy; she was small. The boy was as tall as he was, but Jason was much stronger.

He moved closer and watched the entrance through the darkness. He could cross to it in five steps. They'd never know what hit them. He took a breath and gripped the rock.

This.

This was who he was.

He was the man standing in the rain, soaked, freezing, unable to even have the shelter that was rightfully his. The stone fit his hand perfectly. He only had to step out from behind the tree and go into the cave. If he did that, a chain of events would begin and . . .

Something would be unleashed. Something he had held down for all this time.

He just had to take the first step.

His father would take that step.

He could hear his father, even after all these years. *Are you a coward?*

The boy came to the edge of the cave and stood in the entrance. He looked into the trees right at Jason, lifted his hand like it was a gun, and pretended to shoot.

Jason stared at him. The boy couldn't see him. Of course, he couldn't see him. He was hidden by the trees. Then why this feeling of . . . recognition. Of inevitability. *Yes,* his mind said. *But not yet.*

Jason stepped back. He had to get out of here. He was disoriented and didn't know which way to climb down to find his boat and he couldn't risk it while the kids were still here.

The rain stopped. When the girl left the cave, he watched as she moved gingerly through the trees. The clouds were starting to break up and the moon was visible, so he had to be more careful. It was soon evident what she was doing. He kept distance between them but decided to hurry things along. The tree he was standing behind was half dead. He reached up and snapped a branch off it.

Crack.

It worked. The girl shot up. She said something, then she turned and scrambled back to the cave and soon they were heading back down to their canoe. It took him a long time after that to find his boat. When he finally did, he was filthy, hungry, and exhausted.

There is a line. Every person has a line and tonight, he had touched it. What was beyond? He thought of his father. Once you cross your line, there is nothing to stop you. Arrest, prison, death—none of these things scared Jason. What terrified him was what would happen to his mind. He had seen it in his father. Mental free fall into absolute darkness.

CHAPTER 24

FIONA

2003

The voices came up from below the window. Fiona shifted on her cot but each position only stuck the thin sheet to her a different way. She checked her watch. Forty minutes until she was supposed to meet David.

She'd assumed her dad would leave for his nightlong drive after the memorial, but for some reason he didn't go and instead he was sitting outside. That was going to make sneaking out really difficult. And now, by the sounds of it, Aunt Charlotte had joined him.

Like her father, Fiona marked time on this night, though she only had the vague markers that she had been told about. The car broke down sometime around midnight; the driver attacked her father about twenty minutes after he picked them up. And then there was a gap in time, a black hole that swallowed everything.

Around her, her cousins' rhythmic breathing continued monotonously. They were dark lumps sprawled out on the low cots; everyone on top of their sleeping bags because it was too sticky to want anything touching skin. Fans ran in each corner of the attic but they only circulated the hot air. She lay on her back, pajamas clinging to her in the heat, and listened to the creak of the old lawn chair when her father leaned forward to pick up the beer bottle, and the quiet clink as he put it back down.

Finding the cave and Jenny Glick's ghost were the reasons she gave David for visiting Smuggler's Point tonight, but Fiona had another reason, something too delicate to put into words. She could barely let herself think it. What if . . . what if there was a clue on that island about her mom? It was close to the park where they knew he took her, but the park had been full of people, so maybe he'd got a boat and brought her there. She hadn't run this theory past David because he'd poke holes all over it, but still. There was something about the island that called to her. David wanted to plan the route in the daylight so they'd gone to check it out that afternoon and the moment she'd seen it, she knew it was important.

She checked her watch. Thirty-eight minutes until she was supposed to leave.

At first, her dad and aunt had been speaking too quietly for Fiona to catch what they were saying, but then Charlotte got louder. That happened when she was excited. She was a hand talker. Fiona could picture her waving them around now.

"I mean, all that time alone. I don't think it's natural. It's not. Humans aren't meant to live that way so if you get someone who's messed up. And I hate those trucks. They creep me out. Not just because of, you know—"

Ugh. She'd probably been dying to ask her dad questions and saw this as her chance.

"I hate driving past them, especially at night," she continued. "I've seen strips of rubber come off their tires that could destroy a small car, and sometimes they swerve because the drivers drive too long. Like I've read about it. They're all on uppers, or worse. When I have to pass one, I hit the gas and hold my breath."

Fiona started picking at the scabs from the bug bites on her calves. "Can I ask . . . ?"

She ripped a scab off and the sting of it was briefly satisfying.

"What was he *like*?"

Creak, clink. How many times had her father sat through versions of this stupid conversation?

"I don't know. It was dark. He was wearing a hat."

"Like he was hiding," Charlotte said, the brilliant detective.

"I guess. But it's not like he knew he was going to pick us up. We needed help and he stopped."

"But like, could you sense it? Did you get in the truck and then realize?"

"I was more worried about the car. How much it would cost to fix it. And we'd left Fiona at home with my parents. Ana was anxious to get back to her."

He paused but now Fiona didn't want him to stop. Her dad never talked about that night. Ever.

"We were both tired and stressed," he continued. "I don't even remember what we were fighting about."

"Oh my God, poor you, and then you lost her." There's a sniff. "Oh my God. I'm sorry—I'm just, I'm a really emotional person."

Gag.

They were quiet for a moment. Probably Charlotte was hoping he'd spill more details but Fiona could have told her she was out of luck. Finally, she sighed and said, "I guess I should go to sleep. Callie'll be up at four. Are you staying up for much longer?"

"Yeah, I'll be a while."

After her aunt left, it was quiet down below. She thought—hoped, anyway—that her dad had decided to go to bed, but then she heard the twist of another beer cap coming off. She should have snuck down while her aunt was there distracting him. She changed back into the shorts and T-shirt she'd hidden in her pillow, stuffed the pillow and pj's into her sleeping bag in case anyone did a quick body count, and slowly eased herself down the steep stairs, through the hallway, and out the back door.

She kept to the shadows, moving away from the cottage to the old outhouse and then to the boathouse. They couldn't launch the canoe from the dock either—that would be in direct view of her dad. They'd have to portage over to the beach a few cottages down. Then, it was a thirty-minute paddle out to the islands.

"Hey—" It was only a whisper, but Fiona almost screamed. David stepped out from behind the boathouse.

"You just about gave me a heart attack," she said.

"You're early."

"So are you."

"I saw my chance," he said. "Dad got a call and left, and Mom was watching TV."

"My dad didn't go for his drive. He's sitting outside."

"No kidding. I just about walked right in front of him."

When they got out onto the water, the breeze wicked the sweat off her and was strong enough to keep the bugs away. David steered—he was a natural paddler—and she sat in front and paddled as he directed her to. He kept them parallel to the shore and they moved as quickly and quietly as they could. The moon reflected off the water, its light catching the infinity of ridges. It was one of the things she loved most about the lake. It was always alive, always moving.

After fifteen minutes, they were by the state park, following the shoreline of the peninsula. They could see campfires from the beach that wrapped around the end. Someone was playing a guitar and the sound traveled out to them as they passed by in the dark. Far off to the west, a fork of lightning reached into the water. The wind was stronger out here as they approached the open lake.

The islands came into view, dark shadows rising out of the water. As they got closer, they could feel the current getting stronger. They passed the signs that warned against boating here. They floated between the first two smaller islands and Fiona's paddle hit a rock underwater, making the canoe sway side to side.

"Let me take it from here," David said.

Fiona pulled out her paddle and looked up. Immediately above them, the sky was an explosion of stars. Frogs, crickets, and night birds were the only sounds besides the gentle dipping in and out of David's paddle. The sky to the west was pure black now with the low clouds blotting out the stars. Soon they would cover the moon. They passed more islands. Most of them were so small, they were no more than a collection of pine trees clinging to the rocks. The canoe scraped over another rock on the right and David swore quietly, using his paddle to push them away from it. Then, ahead, a large dark form rose up: Smuggler's Point.

As soon as she saw it, that feeling came back: *here.*

What would it mean if she found something, some missing piece of that night? Would it help or would it hurt? There was a fluttering in her stomach. She couldn't tell if it was excitement or nausea.

The canoe scraped hard over another rock and stopped. "Shit," David said. "Let's get out and swim it in from here."

Carefully, she dropped over the side expecting a rock. Instead, she went all the way under, then came up, sputtering. David slipped in after her and they half swam, half walked the canoe the rest of the way. The rocks underwater were slick, uneven and invisible. Once, she hit her shin and she heard David grunt with pain too, but they slowly made their way to the island's rocky beach.

"I can see why people don't bring boats in here," she said, gasping for breath as they finally pulled the canoe out of the water. There was a gust of wind and trees creaked. She felt her pocket but the flashlight she'd stuck in it was gone.

"I lost my light."

"I've got mine," David said and flicked it on. The beam of light was bright but only lit what it was pointed directly at. Another gust of wind hit them. The air had got cold with the pressure dropping and her teeth started chattering.

"How are we going to get back in this? We're going to have to paddle into the wind."

"It's moving quickly," David said. "It should pass over us. Come on, let's find the cave before it starts raining."

Keeping close together, they followed David's pinprick of light and stepped into the trees. Almost immediately, they were climbing and soon her hands were sticky with pine sap from where she'd grabbed branches for balance. She was breathing hard and she could hear David's labored breath in front of her. She tried closing her eyes and imagined her mind sending out feelers. *Show me where you are,* she thought. Ten years ago exactly on this night, with a storm coming in off the lake just like now, her mother might have been right here. She had felt so sure before.

"What if we can't find it?" She could come all this way, be so close, and still get nothing.

"It's not a big place. We'll find it," David said.

It was impossible to see anything other than the dark forms of trees. Fiona turned and looked out. They were high enough that she could glimpse the open lake between the other islands. We're only half a mile from shore, she told herself, but it felt like they were in complete wilderness.

A bolt of lightning cracked the sky open out on the lake and she screamed. But for the briefest of seconds, it lit everything up and there it was, above and to the right: a black hole. "There!" she yelled. The clouds opened and fat raindrops pelted down on them as thunder rumbled.

"Come on," David called over the wind, "let's make a run for it."

She felt giddy. They scrambled toward the cave, laughing as their sneakers slid on the moss and the mud.

David reached the cave first and then turned and pulled her into it. The first thing that hit her was the smell—it wasn't a bad smell, just damp like moss and earth. They stood in the entryway while the curtain of rain fell across them. They were both soaked and breathing hard.

"We made it," David said. He sounded like a little kid. "Holy shit, we found the Jenny Glick cave. It's real."

Not just Jenny Glick, she wanted to say. My mother might have been here too. But she didn't say anything. Did he bring her here? That feeling she'd had before, why couldn't she feel it now?

Inside the cave was the blackest black she'd ever seen. She touched the wall. It was damp near the entrance but got drier when she took another step in.

"I can't tell how far back it goes," David said. His shone his light back but it just got swallowed up in the darkness.

"I feel like the ground is sloping downward," she said. Roots poked through the ceiling and tickled the top of her head. "Watch your head—"

"Ow," he said at the same time.

"Yeah. It gets low, fast."

Keeping by the walls, they took a few more steps in, each bent over. Then David's light hit a pile of rocks and dirt. She looked back at the entrance and estimated they were about thirty feet in.

"Damn," he said. "It caved in. I wonder when?"

"My dad said there was an earthquake in the eighties. Maybe this is from that. So, when Jenny Glick was here, this might've gone much farther back."

"I think they shot her," David said. "She's probably buried somewhere on the island."

"But if they didn't and she died of starvation, she could be in there. Her and her baby." She touched the pile of rocks that blocked the rest of the cave. "I wonder how far back it used to go. It might go all the way through to the other side."

David moved back toward the entrance where he could stand upright. "Can you imagine, being a smuggler and hiding out up here? You'd have the perfect shot at anybody coming for you." Silhouetted against the mouth of the cave, he raised his arm and pretended to shoot a gun out the cave entrance.

"Yeah, but imagine being stuck here. So close, but no way to get to shore." On a map, it might look like they were close to civilization but being here on the island, she felt like they were hundreds of miles away. She leaned against the cave wall and slid down to the ground. David was still talking about smugglers and hidden guns but she'd stopped listening.

As quickly as the euphoria of finding the cave had risen, it receded. There was nothing here. She was dumb to think she was going to find something. Surely, they'd searched this island. They'd searched all the islands and the park and the lakeshore for miles. Ten years ago, on this exact night, her mother had died. No one knew how. No one knew when. And no one knew where. She was just gone. The finality of that was a stone in her stomach. She had been resisting tears all day but now they came, silent and hot. She's gone. She's gone. She's gone. And it would never stop hurting because she and her dad had to live through August 28 again and again and again.

"I want to go back," she said quietly.

"What's wrong?" David said. He moved back to her, keeping himself bent over. When his light hit her face, he squatted down in front of her. "Hey, why are you crying?"

"You know why."

"Yeah." He flicked off the light and sat down beside her in the dark. She leaned her head on his shoulder. In the past year, he'd gotten bigger than she was. One of the many ways that time kept moving them forward, away from her mom who had been left, frozen behind them. Forever twenty-one. One day, she would be older than her mother had ever been. That was a strange thought.

"I'm freezing," she said.

"Me too."

He wrapped his arm around her and she huddled into his body. It felt good—normal and comforting, but also something else. Something new and fluttery. Aside from a few times like earlier at the memorial, they had each been keeping a little more space between them this summer. It was too dark for them to see each other, but when she turned her head, his breath hit her forehead.

"Fi, I—"

"I have to pee," she said at the same time and pulled away from him and stood up. "The rain's stopping. We should start heading down."

She turned and walked quickly out of the cave. Her heart was beating hard again and her face felt hot, even in the cold damp air. Something had changed between them this summer and she didn't know if she liked it or not. She had seen the looks that had passed between her aunts when she and David came back from their hikes or canoe rides. Those little smirks, but they were wrong. But still, last summer she would have just peed behind the closest tree, assuming the night would hide her. Now she wanted to make sure there was space between them, so she kept walking. The ground was soggy from the rain and when she went under a pine tree, water dropped off the needles, resoaking her.

She was almost done when—

Crack.

She scrambled up, pulling her shorts up, and spun around, blinking into the darkness.

"David?" she called out. She took a step toward the place where the sound had come from but then stopped. What if there was an animal on the island? "Shoo," she called out, but her voice was scratchy and too quiet to carry.

Maybe she'd imagined it. Maybe something had just fallen, dislodged from the rain and wind. But there wasn't any wind now. Everything was still. Silent. That was what was so strange about this island; all the usual night sounds, like birds and bugs, weren't here.

She turned around and started moving back in the direction she'd come, but she couldn't see the cave. Panic clenched in her belly. "David?" she called out again. No answer. Don't be stupid, she thought. It's a small island. If I missed the cave, I'll just go down and end up by the water. Then the clouds thinned and the moonlight shone through and she saw it to the left only twenty feet away. She ran toward it, slipping and sliding on the slick moss and almost crashed into David as he stepped out of the entrance.

"Whoa," he said, reaching out automatically, but she stopped before they made contact. "What happened?"

She was breathing hard. "I'm fine," she said. "Let's go back. The storm's passed."

"Do you want to look around more first? We can actually see now."

"I just want to go."

They didn't talk as they picked their way back down to the canoe. Fiona kept looking over her shoulder but all she could see were the silhouettes of trees and rocks. She felt like they were being watched, but that was just Mikey's stupid stories. There was no ghost of Jenny Glick. When they pulled the canoe back into the water it felt warm compared to the air. They guided it through the maze of underwater rocks and when the water got deep enough they scrambled over the sides. David tried to steer them back out the way they'd come in, but now they were going against the current and kept getting pushed off course and into rocks.

Finally, he said, "If we move with it, it'll spit us out on the other side."

"But then we're on the wrong side."

"We can circle around the island on the open water side. It'll take a bit longer but I can't fight this current with all these rocks."

It was the middle of the night. The thought of being out on the open lake, so far away, made her stomach clench. David turned the canoe and they immediately started moving faster. When they came out of the island cluster, she could see the lights from the houses on Bonasera Bay glittering in the distance. He angled the canoe toward the open water and started paddling them back around the island. On this side, the open lake stretched for infinity. On the other was the dark form of Smuggler's Point rising up like a cliff, scraggly pine trees clinging to its sides.

"What's that?" David said.

"What's what?"

He pointed but all she could see were shadows. "There's a tree that's leaning toward the water. It's behind that."

"An animal?"

"I think it's a boat."

He angled the canoe closer. She could only vaguely make out a dark form sheltered next to high rocks but then the moonlight caught it. It was a silver boat. It bobbed in the water but didn't move so it must have been tied to something. It was empty.

"Maybe they got caught out on the lake in the storm and took shelter there."

"We would have heard the motor," she said. But would they? With the wind and the rain?

"Do you think they need help?"

"I want to go," she said.

David didn't protest.

Thirty minutes later, her arms on fire, they finally saw the lights from her grandparents' cottage. It felt like they'd been gone for hours but a few of the campfires were still flickering on the shore and her father was probably still sitting in his chair, swatting the mosquitoes and holding his vigil. The storm system was so small that it hadn't even made it to shore.

When they got close enough, David guided the canoe so they got out farther away and were blocked by the boathouse. They were almost back when Fiona's dad stepped out of the shadows and ran toward them.

"Go," David whispered to her. She let go of her end of the canoe and ran to meet him.

"Fiona? Where were you—? Why aren't you in bed? I went to check on you and you weren't there and—"

"I'm sorry," she said. "I'm sorry, Dad, I'm so sorry." She kept saying it over and over, but the words were all jumbled with tears.

She was expecting him to be furious but he pulled her into his arms. She didn't struggle to get out of his tight grip. "Don't ever do that again," he said into her hair, but his voice sounded hoarse. "Don't you ever, ever, ever."

Fiona was aware of David moving past them, maneuvering the canoe to the boathouse by himself. She half heard him murmur, "I'm sorry, Mr. Green," but if her dad said anything in response, she didn't hear.

CHAPTER 25

JASON

2003

The lake was dark and empty. It was just him, shooting across the surface. When he turned back, Smuggler's Point was lost in the darkness. But what had happened there, what had almost happened there . . . Maybe it didn't matter that he hadn't done it. Maybe now, it was only a matter of time.

When the Greens' cottage came into view, he cut the engine and used his paddle to pull himself toward the shore a few cottages down from theirs. It was well past midnight, the deadest time of night. The moon was high in the sky and all the cottages were dark. He tied his boat to someone else's dock, hopped out, and moved silently along the shoreline to the Greens. He almost walked right past the man in the chair.

Ben Green.

Are you waiting for me? he thought. All of the exhaustion fell away when he saw him. Ben Green, sitting out front like a pathetic guard dog, empty beer bottles scattered around his feet. His neck was bent back over the edge of the lawn chair at an angle he'd regret in the morning. He was deep asleep. Jason could walk right into the heart of his family, the center of his sanctuary.

Jason crept behind him to the cottage door. The hinges started to creak as soon as he moved it. With one quick jerk of his hand, he pulled it open. Ben stirred in his chair but didn't get up. Jason clamped his hand around the rusty spring and shut the door behind him. He was in.

The place was old. Two squat, plaid couches sat side by side. A clothesline stretched the length of the porch, sagging under the weight of beach towels and bathing suits. The curtains lifted and fell in the breeze. Hanging over the door that led into the rest of the cottage was a painted sign that said THE GREEN FAMILY WELCOMES YOU in swirly cursive with a border of strawberries.

He tried to remember what he had learned about the Greens during the trial. Ben was the oldest, but he had brothers. Jason couldn't remember how many. The Green family had seemed huge back then. They'd taken up several whole rows in the courtroom. Aunts, uncles, cousins—they'd all been there, unified. Jason remembered being more frightened of that huge family behind him than he'd been of the judge or the various police officers and detectives who had come in and out throughout the weeks of the trial. The girl's family had been much smaller, he remembered that too. Just her parents, looking exhausted. They were silent, while the Greens had been a loud group. They cried, they talked among themselves. There were lots of hands on backs and hugs in the hallways, always bustling around each other, calling out across the crowd like they were the only ones there. The Greens had tried to pull the girl's parents into their group—he remembered this now, seeing Mrs. Green try to hug the other mother and how she pulled away. And there were other families there too. Families of the other victims who had come from all over the country. The courtroom was filled to the brim with families and journalists, with more people spilling over into the hallways.

But it was the Greens who were the ones he remembered the best. Impenetrable, unified, circling around Ben Green, the star witness, like a herd of bison, horns lowered.

He and his mother were allowed to enter through a side door to avoid journalists, but no one spoke to them except the lawyers. His mother kept her arms wrapped around herself like she was always cold, even though the heat had been blasting, making the room stuffy and dry. He'd stayed as close to her as he could. Not that she'd noticed. On the breaks, she would go into the alley behind the courthouse and smoke and pace.

He blinked and looked around the dark kitchen. Right under their noses, all of them asleep and here he was, that scrawny kid in the secondhand winter jacket who had sat hunched over behind the defense. The kid who never got to say goodbye to his dad. Instead he had to watch him be handcuffed and shackled. The one time he'd gone to a zoo, he'd seen a male lion. His mane was matted and he stank like piss, but he strutted around that cage like he was still the king, completely unaware that the humans on the other side were gloating over him. Jason's father had reminded him of that lion during the trial.

A half watermelon covered with plastic wrap sat on the kitchen counter, with Tupperware containers stacked neatly beside it. He opened the top container: homemade chocolate chip cookies. Of course. His stomach grumbled, and he was a hungry kid all over again, except now the kitchen was full and he could gorge himself. He shoved a cookie into his mouth and then grabbed three more. The fridge was bursting with more containers of food, vegetables packed into the crisper, three different kinds of juice, two kinds of milk, and bottles of premade baby formula. He tipped the whole milk into his mouth and chugged it until it spilled onto his chin. He tore off a handful of fat green grapes and popped a few of them in his mouth. Every bite he took, an explosion of flavor, made him want more. He opened each cupboard door, one after the other, leaving them open, and stared at all the food. One cupboard had at least seven kinds of cereal. Another had jars of pickles, olives, fire-roasted peppers, artichoke hearts, oils, and vinegars; another was filled with boxes of granola bars, crackers, chips, and more cookies. He pulled a black-cherry soda from a line of them in the fridge and popped it open. The sound was loud in the silence. He waited. Nothing. He drank until it was empty. Cold and sweet and bubbly, he felt the sugar hit him, giving him new energy. He left the empty can on the counter.

Beyond the kitchen was a large central room with more couches and chairs on one side, and a long dining table on the other. Leading off the room were two hallways where the bedrooms must be. Now that he was here, what should he do? He'd come on instinct without a plan. For all this family had done to him, eating some of their food paled in comparison.

He crossed the room to look at a half-finished chess game. What caught his eye were the pieces, which were large and lumpy, made out of roughly carved driftwood. He picked up a knight and ran his finger over it. Whoever had made these had put faces on them; the horse even had a halter. He didn't play chess, but he knew enough about it to figure the knight was probably meant to protect the king and queen. He slipped it into his pocket. Tomorrow, they would get down on their hands and knees and look under all the furniture, trying to find the missing piece.

They would never know that Jason Ward had it.

When he and his mother had moved into the trailer, he'd put his collection in a box and kept it hidden in his bedroom closet. He would take it out and display it again because now he could add to it.

He'd thought breaking into this cottage would feel like a victory. Would his father see it that way? No. All he'd done was eat some cookies and steal a piece from a game, like a child. He had to do something to bring some balance between him and this family, but what? He could do anything to them right now. He thought again about what he'd almost done to those kids on the island, trying to find that feeling again but also . . . also terrified that he would.

He would leave a message, something that Ben would be sure to see when he stumbled inside, to know that he wasn't safe, even surrounded by his huge, loud family. Jason pulled the rock out of his sweatshirt pocket. How perfect.

He found a broken crayon in the junk drawer under the phone and scratched it onto the rock:

FOUND YOU

He put it in the center of the large table where it wouldn't be missed, then slipped out of the cabin, holding the creaking hinge to keep it silent. If Ben Green stirred, Jason didn't see because he didn't look back.

CHAPTER 26

FIONA

Now

There is no Beekman Avenue or Court or Road or Crescent in St. Rose, but there is a Beekman Street in St. Thomas. I know this because as soon as Lily walks away, I put the address into my GPS and drive there.

3324 Beekman is a nondescript brick house on a street of similar postwar houses. They're all bungalows. Some have been added on to, others probably look as they have for the past seventy years. There's no car in the driveway. Overgrown juniper bushes block the bay window, the matching feature each house shares, and there's a collection of soggy newspapers scattered on the walk leading up to it. I park far enough down the road that I can watch the house without being near it and sit there until my hunger pulls me away. In all that time, only three cars pass me. The only other movement is from a skinny gray cat who sits and watches me until it gets bored and skulks off.

I try searching for the address but nothing comes up besides the fact that it's off market and was last sold in 2007. But there's something about this house that is nagging at me. Again, I think about calling David. Again, I don't.

Ever since she left my car, I've been trying to figure out what Lily could possibly have to show me. My imagination has ranged from the innocuous, like some newspaper article she's dug up, to a picture of my mother's body.

When it's almost four, I go back. The street looks the same except now there are a few more cars in the driveways. I'm looking for Lily to come from the main road where I saw a bus stop, but a few minutes after the hour, she steps around from the far side of the house, checks both directions, and then waves at me. When I reach her, she's standing at the side door, jiggling a paperclip into the lock.

"Are you breaking in?"

"It's fine. I just lost my key."

"But—"

"It's my dad's house. I want to show you the collection."

Before I can protest, the lock clicks, and she opens the door. "Come on," she says, and grabs my coat sleeve pulling me inside. My immediate response is to get out, now. Everything about this feels wrong. I push the door back open to leave but she's still holding on to my sleeve.

"Relax," she says. "He's on the other side of the country."

The door slams shut behind us.

"Are you sure?"

She rolls her eyes. "Well, I don't know *exactly* where he is but he left last week and said he wouldn't be home until December. So, do you want to see this or not?"

The air is thick with a combination of smells: old grease and cigarettes and underneath that, something else, something human.

"Your father is not going to want you breaking into his house."

"He knows I come here sometimes."

We're on a little landing. In front of me are a few stairs that go up into the kitchen and to my right, a set of stairs to the basement. I see the edge of a washing machine with boxes piled beside it. When Lily sees me looking down the stairs, she says, "I can show you the basement if you like."

"I don't want a tour. Just show me what you were going to show me, then I'm leaving. This isn't right."

"Fine. Come on." She sounds annoyed, like I'm not enjoying her surprise the way she thought I would.

I follow her into the kitchen. Dishes are piled on the counter, and the garbage is overflowing, which explains part of the smell. The fading afternoon light makes everything shadowed and gray.

"How long is he gone for?" I ask.

"My dad's a slob," she says over her shoulder. "It's always like this."

I want to stay where I can see the door, but she moves through the kitchen into the living room, and I follow. It's almost completely dark because the window is blocked by the bushes. While the kitchen is messy, the living room looks almost empty. There's an old recliner and a television, and that's it. No pictures on the walls, no books or newspapers or signs that anyone spends any time here. It's stuffy and hard to breathe. She pulls out her phone and turns on the flashlight, then leads me into a small hallway.

"Is the electricity off?" I ask.

"I'd just rather not call attention to our visit."

There are three closed doors. It's narrow and my claustrophobia gets worse the deeper we go into the house. She opens the last door and we are in a small bedroom. Through the lone window there's enough light coming in to give some relief from the dimness of the interior. A single bed is on one side and when I step in, I see that the opposite wall is lined with shelves. On them, equally spaced, is an odd assortment of snow globes, knickknacks, and other small things.

"This is my father's collection," she says, moving her phone light over the objects.

I step closer to look at the shelves, but she reaches out and pulls me back.

"Don't touch anything. He'll know."

Each item is covered in a thin film of dust. I'm not seeing how this is supposed to relate to me.

"Your father collects knickknacks?"

"No," she says. "*His* father did. Souvenirs."

And that's when I know why this address feels familiar. I've seen it in a police report. I stagger back.

"This is—"

"This is where my father grew up," she says, smiling. "I was wondering when you'd figure it out. I thought you would have recognized the address. After my grandpa was arrested, it sat empty. People started to vandalize it. My dad bought it so he could take care of it properly."

I look out the window at the backyard. It's surrounded by a high wood fence. The yard is empty. Long dead grass and bare earth— nothing to show what was once hidden there.

"Why did you bring me here?" I'm having trouble breathing again. I need to lean on something or sit down, but I don't want to touch anything.

"Are you okay?" She sounds more curious than concerned.

"I need to go." I start moving toward the door.

"But there's something here that belonged to your mother. Don't you want to see it?"

"Just show me what it is and I'm leaving."

She gestures toward the collection. "Can you guess?"

Ever since we've come into this house, the girl who was sobbing in my car this morning has disappeared. Outwardly, she still looks like a teenager. She's still wearing her huge coat and her hair still hangs limply under her cap, but it's the way she moves in here. She's not guarded the way she's been. Her eyes scan the shelves as if she's looking for it, but I have no doubt she knows exactly where it is.

"Try to find it," she says in a singsong voice. My eyes are moving from item to item but I can't take anything in. I guess I'm moving too slow for her because she says, "So, my plan is to return some of these things to the families. You're the first." She points to an orange pill bottle on the far end. Before I can lean in to get a better look, she plucks it off the shelf and gives it to me.

The label is faded but in block letters it says "PROZAC 40mg." Under that is the logo for Fays Drugs and an address for Syracuse.

"I don't understand," I say.

"*Look.*" She shines her flashlight on it. There, so faint it's almost invisible, it says "LUKAS" with a date for refills under it: "5 refills by 2/6/1992."

"Did you know your mother was medicated?"

"I don't know," I say, but my voice doesn't come out right.

"It's nothing to be ashamed of," she says. "Half the kids at my school are on something."

My mother was on medication. Depression? Anxiety? When did it start? The prescription is for the year after I was born. If my mother went through anything like what I went through and my father didn't tell me, especially when he knows what happened to me with Zoe . . . I can feel the panic in my throat—panic and rage and confusion—and now I'm here, in *his* house—I can't think clearly. None of this is real. I'm not really here. I'm not standing in this house holding this bottle. But I am. Lily is watching me, her head cocked to the side like my response isn't what she was expecting.

"So, I guess your family never told you." She shakes her head. "That's not right."

"How—?"

"My grandfather always brought home souvenirs for my dad," she said.

"Why don't the police know about this collection? This is evidence."

"No," she says. Her voice is sharp. "No. The police don't get to be involved. My father can't know."

"But this could lead to more people. If you're serious about making amends—"

There's a thump from somewhere under us. We both hear it and freeze.

"Hold on," she says and walks to the door then turns back. "Stay here."

"But—"

"Just do what I say," then, "Sorry, it's probably nothing. Old house. Just give me a sec."

She leaves, closing the door quietly behind her. Outside, movement catches my eye and I spin around but it's just a gust of wind picking up dead leaves in the yard. The house is silent.

I go to the door and open it a crack but I can't hear anything. The noise sounded like it was coming from beneath us. Maybe a basement window is open or—

I have to get out of here. There's the front door and the side door we came in and both of them involve crossing through the house. Can I get out the window? I have walked right into the house that was Eddie Ward's graveyard. These shelves are full—there's well over fifty "souvenirs" here. What if they aren't all from Eddie Ward? What if Jason Ward is continuing the collection? And he could have come back—she wouldn't know. He could be here now, about to walk into this room and—

I close my eyes. Breathe. The old pattern a therapist taught me so many years ago: think about trying to soften that jagged ball of acid in my chest.

I reach into my coat pocket and grip my phone, my access to the outside world. Lily won't want her father knowing she's brought me here. I have to wait for her to help me get out. I'm going to open my eyes and take a picture of each item in the collection, one by one. When she comes back, I will leave and I will never see her again. And I'm going to give the pictures to David, even though he will freak out because I've been stupid enough to put myself here.

I open my eyes, take my phone out of my coat pocket, and open the camera.

Three wood shelves held with silver brackets. Each item is evenly spaced. Are these in the order they were received? That could be important. I start at the top left corner.

A snow globe with the St. Louis arch. Two tiny skaters holding hands below.

A pea-green toy transport truck with yellow flames painted on it. Inside a miniature faceless driver—

Another gust of wind outside. My head snaps to the window but the backyard is empty. The house is still silent. I turn back to the shelves.

A glass cigarette dish with a lobster etched into it. "Welcome to Maine."

A rosary made of white and turquoise plastic beads.

A tarnished brass lighter. "Vietnam 68–69." "To Hell and Back" written on the bottom, dirt permanently stuck in the etched letters.

A snow globe with Bigfoot inside wearing a Santa hat. On its base, a snowy mountain forest. It says "Bigfoot Country Christmas."

Another snow globe with a lone wolf, sitting on its haunches, howling. "Bozeman, Montana" written in silver letters around the base.

Where is Lily?

A rabbit's foot key chain with three tarnished keys on it.

A gold medallion that says "The Big Wheel. Austin, Texas, 1990."

A single blue cuff link. "Kentucky Derby, 1792–1992," written in gold. Three tiny horses, necks out, straining forward across the top.

A chess piece carved out of driftwood.

I stop.

It's in my hand before I even realize I've grabbed it. The soft pale wood. My grandfather's rough knife marks, teaching himself how to whittle wood on rainy summer days. And it's here, in this house.

I stuff the pill bottle and the chess piece into my pocket, open the bedroom door, and run back down the hall and through the dark living room. Lily is in the kitchen holding a glass of water.

"Fiona, wait! It was just a window—"

I don't stop. I'm down the stairs and out the side door. I hear it slam behind me. I half expect Lily to come after me but she stays in the house. The street is still empty. There may be people in the other houses but I don't care if they can see me. I run to my car, fumbling with the keys. The feeling of that house. *His* house. His macabre collection. The son of a monster, groomed from a young age. Becoming a monster himself. My father was right all those years ago. Jason Ward was watching us—hunting us. He took this chess piece to add to that horrible collection of mementos. If he's adding to the collection, then that must mean—

That sound. Someone else in the house. He's here. And he knows I'm here.

I've walked right into it.

CHAPTER 27

JASON

2007

Jason parked his car in the driveway and looked at the house. His house. All his. No one could take it from him now. The juniper bushes that grew in front were huge and unruly and with two feet of snow piled on top of them, they completely blocked the bay window, but he liked the privacy they gave. He never wanted to see out that bay window again.

His parents' house.

No, his now.

For the past three years, Jason had been saving money to buy a place that could be his. The new job driving trucks made it easier, especially since he hardly took vacations. He hadn't thought it would be this house, but it made sense. Where else could he go? It wasn't just the money, it was him. He drove all over the country now, but it had been made very clear that this was the only place he would ever be allowed to be. There was no escaping it.

The house had sat on the market for years with no one wanting to touch it. When he'd called the Realtor, the guy thought he was joking, then Jason told him his name and he got real quiet. Probably called the cops the second he got off the phone, "Hey, *son of* is buying the crime scene house . . ." But Jason wasn't doing anything wrong. He'd been taking care of it for years anyway. Ever since he was old enough to drive, he'd come and mow the lawn or shovel snow. Sometimes, it would get tagged with spray paint or eggs or dog shit—so much dog shit—but he always came by and cleaned it up. Now, he could care for it properly.

The Realtor seemed relieved he didn't want to do a tour or an inspection. They met in the office in St. Thomas and the guy was obviously nervous though trying to hide it. He shook Jason's hand hard, but he was sweating and kept trying to pretend he wasn't. There was no small talk, which was fine by him. Ten minutes later, it was done. Now he just had to go in.

After the police finished tearing the place apart, his mother had hired a clean-out company to go through and get rid of everything. She hadn't gone back to it since the day they'd been moved to the motel in the back of the police cruiser. At that point, there were already some media vans parked out front and a lot more came after the bodies in the backyard were discovered. The parts of the fence they'd taken down to get their equipment in had been put back up, but it was sloppy work that would need to be fixed. Treasure seekers had come in over the years to steal pieces of the concrete pad that had covered it. The cops had just left it broken in a pile. They'd filled in the hole, but he'd have to lay down top soil and plant grass seed if he was going to get it to look normal again. That was fine. He could do that.

He took a breath and got out of the car. A few houses on the street still had their holiday lights up even though it was February. The air was bitterly cold. He waded through the snow to the side door and went inside.

He tried to figure out what he was feeling as he stepped into that house for the first time since he was a kid. He could see his breath in the flashlight beam, but he didn't need light to find his way; this was muscle memory. The kitchen window had been broken a while back. He'd nailed boards over the outside but he hadn't been able to go in, so the shattered glass still sparkled across the counter and crunched under his feet. The rock that had been used had skidded to the far corner. It reminded him of the rock he'd left for Ben Green. Had he found it? The summer had ended after that and the following summer, he saw the Greens from his boat but he didn't see Ben. After that, the need to punish them faded. That was in part because of Samantha.

They'd been off and on for three years. After that summer, he'd given up on seeing her again, and then she walked into the auto body shop when she was home on winter break. When he was with her, as long as they weren't in St. Thomas or St. Rose, no one looked at him strangely. They were just a young couple like any other. At first, it felt like he could stop being *son of*. That thing that had risen up inside him had been lulled back to sleep.

But she started asking questions. She wasn't horrified by his family; she was fascinated. What had his dad been like at home? What was he like when he got back from the road? Could Jason sense when he'd killed someone? He almost told her about the collection, but something made him hold that back. Sometimes, during sex, she wanted him to get rough, to role play. And it scared him because he felt how that part of him was just under the surface. But she was also sweet and kind, and he liked how their relationship was a secret. Then, she wanted him to take her to the prison to meet his dad. When he refused, she asked to meet his mother.

The last time he'd seen her was just before the holidays. He'd finally relented and invited her to the trailer. She brought flowers and a box of fancy cookies and had complimented Carole on her handmade afghans. But when he came back in from walking Sam to her car, his mother was waiting for him.

"If you think that girl likes you for anything more than getting close to your father, you're either blind or stupid, or both."

He tried to protest but she wouldn't hear it.

"There are things I haven't told you. I tried to protect you, but what for? So you can run out and jump in bed with the first girl who talks to you? You didn't see how she was looking around? How she asked questions about back then? About him?"

"She's just being polite, Ma. That's what people do."

"Don't talk to me like I'm the dumb one here. That girl is just like everyone else. They want to touch the evil. They want to get that filth all over them. You're the filth, Jason. You and me. But they can walk away any time they want, once they've got their thrills. You can't."

"She's not like that—"

"She ask to see stuff from your childhood?"

"Yeah, but—"

"She ask if she can have any of it? Because you can bet she's going to turn around and sell it. Or she'll go talk to some journalist and sell the story. Make herself rich off us."

"You don't know her."

"Neither do you. You think you can walk away from all this just 'cause you're with her? Well, you can't. Because that girl doesn't want you—she wants *him*."

He shook his head to try to clear it. His mother's voice, Samantha, he needed them both out of his head. That's what this was supposed to be too. A fresh start. A place where he could be alone. What better place than a house no one wanted to touch.

Jason walked through the kitchen into the living room and shone his light at the bay window. As he'd suspected, the outside world was blocked by the bushes and snow. That window was where he'd been standing the last time he'd talked to his father. He'd woken up because his parents were fighting. His dad's truck was outside. He thought he'd seen someone in it but it had been dark and raining. He'd wondered if his dad had a girlfriend. She—he'd been pretty sure it was a woman—had waved at him. Not just a friendly wave, she was waving like she wanted him to see her, but he knew he wasn't supposed to. His dad would be angry—angrier than he already was. Jason had stepped back from the window. Then his dad had called to him and pressed that pill bottle into his hand. "Keep this for me." No hand on the shoulder, no goodbye. Just another piece for the collection.

Jason turned away from the window. The room was empty, cable wires hanging out of the wall where the TV had been. In a corner were some old papers. He went over and picked them up. He recognized the writing as his own at eleven years old. The papers he'd dumped out of his school bag so he could hide his father's collection, no idea of what was about to happen. There were the beginnings of sixth-grade math homework—fractions—and instructions for a three-page paper about local history. Ha. His family had become part of that. He'd written his name in the blocky printing he used back then: "Jason E. Ward." That was the last time that name had just been a regular boy's name, not stained in blood.

Past the living room was a hallway that led to the bedrooms. He knew his parents' room would be empty, but he didn't want to go in. Instead, he opened the door to his old bedroom. There were the empty shelves where he'd put his collection. The window was cracked open and it gave the room the fresh smell of winter air.

This would be his room again, he decided. He'd display his collection as he had before. It wouldn't be right to be in any room but this one.

He was walking back through the living room when there was a knock on the side door. He just about dropped the flashlight he was so startled. One of the neighbors must have seen his truck. If they recognized him, would they give him trouble? He looked around for something to use as a weapon if it came to that, but all he had was the plastic flashlight. The knock came again, and then a woman's voice.

"Jason? I know you're in there. It's freezing out here."

Sam. How had she found him?

After his mother had shared her views of Sam, he'd run out of the trailer to a pay phone. He didn't have one of those new cellular phones, but she did. She picked him up and they'd gone to a motel. All night he'd wanted to ask her if it was true, but he didn't need to ask because he knew as soon as his mother said it that it was. And he knew he wouldn't see her again after this. There had been times in the past three years when he'd imagined the two of them married, living in some little house with a couple of kids and a dog. For the first time, maybe he was done being punished for being *son of* and could have a normal life, the kind of life everyone else got and didn't recognize as special. It was why he was saving his money. Now that would never happen, but he wanted this one night. And maybe it was the way he'd run after her, or the cheesy motel room, or maybe she knew it was the end too, but it felt magical. For a few hours, he was able to push his mother's words out of his head.

And then, sometime around three in the morning as he was drifting off, feeling the warmth of her back pressed against his chest, she said, "I wrote to your father. He wrote me back."

In his head there were a lot of things he did. He smashed, he screamed, he slammed, he punched. But he didn't do any of those things. She kept talking.

"I told him who I was and that we are, you know, kind of getting serious, and I just said that I wanted him to know. And I said that I wasn't going to force you to go see him, but that you were a great guy. I didn't give any details, I just said that I'd be interested in meeting him, with you of course, if that was something that might be good."

He swallowed to make sure his voice sounded steady. "What did he say?"

"His letter was really long. Do you want to read it?"

"No."

"Okay. Well, he told me a lot about what prison life is like. Like their daily routine and he told me about some of the guys. Even a couple of the COs. It sounds like he knows everyone in there. It's like its own ecosystem. And he said that he thought about you all the time and that he was glad to hear you were with me and I sounded like a sweet girl. And he really liked that I was a nurse."

"You told him that?"

"I mean, yeah. It's not a secret or anything. He said it was an honorable profession."

She fell asleep after that but he couldn't. He got out of bed and looked through her purse, but the letter wasn't there. And then he left. He walked the three miles back to his mother's trailer and slept in his car. Sam left messages for him, but he didn't return her calls. And he decided to use the money he'd been saving to buy this house. Because there was no escaping who he was and where he was from. There would be no little house with two kids and a dog. There was just this.

"Jason, come on, please. Just let me in."

Sam was still out there. She must have gone to his mother's house looking for him and she sent her here. His mother thought he was a "dumbass idiot" to buy this house, but he was long past caring what she thought.

He walked through the dark kitchen, down the little stairs to the side door, and whipped it open. Sam was standing there, stamping her feet and blowing on her hands.

"Why are you here?"

"Wow, what the fuck? What did I do?"

"Just get inside." He grabbed her arm, pulling her in more roughly than he meant to. "I don't need any more attention here and now you've announced yourself to the whole neighborhood."

But she wasn't listening. Her eyes were moving all around, trying to take it all in even in the darkness. Not that there was much to see: a set of stairs leading down to the unfinished basement and three stairs going up to the dark kitchen.

"This is it?" she asked.

"This is my house," he said.

"But this is the house where—"

He turned and walked up into the kitchen, not bothering to share his flashlight with her. She followed anyway. "Like I said: This is my house. It was then, it is now. Why are you here?"

"Because I need to talk to you. I have to go back in the morning."

"Well I don't need to talk to you."

"I'm not here about your dad, okay? I'm sorry if I overstepped by writing him."

"Has he written to you again?"

"Does it really matter?"

So, he had.

"Jason, I'm pregnant."

He stared at her. Her face was in shadow but he could see enough to know she was looking right at him.

"I thought you were on the pill."

"It's not infallible."

But it wasn't that. This was another trick, he was sure of it. She was willing to do this just to get further in? Well it wasn't going to work.

"I'm about eleven weeks along, assuming my math is right, which I think it is. Morning sickness is a bitch when I'm on shift, but my friend gave me this natural stuff that helps keep the nausea down, but that's why I think it's a girl—"

"I don't want a baby," he said.

That made her stop talking. He heard her take a breath like she was going to say something, but she didn't. They stood like that for a moment, then she said, "Can I look around?"

She took the flashlight out of his hand and he listened to her walking through the pitch-black house, opening and closing doors, but there was nothing here for her to see. Only he could see the ghosts.

She came back into the kitchen and put the flashlight on the counter.

"So that's it? There's no explanation. It's just 'no'? It's not your choice, you know."

He didn't say anything. He couldn't trust himself. Because still, that stupid, blind, dumb-fuck part of him that his mother saw so clearly was screaming, "Yes, yes, yes. You see? You can escape. You can have a real fresh start. Not this. Something normal. Something pure." He turned and focused on the broken glass, slowly sweeping it onto the floor and then crushing it with his boot.

Sam went outside. He thought she'd left but he didn't hear a car. He went out and saw footprints leading to the backyard. The gate was open. She was standing just inside, looking at the lumps in the snow that showed what was left of his father's graveyard.

"Have you seen enough now?" he said.

She pointed to one of the windows. "That was your bedroom."

He didn't answer.

"Did you see what he was doing back here?"

He didn't answer.

"You knew. I always figured you must have had some idea. Your mom too."

He didn't answer.

She turned to him. "I'm keeping this baby. I'll raise her on my own if I have to. None of this is her fault. It doesn't have anything to do with her."

"Sam, don't, please." He sounded like he was begging. Maybe he was. "This—" he gestured to the lumps in the snow, the house, all of it "—this has to end. *He* has to end."

"What's that supposed to mean?"

"He ends with me."

He hadn't been able to put it into words until they came out of his mouth, but as soon as he said it, he knew it was right. It was the only thing he could do: refuse to continue whatever monstrous DNA his father had passed on to him. He would live in this house and he would die in this house and then it would be over.

Sam had taken a step back from him. "When she's born, I'm going to write to your father. I going to tell him he has a grandchild." And then she turned and walked away.

CHAPTER 28

ANA

They were in a town. For a second her stupid brain felt relief. He was going to take her to a gas station. He had done something to Ben, but he was going to drop her off and she could call an ambulance. Was this St. Thomas? It all looked familiar. She was so close to home now. There were gas stations in St. Thomas. There were people—

He slowed and turned onto a residential street. He turned his lights off so they rolled forward in darkness. The houses all looked identical. Brick bungalows, windows dark, outside lights off. He stopped the truck and turned to her.

"Stay here," he said. He pointed the knife at her again, then clicked it shut and put it in his pocket. He leaned across her—she shrank away from him—and opened the glove box. He pulled out two long plastic zip ties. He took her left arm and zip-tied it to the gear shift. He pulled it tight and she felt the plastic dig into her skin. He got out and pulled open the passenger-side door. The rain had soaked into his jacket. He was still wearing his ball cap, his face hidden. He reached in and grabbed her leg. The feeling of his fingers clamped around her ankle. She was too stunned to react. He zip-tied her ankles together and she cried out automatically.

"Shut up."

He looked at her. "Give me something."

"What?"

"Something of yours. The necklace."

He started to reach for it.

"No!" She cried out louder than she'd expected. Before she'd even realized it, the knife was back out poking into her side.

"Give me something."

"Money?" she asked. "I can get money."

He saw her purse at her feet and picked it up, rooting through it. He pulled out her pill bottle. He shoved it in his pocket, tossed the purse back at her feet, and slammed the door.

A security light came on as he walked to the side of the house and went in. She saw a light go on inside.

She was alone. She was alone and she couldn't move. With her free hand, she tried to open the door but it was locked. She looked at the other houses but no one else had turned on a light. They were asleep. She could scream but no one would hear her from inside the truck with the rain pounding down.

Then, there was movement in the front bay window. A child was standing in the window looking out at her. He or she had pressed their hands to the glass and was looking out at the truck. She lifted her free hand and waved it frantically. She banged on the window and the movement made the plastic on her wrist cut deeper.

"Please! Please help me—"

The child turned and looked behind them, then they disappeared back into the house. "No—"

The man came back out. Did he hear her? He yanked his door open and got back into the truck. He was breathing hard again. He stabbed the keys into the ignition and the engine roared to life but when he went to move the gear shift he must have realized her hand was still attached. He took out his knife. She tried to jerk away but she couldn't move.

"Stay still or I'll cut you here," he said.

He slid the blade between the tight plastic and her skin and flicked it up, releasing her. She hugged her wrist to her chest, massaging it as they drove away from the dark houses. In the last second before it went out of view, she saw the pale shape of the child back in the window, watching them drive away.

CHAPTER 29

JASON

Two Weeks Ago

The call comes through on the landline, which means it can only be from one person. Even the robocalls came on his cell. So many times, he'd thought about disconnecting the landline, but could never go through with it. Jason picks up the phone and waits for the recorded voice to ask him if he is willing to accept a collect call from, his father's voice recorded here, "Edward Ward," at Grady State Penitentiary. Hearing that voice, he's a child all over again. He clenches his free hand. *He's just an old man now . . .*

"Yes," he says, and then he waits for his father to speak. His breathing sounds like air being sucked through an opening that is too narrow.

"Jason." It's not a question, as in "are you there," it is a statement. An expectation.

There are a thousand things this son could say to his father. He could tell him that serving a sentence in a prison with no walls means that it is inescapable. He could tell him what it's like to be forever stained by actions he had no part of; to know when he goes to the grocery store, the dentist, the bank, that people move away from him, avoid eye contact, and then watch him until he leaves. Always the unasked questions. *Could you? Will you?* The only option has been isolation—

to create a barrier around himself. Life necessitates that he work, that he buy food and pay bills, but he could have gone far away to do these things. He could have changed his name and moved to another country and, at least outwardly, erased this version of himself. But it is like the phone line. He wants to sever it, but he never can. He is held to this place, to his mother stewing in her resentment, to his daughter, and even to this man breathing into the phone from his prison cell.

A thousand things he could say, but instead he says nothing.

"I'm dying," his father says. "Come soon." And then he hangs up.

When he tells his mother, her response is "Good." When he says he is going to go see him, she says, "You're a fool." That is the only conversation they have about it.

He expects a room full of hospital beds, but after he gives his name and his visitor's pass to the corrections officer in the hall, he is taken to his father's room and it looks . . . nice? The walls are painted a pale blue instead of the uniform greenish-white of the rest of the prison. It is small with just enough room for a hospital bed, a bedside table, and a chair. There is a cross on the wall. He stands in the doorway looking at the shrunken man asleep in the bed. Another man comes up behind him carrying a small plastic cup with a straw.

"Excuse me," he says. Jason steps aside and watches as the man leans down to his father. He says something quiet to him and his father opens his eyes drowsily. Then, the man gently slides his arm behind his father's shoulders to help him sit up and holds the straw to his lips. After, the man wipes his father's mouth and gently lays him back down on the bed, then he turns to Jason.

"Come in," he says. "He can't see too good, so he won't be able to see you there. Are you Jason?"

Jason nods. He is having trouble finding his voice. The man steps forward and shakes his hand.

"I'm Kadeem. I'm one of the hospice volunteers looking after your dad."

"Hospice?" Jason says.

"It's a new program they're trying out here. We got two hospice rooms in the infirmary. Trying to give our brothers a little more dignity at the end."

"Are—are you a doctor?"

Kadeem laughs. His voice is low and rumbly. "No, but I'm tickled you'd think I am. I'm in here with your father. I volunteered for this. It's a way of giving back, you know?" He nods to the bed. "Someday, that'll be me. We're all going to die in here."

Eddie's eyes are closed again. Kadeem touches his shoulder. "Hey Ed, you going to stay awake long enough to see your boy?"

Eddie keeps his eyes closed, coughs, then says, "Waiting for you to quit talking an' leave me alone."

Kadeem laughs again and shakes his head. "All right, you cranky bastard. But I'll be back later so don't go nowhere." He turns to Jason. "Take your time, son," and he leaves the room.

Jason doesn't sit down. His first instinct at seeing that kindness was to tell him to stop. To leave this man to die by himself. But as soon as Kadeem leaves, he wishes that he'd stayed. His father turns his head and squints at him and he can feel the boy inside him so desperate for this pathetic monster to see him.

"Took you long enough."

When Jason leaves the penitentiary, he drives until he can't see it in his rearview mirror, then he pulls over on the side of the road and turns off the pickup. On either side of him, fields are filled with dried brown husks of harvested cornstalks. Winter will be coming soon; he can smell it.

He takes out his phone. He has four contacts: his mother, his work, his ex, and his daughter. First, his finger hovers over "Sam," then over "Lily," but he throws the phone on the passenger seat. Calling them to warn them will just cause more problems. His daughter is already so curious about her grandfather, but curious enough to come out here on her own? Probably not. A headache is coming on. There is a feeling at the base of his neck that always warns him of what is to come. He closes his eyes.

"I'm not giving them the satisfaction of watching me die," his father had said. "Come back and bring me something to move things along."

"I can't do that," Jason had told him. The hospice room might have pretty paint on its walls, but they were still penitentiary walls. He wished he'd said "I won't do that."

"You think you're not part of this? You are. You're the one with my collection."

"You gave me those things—"

"Don't interrupt." His father was weak now, but he could see the tendons tightening in his neck. How badly he probably wanted to be able to spring out of bed and hit him, and even though he couldn't, Jason instinctively took a step back. Instead, his father reached for the cup beside his bed. When he opened his mouth to suck on the straw, Jason could see the thick greenish-white lining around the inside edge of his lips.

"You still have it." It wasn't a question. "Bring it to me so I can see it one last time—"

"—I can't —"

"But finish it first."

"What?"

"It's incomplete. It's missing the last piece."

He couldn't help himself. "The last piece?"

"A necklace. I should have taken it when I had the chance, but there's a way these things should be done. Figured I'd get it after. And then?" He held up his hands and let them drop. "She disappeared."

"What do you mean?"

"Disappeared. What I said," his father said, a bit louder this time. "You fucking deaf now? The last one—"

"Ana Lukas?"

"Was that her name?"

Jason remembered that huge Green family in the courtroom, all those families, but especially them, and after, how he'd hated them and wanted to be a part of them at the same time. He thought about the news reports, the missing posters all over town, all before he knew that this local tragedy was directly connected to him. He thought about hiding out in that motel with his mother for months—how, in some ways, he and his mother had never stopped hiding. All because of his father and a whim he'd had one summer night, a whim to kill a woman whose name he didn't even know.

"Ana Lukas," his father said her name slowly, like he was tasting it. He was looking past Jason now, at something he couldn't see. "She went into the water and she never came out. They got her. Not me." Most of his body was still slack, but the fingers of his right hand were twitching, pulling at a loose thread in the blanket.

"But I thought you—?"

"Something got her before I could. There's stories I heard. Ghosts in the water."

"So, she just drowned?" Jason said.

"She didn't drown," he spat. "That's why they never found her."

With a jerk, he ripped the thread out. His hand was shaking. "They'd have got me too."

Movement at the door caught Jason's attention and he turned. The corrections officer was in the hall. They made eye contact briefly, then he walked on.

"They're hungry down there in the deep parts of the lake," his father said. He turned and looked directly at Jason. "Finish my collection."

He stared at his father. What was he asking him to do?

"You always were a fucking pussy. Find something special and finish it."

He coughed and his whole body convulsed. The veins in his neck stood out and his hands gripped the metal sides of the bed. When the coughing fit subsided, he spat into a metal bowl tucked in beside him, then he turned and looked at his son again.

"Find something to finish it, or I'll ask my granddaughter. She'll do it if you won't."

Now Jason can't stop thinking about the water, his boat, and the island— *his* island—that's how he's come to think of it over the years. What he needs is the island. He decides that no matter what the weather, he'll take his boat out one last time before the lake freezes over.

His mother must have told Lily that her grandfather is dying because when he gets back from the prison, Lily is sitting at his kitchen table doing her homework. She's made herself a sandwich and not bothered to clean up. He has suspected that she sometimes goes to his house when he isn't there. He also thinks she's borrowed his pickup, though who knows where she's learned to drive. The key is always back in its place, but he found some of her hair in it a few months before. He hasn't said anything because a part of him likes that he's able to give her this.

"Grandpa's dying," she says and then her face scrunches up and she starts crying.

"Don't call him that," Jason says. Something feels off. She isn't even trying to hide that she's broken in, and has he ever seen his daughter cry? The sight of her hunched over her homework at that kitchen table reminds him of his own childhood, all the hours he spent alone in this house.

"Why are you here?" he asks.

"Where else can I go?" she says. "Mom and Grandma will be happy when he's dead. You're the only one who'll understand."

"He doesn't deserve to have people caring about him. Including you."

She looks at him. Her eyes are huge. "Everyone deserves that, even if it's just one person who cares."

"Did he—?" he starts to ask but then stops himself. "You don't know him," he says instead.

"I want to know him. I have a right."

He needs to warn Sam about his father wanting to contact Lily. He wouldn't be able to phone her. Even Sam, for all her curiosity, would never accept that call. But he needs to make sure she's gotten rid of those letters. If Lily, inspired by her mother, had written to him, surely Eddie would have gloated about that.

"Will you take me to see him? Just once?"

"No."

That triggers more crying.

"Tell you what," he says. "How about tomorrow, I'll pick you up from school and show you something better."

When he picks her up outside her school the next afternoon, she is wearing one of his old coats, which means she's been snooping in his closet. It's shabby and far too large for her, but instead of being angry, he's touched she wants to wear something of his, even if it doesn't fit her right. The tears are gone. She's bouncing in the seat like a kid all the way out to the marina until he tells her to sit still and stop fiddling with the radio, but even his abruptness doesn't dampen her excitement.

Most of the boats have been brought out of the water for winter and the marina feels deserted. The lake won't freeze until late December or January but people worry about ice getting into their engines and take them out in October. As soon as they are away from the marina, he opens up the throttle. He glances at her and the look of pure joy on Lily's face is infectious. The spray that hits them is freezing, but neither of them feels it as they fly across the empty lake toward the vast horizon. They are far out when they pass St. Rose, then he angles the boat toward the cluster of islands.

Smuggler's Point has become his sanctuary. In the years since he discovered it, he sometimes spends several days at a time there. He never lights a fire, so as not to draw attention to it. Sometimes he sees people in kayaks or canoes, but most of them only pass by. If they do venture onto it, they're usually only interested in finding the cave and he knows the island well enough now that he can make himself disappear until they leave. The best place to dock is still under an overhanging tree on the open lake side, and since most people approach from the other side, they don't know he's there.

He steers the boat between the underwater rocks, then ties it to the tree that hangs over the water. Lily watches him carefully but knows to stay quiet. He hoists himself up using the tree. The rocks are slippery with moss and lake water but he's done it enough that his hands and feet know where to find their holds. Lily follows him, putting her hands where he put his, and pulls herself up like it's nothing. She's stronger than she looks.

"What is this place?" she asks once they've climbed up a little and are looking out over the lake.

How can he tell her what this place means to him? "It's called Smuggler's Point," he says. "I come here sometimes."

Her eyes go wide. "I've heard about this place. It's supposed to be haunted. A smuggler died here."

"That's bullshit tourist crap," he says. "We're not like that."

She smiles when he says that. "Yeah," she says. "We're not."

Jason knows he has never been a good father. Usually, he tells himself that she's better off without him. He never wanted a child in the first place and has tried to keep a distance between them, but as she's got older and more independent, she has become more persistent. He watches her now, slowing turning 360 degrees to take it all in. He wasn't sure what her response would be. If she'd been like most teenagers and complained or seemed unimpressed, the tour would have stopped here, but she seems as moved by the island as he was his first time.

"Come on," he says. "I want to show you something."

They climb higher. He takes her to the top first. On a clear day, you can see almost all the way to Canada, but this day is overcast with low gray clouds and visibility is reduced. It will be dark even sooner because it's so cloudy so they'll have to hurry. He leads her down the other side to the cave. Her mouth drops when she sees it, and she runs in like a little kid.

"Where do you think it used to lead?" she asks when she comes back out.

He shrugs. "No way to know." He wants to tell her about how he sometimes camps in this cave, and pretends he's the only one who knows it exists. He wants to tell her about how this island has helped him over the years, the way it's worked its slow magic to calm the monster inside him. How if he hadn't found this place and her mother, but mostly this place, he would not be here now. He too would be in prison.

"It could have another entrance," Lily says, peering back into the darkness. "I bet the smugglers could get into it from the water and hide in there."

"I've explored every inch of this island," he says. "There's no other entrance. This is it."

"No," she says. "I bet there's more."

The anger is immediate, but he bites down on it. "Sometimes there is no more. There's just what you've got."

He turns and walks away from her into the trees. Her belief in a secret exit is childish. There are no magical doors in life and no escaping who you are. There's only work and time. Having the discipline to come here and wait it out. But she wants the magic, the quick solution.

He was wrong. He brought her to this sacred place and she doesn't understand at all.

She runs up behind him, but he doesn't stop walking until she grabs his sleeve. "Why can't it be possible?" she demands. "Just because you haven't found it doesn't mean it isn't there."

He spins around, hand raised. She releases his sleeve but doesn't pull back.

"Why can't this be good enough?" he says.

"Dad—"

That word in her mouth stops him.

"This is a special place to you," she says. "I can see that."

He doesn't say anything. He's breathing hard. They stand there, looking at each other: father and daughter. The wind is picking up, and the trees around them sway and creak.

"Did Grandpa show you this island?" she asks.

"*I* found this. He didn't even know about it," he says. "And I told you, don't call him that. He's nobody to you."

"He's part of me because he's part of you," she says. "And I'm not ashamed of that."

"He never would have come here. He was scared of the water. He thought there were ghosts in it." That seems pathetic now too. He turns and starts walking back down to the boat.

"But there are," Lily says. She scrambles after him. "There are shipwrecks all over the lake; lots of people drowned. I'm doing this project on it at school. But someone died on this island too. Maybe more than one person."

"You don't know that."

"I can feel it." She says it matter-of-factly like it's nothing to her. "Did you ever ask him what it was like to watch someone die? I wonder what that would be like."

Jason stops walking and turns to look at her. Her hair is long and deep brown, like her mother's when he met her. The wind is lifting it up and blowing it into her face, but she doesn't brush it away. In her entire life, if he added up all the time he's spent with her, it probably wouldn't amount to a full day, and yet this recognition when he looks at her now is disarming. He needs to teach her how to control these feelings, these questions. But he doesn't know how.

"We should go," he says. "Weather's changing."

The next morning, he leaves on another cross-country run. He'll be gone for a few weeks. Hopefully, by the time he comes back, his father will be dead, taking his threats with him. There might be snow when he returns but he's decided to risk it and left the boat in the water. It's four in the morning and pitch-black outside when he stands in his kitchen making coffee. He'd dug out one of his old winter caps and now he puts it on the counter, thinking of how Lily's hair had blown in the cold wind. He doesn't have a spare house key, but that obviously won't stop her from getting in. He likes that. She's allowed to come in, but she has to work for it. Right before he leaves, he takes two keys out of his pocket: one for his pickup—no more need for her to pretend she doesn't use it—and one for his boat. Maybe, even though he couldn't put it in words, the island will work its magic on her as well. He leaves the keys with the cap where she'll see them the next time she breaks in, and then he walks out.

CHAPTER 30

FIONA

Now

I call David as I'm driving back from St. Thomas. The whole way back, I have to grip the steering wheel to stop my hands from shaking. I was such a fool to think I could just walk up to Jason Ward and demand answers from him. Seeing something from my childhood sitting in a serial killer's collection of souvenirs has made me finally understand what my father knew back then and what David has been trying to warn me about. I've talked to his mother, I've spent time with his daughter, I've been inside his house. I have invaded his life. If he knows, what will he do?

When I get back to the cottage, David is standing outside his car, waiting for me with sandwiches and a six-pack of beer. Tucker comes bounding out of the bushes and jumps on me. I have never been so grateful to see either of them.

"I'm so sorry. You were right. I don't know what I was doing. I thought—she told me—"

"Whoa, it's okay," he says, striding over to me. He goes to hug me, but then we both pull back, and instead he puts his hand on my arm. "Was he there? Did he threaten you?"

"No. I don't know. I don't think so. We heard a noise but Lily said it was just a window and then I ran out."

I explain from the beginning how I ended up at the house and what I saw. I pull up the photos I took on my phone and thrust it at him. "There's so much evidence. You have to get a warrant. There could be things there from victims no one knows about. And he's had it this whole time. Or maybe he's added to it."

"The police tore that house apart," David reasons. "Don't you think they would have found it if was there?"

"So? His father was probably storing it elsewhere. Think of all those other families who still don't know what happened to someone they loved. The evidence could be right there."

"I get it," he says, "but we still can't go sweeping in. There's a procedure. And it's questionable how much information we'd be able to pull from those items anyway. Some of them could be forty or fifty years old. They've been handled by other people, they've been sitting on a shelf covered in dust. And Eddie Ward is dead."

"But his son isn't. What about the chess piece? That's evidence he was in our cottage."

"It's not. It's just evidence that something *from* your cottage ended up in Jason Ward's house."

"Oh, come on. How else would he have gotten it?" I don't understand why David's nitpicking. I thought he'd be excited to see these photos. Sure, they might not all be souvenirs, but my mother's pill bottle is, and there's a good chance other things are too.

"I know it seems obvious, but it won't stand up for a judge."

"Can you at least talk to your captain?"

"Not while we're in the midst of the Ramirez case."

"Every one of the families who lost someone to Eddie Ward was *exactly* like the Ramirez family is right now. They don't matter less because it happened a long time ago." As soon as I say it, I know I've gone too far.

David steps away from me. "Why do you think I've been busting my ass for the past four days. I'm doing everything I can not to have another family end up like yours, but what good has it done?" He turns to walk away. At first, I think he's going to get back in his car, but instead he goes down the stairs to the cottage and stands looking out over the lake. Tucker gives me a reproachful look, then follows him.

I know I pushed him too far, but I also know I'm right. It's something that you can't understand unless you've lived it: there is no getting over something like this. I grab the sandwiches and beer and walk down. David is standing at the top of the stairs to the beach. I come up beside him.

"I'm sorry."

"Maybe I didn't live it like you did, but I have a pretty clear understanding of the stakes." He doesn't sound angry anymore, just exhausted.

"I know you do," I say. "I think we both need to eat. Will you stay for a bit?"

I hadn't realized how worn down he has become in the past few days. He looks older than he did when he picked me up at the airport. "Or, you don't have to if you have to go back to the station."

"Not tonight," he says.

"I probably shouldn't be keeping you up then. You must be exhausted."

"It's been pretty nonstop."

He's deciding if he can tell me something. I know him well enough to recognize this and to understand that he might not. Our days of telling each other all our secrets are long gone.

"I don't want to be inside tonight," I say. "Let's have a campfire."

He laughs. "In November?"

I grab some lawn chairs from the boathouse and carry them to the fire pit on the beach. David brings down an armload of wood and while he's getting the fire started, I raid the cottage for old blankets we can get sand on. Tucker, who seems immune to the cold, splashes around in the lake, then plunks down in the wet sand, his head resting on his paws.

We eat and watch the fire in silence, but it's not awkward. We used to spend hours together without the need to talk. It feels like a connection to old times being able to do it now. Watching the flames is hypnotic. I'm lost in thought when David says, "My chief told me to take the night."

I wait.

"The Ramirez family's here. The parents are okay, they're mainly just in shock, but the sister doesn't think our department can handle the investigation. She doesn't think *I* can. My chief fought for me at first but now it's been four days."

"Four days isn't very long," I say quietly.

"It is in a missing person's case. She's out there, Fi. It's all I've been doing, and I don't have anything to show. He says I need perspective."

"So, you get a good night's sleep and you can go back fresh tomorrow."

"No," David says but then doesn't say anything more. He pokes at the fire. "I'm starting to think the sister's right."

Tucker has edged closer but then a piece of wood pops and sparks fly up. He yelps and jumps back. David reaches out to him and scratches his head. "It's okay, boy. Just stay by me."

We sit in silence for another few minutes, David stroking Tucker's head. The adrenaline has left me and I can feel the beer now. I wonder if he can too.

"My chief worked under my dad. He'd just joined the force the year before your mom disappeared, so he was pretty junior, but they were all involved. He said he admired him—they all did—but as the investigation got bigger, there started to be problems. There were a lot of other people, you know, with so many agencies involved. There's a lot of egos in a case like that, a lot of attention from the press. At first, he said, everyone admired how my father was handling it, how relentless he was, but after a while, it made him lose perspective. Some of the guys thought my dad was getting in the way."

"He told you this?"

"I think it was a warning. That's how I take it."

"Of what? Is this going to become a huge case?"

"The family's pushing to get bigger players involved. They think I'm too inexperienced."

"Is he going to take you off the case?"

"Not off, but I might have to step aside." He pokes at the flames again causing more sparks. "I *know* she's out there. We've done a deep dive in her social media. We've talked to every person who lives within ten miles of where her car stopped, and every person who was at the bridal shower. We've gone through security footage at gas stations for a huge radius, and at the places where she was in Canada—that took some coordination. Was she followed? Was she meeting someone?"

"Do you think this was planned?"

"Nothing we've found points to that. I think it's the most obvious scenario: her car ran out of gas and someone picked her up. And I think it was local. Given where it was, and when, it almost had to be."

"Sounds familiar."

"That's what I can't let go of. The chief intimated that I'm letting that blind me. I don't know, maybe he's right."

"But if it is local like you think, then they have to keep you on," I say. "You're the one who knows this area. Bringing in outside people isn't going to help."

He runs his hands through his hair again and groans. "I can't screw this up, Fi. If we don't find her soon . . . Her sister's in the station all the time. 'Have you done this? What about this?' I get it. She's trying to *do* something. But it's the parents who I can't stop thinking about. They're so quiet but you can see this is destroying them. The mom just looks at me when they come in. She just looks at me, and I feel so fucking useless."

"Hey." I reach out and grab his hand and squeeze it. "You will find her. You will. I bet you're a great detective. It's what you've always wanted to do. As long as I've known you, and I've known you from the beginning. That's a long time now."

"Right here on this beach," he says. "Two fat little babies, stuffing sand into our mouths."

"Speak for yourself. I'm sure I had better taste."

He smiles at me and then in the same second we realize we're still holding hands, and drop them.

I stand up and everything swims for a moment then rights itself. "I found a bottle of scotch one of my cousins must have left. I need something stronger than beer."

The fire burns down to embers, then we stir it up and add another log and it rises up again. At some point, David goes to find another blanket and comes back with what turns out to be a very stale bag of cheese puffs. We take turns tossing them into the fire and watching them melt. It's such a relief to lose track of time. I just want to be here, now. To get lost in this. When we were kids, I assumed, in that deep, sure way you can be certain about things when you're that young, that David and I would always be together; that our lives as adults would pair as closely as they always had. Could they still? I've never felt as close to anyone as I did to him when we were kids and being with him now, I feel those old feelings coming to life again.

"Hey." He's got his hand on my shoulder and is shaking me awake.

"Mmm?"

"I think you fell asleep."

"Did I snore?"

"No, you just kind of drifted away for a bit. Come on." He stands up and lets the blanket drop around him. He leans down and tucks his arm behind me to help me up.

"What are you doing?"

"I'm helping you get up."

"I don't need help. I'm sleeping here."

"Come on, I've sworn an oath to help civilians."

"This civilian is perfectly happy where she is."

"You can't sleep outside in November. If you die of hypothermia, it'll be my fault."

"Remember how we used to beg to sleep on the beach? Why didn't we ever do that? We could have in the summer. My dad always made me go back into the cabin."

"I don't think it would be as comfortable as you're imagining."

"We have enough blankets. It'd be cozy. It's so strange being in that big cottage all by myself."

"Come on. Up you get."

He's leaning over me. I can smell him. It's a familiar smell but also there's some kind of cologne in there. Our faces are so close. How many times have I wondered what it would be like to kiss David. My hand goes up to his face and touches the stubble on his cheek. He puts his other hand down on the chair to support his weight and the rusty metal creaks in protest. The gap between us closes. His mouth is so soft. I reach up to pull him closer and suddenly Tucker is up, barking.

"Whoa, Tuck, it's okay." David stumbles back up and grabs for him but the dog is focused on something up beyond the cottage and then he's off, bounding back up the steps and barking the whole way.

"What the hell?" David says and before I've even stood up, he's following his dog, all signs of exhaustion gone.

When I finally catch up to them they're in the parking area above the cottage. David has a flashlight in his hand and is searching the ground for something. Tucker has calmed but is pacing and sniffing.

"What was that about?" I ask. "An animal?"

"If it was, Tuck scared it away. I didn't hear anything, did you?" Then his light catches something on my car and he walks over and pulls a piece of paper out from under the windshield wiper. He opens it. "What the fuck?"

"What is it?"

He holds it out to me and shines his light on it.

Sorry about today. Need to talk. Meet at 3 behind school. Please. xo—Lily

Instinctively, I go to grab it but he pulls it away from me. "Don't. Prints." He goes to his car and comes back with an evidence bag and slips the note in then shines his flashlight back over the ground. "There are tire tracks, but those could be ours. Of all the people for you to become friends with."

Whatever happened between us just a few minutes ago is gone.

"We're not friends," I say. "She just showed up."

"You've hardly discouraged her."

"I get that you don't trust her father, but I don't think it's fair to assume that Lily is anything like him, or her grandfather. She never even met him and according to her mom, she barely has any contact with Jason Ward."

"She brought you to his house today."

"But she doesn't have a key. She had to break in."

"You broke into his damned house? What were you thinking?"

I can't explain it to him in any way that will make sense.

"She can't help you find out what happened to your mother, and that is what you want to know, right? There is an active investigation going on right now—"

"That involves them?"

David doesn't answer my question.

I look all around, half expecting to see Lily walk out of the woods smiling at me. Everything around us is pitch-black. Woods, dirt roads, empty cottages. There are a million places a person could hide and watch if they wanted to.

"Could she have put that on your car before, when you were at the house?" He asks. "Maybe you didn't notice it when you drove home."

"No, I'd have seen it. And I used my wipers. She knows about the cottage, but I didn't tell her where it was. These old places are impossible to find—"

"Unless you've been here before."

I'm about to protest that Lily has never been here, but Lily isn't who he's talking about.

"I think you should stay at my place tonight," David says. "Or you can stay at a motel. Just not here. You have to be somewhere where he can't find you."

CHAPTER 31

JASON

Now

Jason is in Nebraska when he gets a call from his neighbor, Roger. The old man is a son of a bitch who more than once has threatened to shoot people on the street he thought were trespassing. But over the years, he and Jason have found a sort of mutual respect for each other. Jason helped him once when his son-in-law needed a reminder that debts should be paid and just 'cause the old man couldn't personally kick his ass, didn't mean he couldn't still make trouble. In exchange, Roger keeps an eye on the street and on Jason's house in particular. It has been years since people tried to break into the backyard or tag it with spray paint, but that doesn't mean it couldn't still be a target for people feeling nostalgic.

Roger calls him to say his daughter is coming and going from his house.

Jason says that isn't a problem; Lily goes there sometimes when she needs a break from her family. She's probably upset because her grandfather died.

No, he insists, she had someone with her. Couldn't tell who but they looked drunk. Could barely stand. Middle of the night. Maybe it was a boyfriend. He—Roger—wasn't one to judge if the girl was turning into a little slut, that's why he hadn't said anything at first. But then this afternoon, he'd seen a woman go in the house too. She went in with Lily but she ran out a bit later looking like she'd seen a ghost.

Jason pulls off at the first exit he can find, turns his truck around, and starts driving home.

CHAPTER 32

FIONA

Now

David sets me up in his apartment, then goes back to the station. I didn't think it would be possible for me to sleep, but I must have drifted off sometime in the early hours of the morning. I wake up to the sound of him getting home and Tucker whining anxiously.

"Have you slept at all?" I ask.

"No," he says. "I just came back to walk Tuck. There's something you should know, though. We picked up a glove on the side of the road where Angela's car was. It took a bit, but they were able to get some DNA off it. It was Jason Ward's."

I sit down hard on the couch.

"So, he's now officially a suspect."

I can't tell whether he is excited about this or upset because he's moving around too much for me to see his face. He goes into the kitchen and comes out with an apple, then goes into the bedroom. I stay on the couch.

"That's a big find," I say, finally. "You said you didn't have any leads."

"Now we do. But we have to find him." He comes back out, pulling a fresh shirt over his head. "But, I don't think you should go back to your cottage. It's too dangerous. This has to be connected to his father dying; it's too coincidental otherwise. It's pushed him." He grabs Tucker's harness and starts to attach it.

"What about Lily? Do you think she's in danger?"

"Why do you care?"

His sudden anger comes out of nowhere and I can feel mine rising to meet it. "'Cause she's a kid whose father might be violent."

"Isn't this enough for you to stay clear of that family?"

"I didn't say I was going to go tell her. I just think she should be warned. So should her mother."

"This isn't your case. Just leave it. You should go home, Fiona." I want to say something about last night, but maybe that was just alcohol and circumstance. "There's too much going on. I can't protect you."

"I don't need your protection."

"Oh no? Because yesterday, you walked into the house of a man who is now our number one suspect in an abduction. A man who has targeted your family before and who clearly knows where you're staying."

I start to protest but what am I supposed to say? I turn and walk into his room to grab my bag. He follows me to the bedroom doorway.

"Were you even going to tell me about your daughter?"

It's like someone has just punched me in the stomach.

"I-I wasn't trying to hide her from you."

"Really? Because you've been here for almost a week. I mean, Christ, Fi. That's kind of a big thing. And I have to find out from my father?" Off my look he says, "I talked to him last night about Jason Ward. He's still in touch with your dad, who, by the way, was not happy to hear you'd come back."

"I'm not with her father. We were together briefly but—"

"But why wouldn't you tell me about her? Don't you think I'd be happy for you?"

"It's not like that, I swear."

He turns and walks out of the room. I hear a cupboard door slam, then the water running but when I come to the kitchen, he's just standing in front of the sink holding an empty glass. Tucker whines and moves back and forth between us.

"Why did you come back?" he says. He's still not looking at me. "I know you were going to talk to Ward, but surely you knew, even if you did talk to him, he wasn't going to give you back your mother."

"I thought if I could find out what actually happened then maybe, by some miracle, it would help me figure out how to fix myself." It sounds so pathetic when I say it out loud. Like magical thinking. "But I haven't learned anything other than she was messed up too. I didn't think I would ever become a mother, but when I got pregnant, it felt like maybe a baby would . . . I don't know, fix the part of me that was broken. But I was wrong. I was dangerously stupidly wrong."

"You're not broken," he says.

"No, David, I am."

He turns and looks at me.

"And now, knowing what I know about my mother, that maybe she *left*, it confirms it."

"Nothing you've found out proves that. Just because your mom was on antidepressants, doesn't mean she wasn't a good mother. If anything, it proves she was trying to be."

"Do you remember my grandma Lukas? How cold she was? She still is. I am her connection to her daughter, and she barely wants anything to do with me. That's messed up. But maybe there was something wrong with her. This sort of thing can be genetic. And now I know my mother struggled with me too."

"You don't know that. There's no way to prove that."

"Okay, but I do know the terrible thoughts I have had. I know what *I've* almost done—"

"What did you do?"

The baby carrier on my chest. The icy ocean water coming higher and higher, dogs barking in the background. I have replayed that day so many times in my mind. I can't tell him this. Never, ever, ever.

"I've thought about just disappearing too. Many times," I say instead.

"You think that's what she did?"

"If she was in the water and she was alive, which we now know she was, then she should have made it home. She was a mile away from our cottage."

"In a storm. At night."

"My mother could swim fifty miles. The only reason we never saw her again was because she didn't want to be found."

"So, what, she saw her chance and swam to Canada? Come on—"

"People don't just disappear. You said it yourself."

"Have you ever seen the full file of the investigation? Because I have. They knew she was a good swimmer. Good swimmers drown. It happens. I know people don't just disappear into thin air. They are somewhere. But that doesn't mean they are ever going to be found."

He walks past me like he's going to leave, but then he just stands in the middle of the living room, lost.

I walk up behind him but keep a space between us.

"David?"

He doesn't turn around.

"My daughter's name is Zoe. She'll be two next month. Her father and I were only together for a bit but we're friends. He's a good man. Aaron married another woman named Jenna. Zoe lives with them. She was with me for the first year but it didn't work. Jenna is a better mother than I could ever be, and with her and Aaron, my daughter will have a stable, normal family. And she will be safe because I am going to give up my parental rights."

He turns and looks at me.

"I'm doing the best thing for her. The best thing for her is keeping her far away from me."

When he speaks, his voice is quiet. "You are chasing a ghost. If you'd trusted me enough to tell me what was going on, I never would have encouraged you to come back. This whole time, there's a child who needs you and you're just giving up." I'm expecting anger but he looks so sad. Like the boy I used to know. "Fiona, you of all people would do that to your child? I don't even know who you are anymore."

I grab my bag and walk out.

The last connection I had to this place, to the person I used to be, has now been severed.

I am free floating.

I am lost.

CHAPTER 33

JASON

Now

Jason drives through the night and into the next day, but his house is empty when he gets there. Empty, but Lily has been there. His truck isn't in the driveway and the boat keys are gone as well. The kitchen is a mess with dishes everywhere and there's a strange smell in the house.

In the living room, he finds her school bag. It's the day before Thanksgiving, so she's not in school, but why did she leave it here? He opens the bag and dumps it on the armchair. A math textbook, binders, and loose papers fall out, and then he sees it: a stack of folded papers, held together with an elastic band. He picks it up and turns it over. Attached to the stack is a note in his daughter's loopy writing:

Fiona, I know you wanted to know him. I did too. Maybe these will help.
xo Lily

He opens the package and there is his father. Years and years of letters. His father's threat to contact Lily made real. It takes him a moment to realize they are addressed to Samantha.

He hurls the letters across the room but they just flutter pathetically to the floor. He doesn't know who he's angrier at: Samantha for writing to his father and giving these to Lily, or Fiona.

Fiona has to be Fiona Green. Ben Green's kid, all grown up. There is no one else who would want to "know" his father. He does some quick math. She must be in her thirties now. He thought she and her father had moved away but has she come back? His mind is moving too fast—the memories of that summer—the first summer he had his boat, when he found their cottage, how he'd followed those kids to the island, how he'd almost—

So much time has passed since then. He has worked so hard to make a space—a tiny space is all he has asked for—to insulate himself. And his daughter is now communicating with Fiona Green? Sharing these letters with her? Lily is a child. The only way they could have met is if Fiona Green found her and is pretending to be friends with her.

But why?

The answer is obvious: to get to him.

He thinks of what Roger told him: how he saw Lily come here with someone who was drunk. And then Fiona came back yesterday? But there's nothing here that has to do with her mother.

No, that's not true, is it.

He goes into his bedroom. He knew Lily snooped, so it was obvious that she would see his collection. But it was largely a collection of trinkets and knickknacks, mementos from truck stops across the country. Unless you looked closely. And Lily, his curious daughter, his daughter who has been fighting for a connection to him ever since she was born, has obviously examined it very closely. She hadn't asked him about it, because she knew he wouldn't answer but that didn't mean she didn't ask her grandmother.

His eyes scan the shelves. He's stared at these items so many times, he has to force himself to look slowly, to catch any gaps. The light is dim so he pulls up the flashlight on his phone. There are two small marks where there is no dust: one is round like a pill bottle and one is square.

That's it.

The shape of a chess piece. The one item he added.

Fiona Green is going to rip it all apart, unless he can stop her. He just has to find her first.

CHAPTER 34

FIONA

Now

I go back to the cottage because there's nowhere else to go. There's no point in going to the airport the day before Thanksgiving. I'll just have to wait it out. If Jason Ward is going to find me, so be it. I sleep for most of the day. Images flood my dreams. Old dreams: waves hitting rock, pine trees overhead. The dream shifts and now I'm with my daughter. The waves are huge. The tide has come in quickly and she's going to be pulled into the water. And then I realize that the little girl is me. My perspective changes. I'm in the water and my mother is on the beach. I turn and watch. She's yelling something to me but I can't hear her over the crashing of the waves. She changes again. Now she's Lily. She's trying to tell me something, to warn me. I turn and see a wall of water rising behind me and—

When I wake up, I'm covered in sweat but the cottage is freezing. It's half past four in the afternoon and quickly getting dark. I've missed my meeting with Lily, though I wasn't sure if I was going to go. I know I have to stay away from her, but she needs to be warned about her dad. But how do I warn her and not alert him that he's a suspect? Could she know what her father has done to Angela Ramirez?

I throw on more warm clothes and grab my keys. I need food, but most of all, I need to make sure Lily is safe. I'll go to her mother's and talk to her there. And if she isn't there, maybe I can find a way to get the message through that she needs to stay away from her father.

I've been lost in my thoughts as I drive the windy road into town, so I don't know how long the pickup truck has been behind me. I become aware of it when the driver switches on the high beams and blinds me in my rearview mirror. I speed up to put some space between us but the truck stays on my tail.

"Asshole," I mutter, and take my foot off the gas. "Go around me if you're in such a hurry." There's no one else on the road. The truck could pass me but is obviously wanting to make a point. I've run into drivers like this before. They're usually young guys who have huge tricked-out trucks they can't afford trying to intimidate other drivers.

"Fine," I say. I tap my brakes and put my blinker on to pull over so he can go around me. The truck roars past and I let out the breath I've been holding as the taillights get smaller in the distance. I pull out to continue but then I see the glow of brake lights in front of me. The truck is sitting in the middle of the road. I come up behind him, stopping a good thirty yards away. My hands tighten on the wheel. My phone is in my purse on the passenger seat but even if I call someone now—and who would I call, David?—how long would it take them to get to me? We're both just sitting, waiting for one of us to make a move.

I flip the lock on the door but the car is already locked. I turn the radio off and use one hand to dig through my purse for my phone, keeping my eyes on the truck. All I hear is the *swish-swish* of the wipers and beyond that, the low rumble of the pickup's engine. I could get around him, but that might be what he's expecting me to do and he'll ram me from the side as I try to pass. My only other option is to drive in reverse as quickly as I can but the road is narrow and it's gotten dark, fast.

The interior light goes on in the truck and a door slams. My headlights just catch a figure moving in the dark toward me, trying to stay out of the light until he's at my door. I see just enough to know it's a man. He's taller than I am and wearing a baseball cap, and he's covering the distance between us quickly. The response is automatic. I slam my foot on the gas. My tires spin for a second, then grip the road and I shoot forward, swerving to the left into the other lane. The man jumps out of the way. I fly past the truck and don't slow down. My eyes keep flicking to my rearview mirror, expecting to see the headlights bearing down on me again, but the road stays dark.

I pull into the first place I come to, which is an auto body shop on the outskirts of town. It's closed. I'm half a mile from the center of town so why does it feel so desolate here? Five minutes pass. Ten, fifteen, but I don't see the truck. Finally, my eyes flicking up to the rearview mirror every few seconds, I pull back out and drive to Lily's house.

CHAPTER 35

JASON

Now

Everything that was so carefully stitched together is coming undone. The line that he has scratched in the ground with his bare fingers has disappeared. Once you cross the line there is nothing to stop you. You are in free fall. Twenty years ago, Jason stood outside a cave holding a rock in his hand and knowing that the only thing that kept him from becoming his father was that line and to cross it would only take one step. That time, Fiona Green and her friend took the place he'd named as his own. Now, she's messing with his daughter.

He borrows Roger's pickup truck and finds the Green family cottage. He knows roughly where it is, having seen it from the water, but finding it in the tangle of barely marked roads that lead to those old cottages takes a long time. Add to that the growing dark and fog. But he does find it. He parks his truck farther back on the road and walks in. A lone purple Jeep sits in the parking area up the hill from the cottages. It's got out-of-state plates. He'd known Ben Green and his kid moved away; this seems like the sign that she's come back. He descends the old wood steps that lead from the parking area down to the lawn as quickly and quietly as he can, but there's no sign of anyone being around. He's not entirely sure he's found the right place until he walks around the larger cottage to the side that faces the lake, then he recognizes the screened-in front porch with the same lumpy furniture he saw twenty years ago and over the inside door is the same cheery sign with its strawberries. He tries the porch door but it is locked, so he steps around the side of the boathouse and watches.

He's just about to give up when a light comes on in the main room. A woman, Fiona Green he assumes, moves around the cottage. She is alone.

The line, he's back at the line. And this time . . . ?

Realizing that makes it hard to breathe.

And then she puts on her coat and looks like she's planning to leave, so he decides to follow.

He cuts through the trees to the road where he parked his truck, moving fast now, not worried about noise. He gets in it just as she drives past, but he's parked off the road and she doesn't seem to see him. He gives her a moment to get ahead, then turns the truck on and follows. He's moving on instinct with no plan. When he catches up to her, he follows for a bit then turns on his high beams.

At first, she speeds up but he stays close behind. When she pulls over, he passes her but decides the message needs to be made clear, so he stops the truck in the middle of the road. Her headlights come up behind him and she stops a little ways back. He is having trouble thinking clearly. He has been having trouble thinking clearly ever since he realized he was back at his line. He opens his door and gets out, stepping to the side to avoid her headlights shining directly on him. He is holding his gun but he doesn't remember picking it up.

He is going to kill her.

No.

He is going to talk to her.

No.

He is—

Spinning, free fall, not able to think.

She guns her engine and comes straight at him. He jumps to the side and watches as her taillights disappear down the road.

Everything could unravel tonight. Everything could be destroyed tonight. Years of careful hiding in plain sight. Years of building that protective barrier. He's been awake for a day and a half, and the exhaustion is making him too weak to stop the raging part of him that wants to hurt.

He will call Samantha and tell her to keep Lily at home, away from Fiona Green. And he will go to the island. It is the only safe place— the place where he can be safe from himself, from the line, and what beckons beyond it.

So, he lets Fiona Green drive away and goes to the marina instead.

His truck sits in the parking lot. His boat is gone. Now he knows where Lily is.

CHAPTER 36

FIONA

Now

It's a relief when Sam answers the door, but as soon as she sees it's me, she doesn't open it any wider.

"Why is my ex telling me to keep Lily away from you?"

"What?"

"Lily's father just left a message telling me to keep her away from you. What the hell is going on?"

"I was coming to tell you to keep *her* away from *him*. He's the prime suspect in an abduction." I probably shouldn't say it but at this point, I don't care.

Her face blanches. "Oh my God." She opens the door all the way. "Come in."

It's obvious I've interrupted again. This time, she's wearing a kitchen apron and there's a spatter of tomato sauce down the front. The smell of garlic and spices wafts out of the kitchen, and my stomach lurches.

She turns and calls up the stairs. But there's no answer.

"She probably has her earbuds in. Just a minute. Sorry," she says, indicating the apron. "I've got a houseful of guests tomorrow and I'm trying to get ready, and now this."

She goes upstairs and immediately comes down, followed by Maisy, who is wearing tights and a leotard with her hair pulled up in a bun. Sam has ditched the apron and is typing into her phone.

"Mommy, we have to go. I can't be late again because then I have to stand at the back and I can't *see*."

Sam looks at me. "I've texted her, but I doubt I'll hear back. She never responds unless she wants something." Maisy is tugging on her arm. "Just a minute. I have to call your father."

Wherever Lily's stepfather is, tinny music is blasting through the phone as soon as he answers.

"You didn't think to tell me that she wasn't home?" Sam says. He says something then she interrupts. "I can't do this, Brent. You were here. You were the one who was supposed to—Well, when are you going to be home . . . No, because she has the *Nutcracker* rehearsal. Yes, the day before Thanksgiving." She looks at me and shakes her head. "I'm not overreacting—I can't *explain* now. I need you to come home . . . Well then meet us at the studio because I have to go find Lily." She hangs up on him.

Sam yanks her coat off the hook. "Apparently, Lily hasn't been home all day, but my husband decided not to mention it before he rushed off to the gym. How did you hear about Jason?"

"My friend is the lead detective."

"Mom, we have to leave now."

"Get your coat on. I just have to make a phone call." Maisy groans in protest but her mother ignores her and goes into the kitchen.

The little girl looks at me suspiciously. "Lily's weird. You shouldn't be friends with her," she says.

"That doesn't seem like a nice thing to say about your sister."

She shrugs. "Everyone says it. And she's only my *half* sister. Did you know, her grandpa's a murderer? Britta asked me if I was scared of her." She lifts her arms and does a pirouette. "Did you know I'm going to be a mouse in *The Nutcracker*?"

Sam rushes back in. "Carole isn't answering, but that's nothing unusual. Lily's probably gone there again. She's been practically living out there lately. I just wish she'd have the courtesy to let me know."

"Mom, come on."

"Could she be at a friend's house?" I ask as we get outside.

"Lily doesn't have any friends," Maisy says matter-of-factly.

Her mother looks up from where she's been frantically digging through her purse. "Maisy Grace, that is not a nice thing to say."

"I'm not saying it to be mean. I'm saying it 'cause it's true," Maisy says to me quietly.

"She told me about her friend, Reilly," I say. "They were doing a school project together. Could she be with her?"

Maisy looks skeptical. Her mother turns to her. "See? Your sister has friends. And if people say unkind things, you ignore them, okay?" Then to me, "I don't have that girl's number. But maybe she's there. Did you text her?"

"I don't have—"

"Reilly's sister's in grade three and she said that Reilly thinks Lily's weird too," Maisy says as her mother bundles her into the car. "She didn't want to work with her, the teacher made her."

"Okay, that's enough," Sam says, closing the car door and turning to me.

"Samantha." I reach out and grab her arm before she can get in the car. "In those letters you wrote to Eddie Ward, did he ever give a reason?"

She looks at me. I can't tell if it's with pity or shame. "He wanted to be seen. To be known."

"He told you that?"

"Those weren't his words, but yeah. He didn't have some grand theory. It was so . . . ordinary. I mean, my seven-year-old wants to be seen. We all want to be." She glances at Maisy, then opens her door and turns to me. "Thank you for the heads-up. I'm going to go get her from her grandmother's. I can't think of where else she'd be. I'll send you her number as soon as we get to ballet. Maybe she'll answer your call because she certainly doesn't answer mine."

CHAPTER 37

ANA

August 29, 1993
1:30 A.M.

They drove away from the houses, from the empty fast-food restaurants and the gas stations. They drove on small roads that led to more small roads. It should have all looked familiar but something had happened to Ana's mind and she was watching all of this from far away. Then, the truck turned onto a gravel road. Tree branches scraped the sides of the cab. She could see the dim image of the two of them reflected in the window in the bluish glow of the dashboard lights. He had no face. Only the baseball cap pulled low.

They stopped.

He turned off the engine and she heard waves crashing onto the shore.

The lake. As soon as he opened his door, she could smell it.

He pulled her door open, the knife in his hand. It didn't matter. All she could focus on now was the sound of those waves. If she could just get to the water.

He leaned in and sliced the plastic tie around her ankles. He nicked her skin but she only registered it distantly, like it happened to someone else's body.

He grabbed her arm with his free hand and pulled her out. The rain was driving down. She stumbled. Her feet were numb, but the knife was poking into her back and so she made herself stand up.

"Walk."

She lost a shoe. Her feet were all pins and needles now as the blood came back into them. Broken bits of shells were sharp in the sand but it didn't matter. The lake was right there. She just had to get into the water, then her body would know what to do. It always had.

She stepped into the water. He was still behind her, the knife touching her back. Was he pushing her or was she leading him? She didn't know. The wet sand sucked off her remaining shoe. A wave hit them, and she heard him curse, but she kept moving. She knew how to move in rough water. He didn't. She was up to her knees, then her thighs. Go slow, she told herself. He can't know she wanted to be there. The water was at her waist. She felt the next wave coming.

"Stop," he said.

The lake was going to help her.

She stopped.

She saw the rise of the next wave.

"Give me the necklace."

He was going to stab her, or grab her hair, or, or, or—

"I said—"

His fingers were probing her hair, trying to find it. He was so close. The wave crested and she dove.

The knife slashed deep into her calf as her foot made contact with his body. She kicked off him and pulled herself forward staying under the water. Pull, kick, pull, kick, her lungs burning for air but she had to go farther before she came up, pull, kick, pull, not yet, not yet. She was trailing blood but the pain in her calf was a distant thing.

Just like a little fish, swimming below the wild surface, where it was calm and dark. She could hear Dad's voice in her head: "Swim, Little Fish, swim."

So she did.

CHAPTER 38

FIONA

Now

When I get her number, I text Lily and hope it's enough. Stay away from your father. Will explain later.

I wait for a response, for her to demand an explanation, but there's nothing. For hours.

A little before ten, my phone rings.

"Fiona? Are you there?" Her voice is an out-of-breath whisper.

"Lily? Where are you?"

"You have to help me." Her voice is muffled, like she's holding a hand over her mouth. Behind her there are other sounds but it's hard to place them. She sounds like she's outside.

"Where are you? What's happened?"

"It's my dad. He's brought me here and I'm so scared he's going to—" There's a thump like the phone has been dropped, then there's scrambling and it's picked up again. "Hello? Are you there? Shit. There's barely any reception here."

"Tell me where you are. I'll call 911—"

"No— He has a gun and he'll—"

"But where are you?"

"That island, with the cave— Come quick—"

And the call is dropped.

He's taken Lily to Smuggler's Point. He'll see the police coming. It's a trap.

I don't know if David will take my call so I text him. Jason Ward has Lily on Smuggler's Point. Has gun.

I give him a minute to respond. I'm about to call 911 when his text comes in.

Lily Ward does this. False alarm.

???

Give me 5. Don't do anything.

I don't want to give him five minutes. If she's in danger, I need to go now. I'm tearing apart the kitchen trying to find a large knife or something to be a weapon when David calls.

"She's done this before. Last year she claimed her father kidnapped her and was demanding $5,000. It was a lie. She had run away from home because she'd had a fight with her mom and stepdad and wanted the money for herself."

"Come on, she wouldn't—"

"I'm telling you, she would," he says. "She's a compulsive liar. I've talked to her mom. I promised her I won't get the police involved unless they need to be."

"But this is different. He's your primary suspect—"

"Fiona, you've got to trust me on this."

"Someone followed me tonight on the road. I think it was him. He tried to approach me and—"

"What? Why didn't you call me? Where are you now?"

"I'm at the cottage."

"Okay. Listen—" I can hear him starting his car. "I'm going to get a patrol car out to you. You have to stay there. Please. Promise me you won't go anywhere."

"But—"

"You have to just stay put. If this is real, there's nothing you can do. Jason Ward is not someone to mess with."

I promise to wait here and we hang up.

I'm not keeping that promise.

I realized tonight why I'm drawn to Lily; I see myself in her. I know what it's like to be that age, to be carrying so much and have no one who can help you lift it. And she's trusted me from the moment she met me. I'm not naive enough to think that if I do right by her, I can somehow fix things with my own daughter. But I can help her—me, not anyone else.

There's a motorboat in the boathouse but even if I could get it into the water, I won't be able to get it close enough to the island without alerting him that I'm coming. I choose the smallest canoe, hoist it off the storage rack, and portage it down to the dock. I'm checking my phone every minute but it's silent. I've never canoed in November, but as long I don't get too wet, I should be fine. The night has cleared and the water is calm. I point myself toward where the islands will be and set off. I'm far offshore when I see the lights of the police car arrive at the cottage. They'll see the boathouse door open. David will know where I've gone. Hopefully, if not for Lily then for me, he'll come after us. He knows this water and these islands better than I do. I have to trust that he'll be able to get to us without getting hurt.

It's cold but it doesn't take me long to work up a sweat, and soon I see the long silhouette of the peninsula. I follow that until I see the cluster of islands a half mile off its tip. It's been twenty years since I've done this, but I remember that night with David. The only way onto Smuggler's Point is from inside the island cluster, but to get there, I'm going to have to navigate underwater rocks. And somewhere on that dark island is a man with a gun. But a canoe is silent and if he doesn't know I'm coming, I at least have surprise on my side.

I spend a lot of time canoeing and kayaking, but my arms are burning when I pass between the first two small islands and enter the cluster. Now, I have no choice but to slow down. Smuggler's Point looms ahead of me, rising up out of the water with its pine trees like quills sticking out of it. The only sound is the quiet dipping of my paddle into the water and my breathing.

I'm almost at it when I hit a rock head-on. The canoe stops abruptly and I fall forward before catching myself. The *thunk* of that hit seems loud in this silence and I hold my breath, but I don't hear anything. I slip out of the canoe into the freezing water, so cold it hurts. I get out on a rock where it's only up to my waist, but in another step I plunge under and come up sputtering. My down jacket is a sponge and my boots are heavy and cumbersome but I keep moving.

Slowly I make my way from rock to rock, one hand pulling the rope that hangs off the canoe, the other thrust out in front of me, trying to feel the rocks before I hit them with my knees. There's no sign of anyone on the island. From here, it looks huge. They could be anywhere. As soon as I reach the rocky beach, I'm fully exposed. I pull the canoe up onto the beach as quickly as I can, then move to the trees. My body is shaking violently. I don't know whether it'd be better to ditch my sodden coat or keep it on. I have spent my life in water. I am well aware of the signs of hypothermia and the speed that it can come on. I take the coat off and with freezing hands, wring it out as best I can, and then put it back on and start to climb. I have to hope that I can keep myself warm through physical exertion.

The most obvious destination is the cave, but I have no idea how David and I found it last time. I just know it was up. There's enough moonlight that I can make out what is immediately in front of me: rocks and trees. I start climbing.

I've almost gone past it when I see the opening of the cave, only slightly darker than everything around it. There's a small clearing immediately in front of it. My breathing seems so loud I can hardly hear past myself. When it's slowed a bit, I close my eyes and listen. Nothing. The island is silent. Too silent. I have to do something but I don't know what to do. If he's in there, he could shoot me as soon as I step out from the trees, but I can't just stand here. All I can do is hope that I can get into the cave, find Lily, if she's in there, and then the two of us can make it down to my canoe and away. This was an idiotic plan—no not a plan, an impulse. Two people, unarmed, in the freezing dark, against a man with a gun. But still I have to try. Because what else am I going to do?

I step out of the trees and stop, waiting for a sound, anything to show me that someone has seen me. Nothing moves. I take another step. I'm a few feet away from the cover of the trees, thin as they are. Still nothing moves. I want to run but I make myself walk, five, six, seven steps and I'm standing at the cave's mouth. I step into it and push myself against the wall. Inside it is pitch-black and I don't dare use the flashlight on my phone yet, not until I know who's in here. My eyes strain to adjust, to make out anything, but they can't. I take another step along the wall and then—

A sound. A groan or a breath, I can't tell, but it's coming from further into the dark.

Lily.

I take another step in and roots brush the top of my head, making me instantly duck, my hand shooting up above me. I forgot how quickly the ceiling slopes down. Now I can hear breathing, labored and thick.

"Hello?" I whisper. My voice cracks so it's barely audible but the breathing stops. "Lily?" I whisper a little louder this time.

"Help." The voice is rough and dry and so, so small.

I creep along the wall slowly, trying to feel what I can't see.

"Where are you?" I ask.

"Help," the voice says again. How badly hurt is she? Can I get her down to the canoe? Lily is tall but thin. If she can walk, I can support her.

I squat down and crawl forward, reaching out blindly with my hands. "Where are you?" Then my hand makes contact with part of her—her arm. I feel long hair filled with grit. I move closer, but I still can't see her. She's lying on the floor. Her head is toward the opening, which means she's facing the utter darkness of the rest of the cave.

"Lily? It's me. Are you hurt? Can you move?"

"Help me," the voice says again. My hand follows her arm but then I reach her wrists, held together with a plastic band and she flinches when I touch them.

"Oh, God, what has he done to you?"

"Help me," she says.

"Can you walk?" I ask. I try to slide my arm under her to help her sit up but she cries out in pain and I pull my arm back. "I'm sorry. I have to get you out of here. I have a boat, but we have to walk. Can you get up?"

There's no answer, just that labored breathing. Whatever he's done to her, he's probably drugged her too.

"I knew you'd come," another voice—a girl's voice—says from the darkness. Suddenly, light hits my eyes and all I can see is white.

"Oh, sorry." The light moves away. I blink a few times, trying to get my eyes to stop seeing stars and focus, then she shines the light on herself.

Lily is sitting on the opposite side of the cave. Her face is dirty, her hair disheveled.

"Lily?" My brain isn't working fast enough. If Lily's there—?

She moves the light to the person on the ground. It's a woman but she's blindfolded and her wrists are tied with the plastic bands that I felt. The part of her face that I can see is puffy and slack. Lily flicks the light off and everything goes pitch-black again.

"That's Angela," Lily says. "The one your friend is looking for." Her voice is flat, almost sounding like she's bored. "Honestly, I don't know what to do with her. That's why she's here. My dad came home early. If that old bastard next door hadn't started yelling at me, I wouldn't have gotten her out on time. I ran out of pills anyway, so I was going to have to do something with her."

"Pills? What—?" My body is shaking violently again.

"I'm trying to tell you."

"You're not making sense—"

"Keppra mainly. My sister's epilepsy pills. I gave her the Prozac I found from your mom, but that's so old, it didn't do anything. There were some painkillers from my grandma but I couldn't take too many or she'd notice. I got some stuff from these stoners at my school. I just sort of mixed and matched. My stepdad has the really good ones but my mom keeps those locked away after last year because she's paranoid. Oh, and I had some diazepam spray, but it's the kid kind so that doesn't do anything except make her throw up and she already stinks. Can't you smell her? I feel sick just being close to her."

I'm backing away from Lily but then she shines the light in my eyes again. My hands instinctively shoot up, but it's not soon enough and I'm blinded again. She shuts the light off.

"Please stay. I need you." She says it with a sad voice, like a poor imitation of a child. I feel her hand on me in the dark.

"What the fuck, Lily—" I jerk away but accidentally make contact with Angela. She cries out and recoils from me, then starts to cry.

"Oh, shut up," Lily says. "She's not going to hurt you. She came here to save us, right?"

"But why are you helping him?"

"Helping him? Who, my dad?" She laughs. "This is all me."

"But why? After everything—"

"My grandpa died. This whole part of me I'm supposed to pretend doesn't exist. My dad called my grandma. She probably wouldn't have even told me if I hadn't been there. No one cares but me. I didn't know what to do, so I went for a drive. And there was Angela on the side of the road. And I thought, what if I do it too? And so, I did."

The woman whimpers.

"Shut up." I hear an impact of a kick and Angela cries out again.

"Stop—" I swing my arm in her direction but all I hit is air. "Lily, you can't do this."

"But I can. That's the thing. And some people just ask for it. Like your fucked-up mother. What was she doing going to a college party with a kid at home? I think my grandfather sensed that, you know? And now you have a kid too. Zoe, right? But where is she? Far, far away."

I can't breathe, I can't think clearly, I just know I have to get out of here but I'm not sure if I can trust my legs to move properly. I'm closer to the exit than she is. I get up fast and stagger to the front, bent double so I don't hit my head. Lily lunges for me, but I've caught her by surprise and I'm almost at the entrance when a man steps into the mouth of the cave and I crash into him. His arms go out and he grabs me but I haven't stopped moving and even though I'm smaller, I have momentum and surprise on my side. His balance is knocked off and he staggers back. I push past him and I'm out.

"Dad, don't let her go—" Lily yells, but I'm already crashing into the trees. I have no idea which way to go, but as soon as I can feel the land sloping down, I follow the slope. I'm slipping and sliding, ricocheting off trees, trying to catch myself but I can't stop. The motion is forcing my blood to move. I know they're behind me but I can't hear anything except my own breathing and my feet hitting the ground, as I zigzag downward. I catch sight of moonlight reflecting off the water through the trees. What if I'm on the open lake side? Can I jump into the water or will I be smashed on a rock?

I can hear someone behind me now. Branches cracking as they run through the trees after me.

"Fiona!" Lily yells. "Fiona, stop."

"Lily," her father roars but he sounds farther away.

A part of my brain registers all of this while I'm still stumbling through the trees, down, down. And then I see the little beach and my canoe on the far side of it. I'm about to step out of the cover of the trees when Jason Ward crashes out of them on the opposite side. I freeze. He can't see me but he sees my canoe. I can hear him swearing, then Lily runs out, closer to me but still far enough away that she can't see me. They're both bent over and breathing hard and it takes her a moment but then she stands upright again and starts scanning the trees, looking for me. Her father moves closer to the canoe; he's hobbling. Lily says something to him. I can't hear them, but he's clearly angry.

"But I did it for you," she says. "All of this is for you."

He stands to his full height. "Why would I want this?"

"It's what you've always wanted," she says. "It's who we are."

I was wrong. I got it all wrong.

He turns and walks away from her.

"Where are you going?" she yells after him.

He disappears into the trees and Lily runs after him so I can't see her anymore, but I can hear her. "You can't do this to me. You don't get to cut me out. Daaaddddd—" she wails.

I sprint for the canoe. I reach it just as she comes back to the beach.

"There you are." She runs toward me.

I hit the canoe at a run, grab it, and begin to drag it to the water but I can't move fast enough. She grabs the other end and pulls it back so I let go and she falls backward. There is no time to think, to make a decision: I run into the water. As soon as I'm up to my waist, I dive under. My foot kicks a rock but I keep going. When I come up for air, I can't see her, so I dive under again and swim farther but my body isn't moving the way it usually does because of the cold and when I surface again, I've barely covered any distance. Lily's got the canoe in the water now and is climbing in. I swim farther out. She is using the paddle to push herself off the rocks. The canoe scrapes over something but she keeps going. My coat is pulling me down, making it hard to move my arms so I clumsily unzip it and it sinks below me, taking my phone with it. Now, I have my arms free but the cold intensifies so much it hurts. How far can I go? Can I make it all the way to the park? And then what? It's November. The park is empty. I'm miles away from people— No. Don't think about that. I know how to move in water. It's in my DNA. I imagine my mother telling me, "Swim. Just swim." So I do.

When I come up the next time, I'm farther away and Lily's facing the wrong direction. I take a gulp of air and dive under again. I'm past most of the rocks now, which means I can move without fear of hitting one, but it also means she can too. I need to breathe. I come up and gulp air too fast, taking in a mouthful of water and start to cough. She aims the canoe right at me and when I try to swim again, my body doesn't obey. She's ten feet away and could reach me in just one stroke. I'm breathing so hard, I can't go back under yet.

"Fiona," she says in that singsong voice, "you know you can't stay in the water. You'll get hypothermia."

"Lily—" It's hard to talk. "Why—?"

She looks like she's actually thinking about the answer. "At first, with her—" she gestures back toward the island "—I wanted to see if I could. But now . . . My dad always said there's a line. Everyone has one. And if you cross it . . . well there's no way back." She puts the paddle in the water and with one strong pull she's beside me. She reaches out to grab me—

Then, the roar of a boat engine. We both turn to look at it. There's a silver boat coming toward us at high speed, Jason Ward standing at the wheel. Lily half stands, screaming at him, but I can't hear her over the sound of the engine. At the last moment, he turns the boat sharply which makes a wake that hits us. As I swallow another mouthful of water, I see Lily fall out of the canoe. I come up, coughing. The empty canoe is floating away. Her father is leaning over the side of the boat yelling, "Lily! Lily!"

For a second, I think of how she sank in the pool, the way her body just fell. I have to get to the canoe. My arms are stones but I force them to move. My hand grabs the rope dragging in the water and I pull. I've grabbed the lip of the canoe to haul myself in when Lily clutches my leg and starts pulling me down. The canoe slips out of my grip and I go underwater, kicking and punching blindly. She loses her grip and I come sputtering back up, getting more water in my mouth, then she grabs my shirt and is climbing on top of me, pushing me under. We are a tangle of arms and legs. My foot makes contact with her stomach, and I kick her away from me. I can hear another engine. There are lights on the water, blue and red blinking on the surface, a voice on a megaphone, a dog barking. I rise up trying to call for help, but Lily grabs my hair and pulls me back under, and I can't get out of her grip. Something bites into my arm but the pain is disconnected because there is no air—no air—no air. There's an explosion of a gunshot, but it's muffled and far away; something happening in someone else's life. All of this is someone else's life, someone I don't know, but it's almost over now. Of that I'm sure.

Because I am sinking. My lungs are squeezing, desperate for air. My head feels like it's going to explode.

In some part of my brain, a deeper animal part, I must have known I wouldn't go back home. Before I flew away, I went to Aaron and Jenna's house. Big windows. House high on a hill. Money I don't have. I could see Zoe playing on the living room floor. Carpet thick enough to sleep on. How much I wanted to go up to that house and take her home, but I couldn't. I thought it would be better if I was gone but—

Above me on the surface, light flashing red, a body sinking, blood in the water—

My lungs—my throat—my body is collapsing in on itself—

"When you get tired, just float. Let the water carry you."

"Some people just ask for it."

Zoe.

And then, darkness.

CHAPTER 39

JASON

Now

Jason Ward is in the water. Everything that had been so carefully stitched together has come undone.

Jason had broken into the marina office, stolen a spare set of keys, found the boat they belonged to—easier now that there were only a few left in the water—and now he has come to his island. He found his boat, hidden in the same spot he'd shown Lily when he brought her here two weeks before. And then he found his daughter in the cave and she was with a woman—not Fiona Green as he had been expecting, but a stranger—and that stranger was dying.

Is dying. Where is she now? Too late to think about it now because he's dying as well.

When he found his daughter, he realized that she was at her line too. He tried to get her away from that dying woman, but she stayed put. She said she was waiting for someone and she begged him to stay too, but he walked out of the cave. He needed to think. He needed the island's calming magic to slow his mind down and he couldn't feel it with his daughter so close.

He walked all over the island and then he went back with the gun in his hand. At first, he'd thought maybe he could take the dying woman away—get her to a hospital—but if she lived, she would accuse Lily and it would start all over again. So, he could go in there and kill the dying stranger, put her out of her misery, then help his daughter bury her. But would that stop Lily from doing it again? If she had crossed her line, there was no way to know.

He was just about to step into the cave when someone—the Green woman, he realized a second too late—came running out and plowed into him, knocking him over.

"Dad, don't let her go," Lily screamed at him, but everything was happening too quickly for him to understand what was going on. Had Fiona Green been in the cave before and he hadn't seen her? Was she involved in this? None of it made sense.

She ran into the woods and he tried to follow, but he was tripping, moving blind. He fell and his knee smashed into a rock, but he got up and kept running until he stumbled onto the beach. There was a canoe that must belong to her. Why was she here? If she hadn't come with Lily, then why? Then his daughter came tumbling out of the trees and ran to him.

He tried to grab her, to shake her out of it, but she dodged him and he couldn't move fast enough with his busted knee.

"What are you doing?" he gasped at her. "Did he tell you to do this? Did he tell you to finish the collection? Did he do that?"

"I did it for you," she said. "All of this is for you."

"Why would I want this?"

"It's what you've always wanted. This is who we are."

No, no, no, no, no. This couldn't be who she was, who he was.

It was all supposed to end with him. He turned and walked away. Every step hurt but he kept moving through the trees even as Lily screamed after him, "You can't do this to me. You don't get to cut me out. Daaaddddd—"

How to fix this? The woman dying in the cave, his daughter on the beach, Fiona Green somewhere on the island. He didn't know how to fix any of it but he couldn't just leave. He got back to the stolen boat and steered it carefully around the island so he could see the beach. The canoe was in the water now with someone in it but he couldn't tell who from this distance. He roared the boat toward it, not caring about the underwater rocks, and then he saw it was Lily in the canoe and Fiona was in the water. He tried to swerve but the wake from his boat caused the canoe to rock, sending Lily overboard. When she came up, she was trying to drown Fiona and he finally made his decision. Lily was in free fall. She had crossed her line. He could do one good thing. He could finally stop this. Stop this thing that had been inside his father and was inside him and had passed through him into his child. So, he would stop it now.

He pulled out his gun, barely registering the police boat roaring toward him, its lights flashing, the dog barking, the voice over the megaphone telling him to drop his weapon.

He pointed the gun at the two bodies in the water. He had to aim carefully but they were tangled together.

He put his finger on the trigger and a shot rang out—

The gun fell from his hand and he tumbled over the side of the boat.

Jason Ward is in the water.

He is sinking. He looks up and sees the light from the police boat and the blood from the hole in his chest swirling into the lake in plumes. Beautiful. Through that, he can just make out the island. The rock rising out of the water with the trees stubbornly clinging to it. Just like his snow globe.

He reaches for it and closes his eyes.

CHAPTER 40

FIONA

Now

I wake up to something warm and wet licking my hand. I open my eyes slowly, then squeeze them shut again when bright light hits them.

"Oh, sorry, let me get that," a woman's voice says.

When I open my eyes again, more slowly this time, the room is dimmer. I'm in a hospital bed. Tucker is licking my hand and David is smiling down at me. I open my mouth to speak but my throat seizes and nothing comes out except a choked cough.

"Here," David says. He holds a cup of water and gently guides the straw to my lips. "They said you'd be thirsty when you woke up but you have to take it easy. Your throat's going to be sore."

I have nasal prongs in my nose and a tube running across my face that I instinctively bat away.

"Try to leave that," he says. "You need all the oxygen you can get."

The water feels like relief but it hurts to swallow. I move my fingers and scratch Tucker under his chin. He nuzzles into my hand, then licks my fingers again. "Wha—" is all I can get out before my throat seizes again.

"Maybe don't try talking," David says as a nurse, the one who's just dimmed the lights, comes over and checks the beeping machines beside me. She smiles.

"I'm going to get you a Popsicle," she says. "It'll be easier on your throat than the water and you need the sugar. Orange or lemon?" she asks.

I open my mouth to answer but nothing comes out.

"Never mind. I'll bring you one of each," she says and bustles off. David moves his chair closer to me.

"You're at the Mount Jerusalem Hospital in Syracuse," he says. "It's—" he checks his phone "—oh, it's almost four, which means you haven't missed dinner." On my confused look he continues, "Thanksgiving dinner, hospital style. Should be good."

I shake my head.

"Yeah, you're right. Better to stick with the Popsicles." He takes my hand and squeezes it. I squeeze back.

"I—" He swallows. Takes a breath. "Sorry. I, uh, am really glad you're okay."

I squeeze his hand again and Tucker woofs, whether in sympathy or to remind us that he wants to be a part of this. With his other arm, David draws him in. "You too, you big baby." He turns back to me. "Do you remember what happened?"

I close my eyes to think. I was in the water. Lily was there and she was drowning. And someone else—Jason Ward. There was a gunshot—

I open my eyes. I nod.

David looks relieved. "They said you might be pretty foggy for a bit. You don't have to do anything yet, but when you can, we're going to need to talk to you about what happened."

I point to my throat.

"You've been out for about sixteen hours. You were in a medically induced coma because they intubated you. That's why your throat's sore. You were starting to come out of it, so they pulled it out and gave you the nasal cannula instead."

The nurse comes back in and Tucker goes over to her, blocking her from getting near the bed.

"Tuck," David says.

"You know me, silly," the nurse says, holding out her hand for him to sniff again. She hands me the Popsicles in a plastic cup. "Go slow," she says. "The doctor will be by in a bit. I've let her know you're up."

Tucker has a bandage around his front leg and though I can't ask the question, David sees me looking at it.

"Someone doesn't know he failed K-9 academy and tried to be a hero last night. He jumped into the water before I could stop him." He reaches over and pulls Tucker to him, burying his nose in his fur. "Don't ever do that again, okay, buddy? That was too close a call." He turns back to me. "Luckily, that's just a bad scratch. He was trying to get the Ward girl off you but he got the wrong arm. That's how you got that." He points to the bandage on my arm. "You were underwater for . . . well, I don't know how long. It was too chaotic. But when we got you out, you weren't responsive. And you had hypothermia."

"Angela—" I croak.

"We got her out." He points across the room. Sitting in a chair opposite me is a large blue teddy bear with a "Get Well Soon" balloon tied to its arm. "That's from Veronica Ramirez, Angela's older sister. She's in the ICU—Angela, not Veronica—but they think she's going to pull through. She was badly dehydrated and Jason had her on a weird cocktail of drugs so they're trying to get those out of her system."

I shake my head adamantly. "Not—" My voice cracks.

"We've searched his house. It looks like he had her in the basement before he took her to that island."

The noise I heard. The smell coming up from those basement stairs. "Lily," I croak. My throat squeezes in protest.

"Lily's upstairs. She's in rough shape too. We don't know what her role was in this—"

This time I reach out and grab his arm. "What is it?" he asks.

"Lily—"

"Lily's the one who told us she was up in the cave. It was the first thing she said when we got her out of the water." On my look, he sits forward and puts his hands on his legs. "Are you up for this?"

I nod.

"Okay, so, from my view, here's what happened. When I got there, I saw Jason Ward in a boat. He was yelling into the water and when I got closer I could see that there were two of you in there and Ward had a gun pointed at you guys and . . ." He swallows. "Then Tucker jumped in to try to save you and—" He closes his eyes, then opens them again. "I shot Ward." He looks off. He suddenly looks so young, so lost. "I shot him. He's gone. I thought I was ready for this, for experiencing that, you know? It's going to take a bit." I reach over and put my hand on his knee. He covers my hand with his. "There's a process I have to go through, like officially, it's not, like I'm not in trouble or anything. It was clear he was about to kill one of you. But, yeah."

"Not Jason." This time it comes out.

"Not Jason?"

I mouth, "Lily took her."

"What do you mean?"

"She told me. In the cave."

David's face goes pale. "You're sure about this?"

I nod again.

It takes a beat, but then he gets up. "Hold on. I have to make some calls. This just got more complicated."

He steps into the hallway as the doctor comes in.

I like this doctor right away. She moves with the grace of an athlete. She introduces herself while she listens to my chest.

"So," she says when she's done her examination, "the detective tells me you're a swimmer."

I nod.

She smiles. "Me too. Actually, I think that's what prevented this from being a lot worse. From what he's said, you were underwater for a while. Do you practice breath control?"

I've never given it a name before but I guess that's what I do. I nod again.

"So, there are some who believe, and I'm one of them, that we can train ourselves to hold our breath longer. If you've been practicing that, then presumably you could've been underwater longer before you panicked and took an involuntary breath. We did a CT scan of your lungs when you came in to see if there was inflammation. There's a bit, but it should go down on its own. You also had hypothermia. I'm guessing you knew that."

I nod again.

"November's a bit chilly for swimming in these parts," she says. "Do you know how long you were in the water for?"

I have to talk slowly, but I manage to tell her about getting wet on my way to the island, and then again after.

"The detective said that your pulse was hard to detect when they got you out of the water. That might have been because of the hypoxia, or the hypothermia, or both. The good thing was, they found it and didn't start chest compressions. Saved you some broken ribs, among other nasty things."

She picks up my chart and scans it, then says, "I'd like to do a follow-up CT scan and we're going to keep you here for a little while longer, but I'd say, given what you went through, you're pretty lucky." She smiles again. "I'll be back later. I like your dog, by the way."

I try to say he's not mine, but of course nothing comes out.

When David comes back in, he's lost some of the excitement he had before. He shakes his head. "Lily's in pretty rough shape, like you. There's a detective up there but it's more complicated with a minor. She's the one who told us about Angela. She was so adamant we get to her in time. That's why we assumed her dad—"

I shake my head again.

"So, you're saying she's the one who picked Angela up?"

I nod.

"At the house," I croak. "There was a noise. It sounded—" I have to swallow to keep my throat from seizing. "It sounded like it came from the basement."

He nods. "Okay. Okay. Well, we'll get all the pieces put together. Angela's coming to, so hopefully we can get her statement. Lily basically shut down when she learned about her dad. It'll take some time." He looks at me and smiles. "But you don't need to worry about that, okay? Just focus on getting better."

The friendship bracelet Lily gave me is still on my wrist. I pull at it but it's too tough to break. I hold my arm out to David. "Scissors?"

He pulls a utility knife out of his pocket. "Is that thing bothering you?" I nod.

Gently he puts the blade under the bracelet and with one smooth slice, it's off. I pick it up and drop it in the waste basket next to my bed. My feelings about Lily are . . . complicated. Part of me is still stuck in the old story that she's a young girl in need of help, caught up in something so much bigger than herself, but last night I saw the person she was willing herself to be. No matter who she is, our connection is now as severed as that bracelet.

There's noise in the hallway and we both turn to the door as Aaron walks in with my daughter squirming in his arms. My father follows. Aaron puts Zoe down and she runs over to me.

"Mama," she says. She's trying to get up on the bed. The moment I see her, I can't talk again but now it's because I'm crying. Zoe scrambles up on David's chair and crawls onto my lap. She touches my tears. "Mama 'kay?"

I nod and squeeze her into me. That lasts for a moment and then she's wiggling out and looking around. She sees Tucker and reaches for him. I'm about to stop her but Tucker sniffs her fingers and then licks them and she giggles. Then she sees the stuffed bear. She turns to me. "Bobo?" she asks.

"No, sweetheart," I whisper. "But you have it." David goes and gets it and gives it to her and she hugs it to her chest.

"Bobo fend," she says.

I reach out and touch her curls. They're springy and soft, like Aaron's were when he was this age.

My father comes closer and stands by the bed. Aaron stays by the door but he's smiling. They both look exhausted. Dad leans down and pulls me into him, then he whispers in my ear. "I thought I lost you. When David called . . . We got on the first plane we could." His voice is rough too. It feels so good to be held by him, to feel his scratchy whiskers on my cheek. It's been a long time since I've let my dad hug me this way. In that hug there are so many words, all the years of it just being the two of us, each living in our grief side by side but so often—too often—not seeing the other. Thinking we were alone.

After another round of Popsicles, which I share with my daughter who's thrilled to get treats, my throat starts to loosen a little. David does most of the talking at first, catching Aaron and my dad up on what we know so far. My father's reaction to Jason Ward being dead is complicated, like mine is. The old bogeyman, but maybe some of that fear was misplaced. There are more tears when I tell him what I have been searching for out here, but talking about it with him, I don't feel that pain that made me want to shut down so many times before. It feels good for us to finally be able to openly mourn together after all this time.

The Ramirez family—parents, sister, and a cluster of aunts—come in to meet me. Names are tossed around that I have no hope of remembering at this point, but there will be time. Angela is awake and giving a statement to the police.

Seeing their faces, the sheer relief, the hope that has been answered despite the odds, I am happy for them, but I also know that this will shape all their future decisions. How do we trust we can send our children, even adult children, into the world, knowing how vulnerable we all are?

In all of the people coming and going, David keeps himself in the background, but he never leaves. At certain points, my eyes meet his and that's enough to know that we're both here.

Finally, everyone starts to go. I can feel myself being pulled back into sleep. My father has gone to see his parents, and will bring them to visit tomorrow. David and Aaron step into the hallway to talk and it's just my daughter and me with Tucker going back and forth between the bed and the doorway, trying his best to keep track of everyone. Zoe cuddles into my arms, holding her new bear tight to her chest, and within a minute, she's asleep. The weight of her on me is a miracle.

Aaron comes back alone, sits down next to me, and takes my free hand. It's the first time we've had a chance to talk.

"I missed her," I say quietly, stroking her head with my other hand.

He nods. "She's been asking about you every day and then when your dad called to say what had happened—" He shakes his head. "I couldn't leave her behind. She doesn't know what happened obviously, but she could sense something was wrong. It's amazing how intuitive such a little kid can be."

"How's Jenna?" I ask.

"Her mom and sister came a few days ago. They've told me they're staying until the baby is born." He gives a smile that says "what are you going to do?" I've met his mother-in-law and know that as soon as she's on the scene, she's in charge.

"I —" I start to say, then stop and swallow. I focus on the weight of Zoe asleep on my chest. I am not sure if I have the words to say what I need to say. Maybe not yet, but I have to try.

Because in those last seconds in the water, something changed for me. I wasn't thinking of the past, of my mother, of all that I have lost, I was thinking about Zoe.

"I want . . . " I swallow again. "To talk about . . ."

Aaron smiles at me. "Us too."

"But Jenna?"

"She agrees," he says. "We'll do whatever you want to do. We can put the adoption conversation on hold for a while."

"I want her." Zoe shifts in her sleep, and her hand moves onto the bandages on my arm. Aaron reaches out and carefully moves it. "I'm still seeing my psychiatrist. I'll keep seeing her. But I think I can . . ."

"We talked to the lawyer," he says quietly. "It's just a matter of filing some papers. If you want, in the future, we can revisit it. Or we can just . . . forget about it. Keep going as we're going, take things as they come."

I nod because my throat is too constricted now to speak.

He leans over, kisses me on the forehead, and then gently, done as a parent who's had a lot of practice, he scoops Zoe and her bear up without waking her and carries her out of the room. She snuggles into her dad's shoulder and stays asleep.

David comes in. "Stay?" I ask him. My eyes are already half-closed.

"I'm not going anywhere," he says.

When I wake up again, the hospital is quiet. Nurses walk past but all I hear is the soft squelch of their sneakers. David's sprawled out in a reclining chair that looks incredibly uncomfortable but I can tell from his breathing that he's deep asleep. Someone gave him a blanket and pillow. Tucker is asleep at his feet, his ears twitching.

When I look at my nightstand, I realize what woke me up. A nurse was just in and left an envelope on the bedside table. I turn up the light over the bed and reach for it. On the envelope is a note:

Fiona
Just got in. Wanted you to have these when you woke up. See you tomorrow.
Love, Grandma L.

I rip it open. Inside are old family photos I've never seen. I dump them onto my lap and something else falls out. It's a delicate silver chain with a half heart on it. Engraved on the heart are half of two names: "*Ade & An*," Adele and Ana, my grandmother and mother.

My dad told me that my mother had bought the necklace we shared when she was pregnant, and that she always wore her half, but he never mentioned her wearing one from her own mother. There's a story here that my grandmother is trying to tell me. I close my eyes and imagine it: my mother, still in her first year of college, telling her parents—her mother an ambitious academic, her father a sought-after swim coach—that she's dropping out of school and quitting swimming to have a baby. My father said that they were furious, that whatever got broken that day was never repaired because they were distant even before my mother died. Maybe they'd all thought there would be time to fix it, but then there wasn't. I can imagine my mom taking off the necklace from her mother and leaving it at home as an act of protest. But she bought one for me. She continued the tradition, just like I have bought one for my daughter.

Since I've woken up here, more of what happened has come back to me, Lily's words in the cave. What hurt so much is that somewhere deep in my heart, I've always wondered if, like Lily claimed, my mother had done something that drew him to her. Predators are drawn to the weak. If my mother was weak, was it because of me? But Zoe isn't the cause of my weakness; she's the reason I want to be strong. Maybe it was the same for her.

I pull off the necklace that I always wear and lay the three half hearts on my lap.

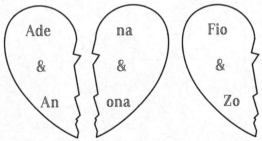

Ade
na
Fio
&
&
&
An
ona
Zo

I've always felt like there was an unbridgeable chasm between my grandmother and me, but my grandmother is trying to reach across it. Tomorrow, when my grandparents come to see me, I will reach back.

Drowsily, I look through the photos: baby pictures of my mom, a toddler on the beach, a second-grade school photo with the requisite missing teeth. All so wonderfully ordinary—not a victim, just a girl growing up. I stop on one of my mom as a teenager with my grandpa. They're in a boat and wearing diving gear, but it's the background that makes me look more closely. Behind them a rock reaches up out of the water with scraggly pine trees clinging to the side of it.

I turn it over. On the back, my grandmother has written

1989—Smuggler's Point—cave diving.

CHAPTER 41

ANA

August 29, 1993
2:40 A.M.

The storm clouds were breaking apart and she could see the island rising out of the water like a shadow. Ana remembered it from four years ago when she and her dad found the cave. They'd been looking for shipwrecks because she'd grown up with him telling her ghost stories about smugglers using this island. When they'd found the underwater cave instead, it felt like a secret place only they knew about. The entrance was a few feet under the surface in a place where the rock had been cracked in two.

Four years ago, she and her dad had diving gear and flashlights. Now, she just had the moonlight fighting its way through the swiftly moving storm clouds. No, she had more than that. She had a will, a strength she'd never known she had. In the past hour, she had swum for her life through a storm, through injury, through terror. It was the hardest swim she'd ever done, but as she put her hand on the hard rock of the island she knew she'd made it. That rock was the first solid thing she'd touched and what it promised was rest, safety. She loved her life, even though nothing had happened the way it was supposed to, but still, it was hers. Maybe all of her worry about her daughter was just what love was—terrifying, suffocating even—but it was also the smell of her daughter's head when she was deep asleep, and her little hands reaching up to hold hers, and all the messy unfinished chaos of her life. She would go back to school, not yet, but soon. She would get back on track. But first, she needed to rest in a place where the man with the knife couldn't find her. She didn't know what had happened to Ben. She had to return. She would not leave that little girl alone in the world.

It took some time, but she found the crack in the rock that marked the entrance to the cave. The first time she dove, she didn't make it through the narrow passageway and in a panic had to back her way out. It was hard to get a big enough breath because her body was so exhausted. She tried again and again had to back out, panic in her throat. The third time, her lungs squeezing tight, fingers gripping the slick algae that coated the stone walls, she fought her way inside the cave.

She surfaced in darkness and gasped in oxygen. It took a moment for her eyes to adjust. It wasn't pitch-black. High up, there was a small opening just big enough to let a little moonlight through. She was in a small pool. She knew from when she had come here before. She felt her way to the rocks on the other side and climbed out.

She lay there, feeling her chest rise and fall.

Minutes passed, or hours. Time had lost all meaning tonight.

Her eyes and ears got used to the enclosed space after the wild vastness of the open lake. The pool was perfectly still in the moonlight. A place of mermaids. Maybe someday she would bring her daughter here.

Her body was heavy as the adrenaline that had got her here drained away. Her clumsy fingers felt the gash in her leg. The skin was swollen and waterlogged around the opening and she couldn't tell if she was still bleeding. The pain had turned into a throbbing that radiated out from her calf.

She closed her eyes.

The air in the cave was cold.

She saw her little girl swimming in the lake. How was that only this morning?

Fiona had disappeared, but now she knew her daughter was just swimming underwater, like a mermaid. Her eyes were open and she was looking for shells. My brave girl, she thought. She isn't afraid of the water at all. She couldn't wait to tell Ben . . .

So cold now, and so tired, but the water was warm.

She got back into the water and floated on her back, looking up at the hole. She would stay here until she saw the sky lighten, then she would swim to the state park.

The beach was close. The cottage was close. Her daughter was close.

She just needed to rest. She closed her eyes.

CHAPTER 42

FIONA

Three Weeks Later

The water that hits my face as our boat bounces over the waves is so cold it's like tiny needles on my skin. I could go inside the little cabin but I want to be out here at the bow with my grandfather. As we get close to Smuggler's Point, it towers over us. I've never approached it from this side. The rocks rise almost straight up from the water. The trees that have managed to grow stick out at strange angles, permanently bent from years of wind and weather. Grandpa signals, and David slows the boat as we come to a low rock overhang. He points below the surface. The cave entrance is down there.

He looks at me. "You s-sure?" Grandpa asks.

I nod.

Although it took some convincing, I am going in first. I'm not an experienced diver, but the passage into the cave isn't deep enough that I need an oxygen tank. I have a rope tied to me that will connect me to the boat and even though the water is hovering just above freezing on this December day, I'm wearing a dry suit, so as long as I'm not in for too long, the risk of hypothermia is low. If I run into trouble, I pull the rope. David and my father, each wearing diving gear of their own, come out of the cabin, lower the anchor, and then look down into the water. The entrance isn't visible from here. Five feet below the waterline, the rock splits wide enough that a person can get through. It will be narrow, but Grandpa told me the passage isn't too long, and then I should come up inside the cave. There had been some debate about just sending in police divers, but it's such a long shot. If I find anything, the police will get involved, but right now, it's just me.

My dad looks anxious but he doesn't say anything. Instead, he watches me put my goggles on, gives me a quick squeeze on the arm, and steps back. My grandpa is standing by the side. I can see his fingers gripping the boat, hard. I know he won't loosen that grip until I resurface. David gives me a thumbs-up. We decided not to bring Tucker, in case he attempted another water rescue. With one last look at these three men who I love so dearly, I jump off the boat.

The water is a shock, but I can feel how the suit is protecting me. I have gone through this in my mind a hundred times, ever since my grandmother shared that picture with me and the idea began to form.

"Could she have found it, in the dark, in a storm?" We were examining a map of the peninsula with the approximate location of where we think my mother went into the water, and where Grandpa thought the cave was.

"She probably didn't swim straight there," he said. "We d-don't know what state she was in when she got into the water—she could have been badly injured—but if she was able to swim, she'd be able to make it that far. Even in rough water."

The hardest part, we agreed, would have been getting oriented. From water level during a storm at night, it would be almost impossible to see and easy to swim straight into the open lake. These past few weeks as we've been planning this dive, I've been trying to tamp down my expectations with this reality.

"She would have been trying to hide," Grandpa said. "We'd talked about it when we found the cave. We were talking about the smugglers using it, but maybe she remembered it that night. If anyone could do it, it was her."

I look up at the boat. Grandpa is peering over the edge, watching me closely. This is probably how my mother saw him on countless swims as he helped her train for her lake crossing. He still has the tremors the stroke left behind, but the more time I've spent with him and my grandmother, the surer he's become, or maybe the change is me, learning to see his strength. Last night, my grandmother warned me he might not be able to join us—it's the first time in thirty years he's been out on the water—but this morning when they arrived at the cottage, he walked straight onto the boat without any hesitation. Now, Grandma Lukas and my other grandparents are back there waiting and watching for our return. Just the three of them sitting together, binoculars in hand, is a kind of healing.

I take a huge breath of air, and dive. The noise of the water hitting the rock, the boat creaking, the wind, all become muffled and I'm in a silent world. My headlamp shines on algae waving gracefully off the side of the rock. Above the waterline, the split just looks like a crack, but when you get underwater, it's actually an opening. It's so narrow, I can touch both sides to pull myself along but I won't be able to turn around, so if I can't make it through, I'll have to back out. That gives me a second of panic but I can feel the rope around my waist and my headlamp is showing me that I'll come out in just another few feet. And, as I know well, I can hold my breath for a long time.

I come up inside the cave. The dampness on the cave walls reflects my headlamp's light, and I can see a ledge of rocks on the other side to rest on. High above, there's a hole in the rock and a beam of light shines down onto the water. On the open lake, the water is choppy with small whitecaps, but in here the pool is still and the cave has an echoey silence to it. I pull myself out and sit on the rock.

Next to me is a pile that looks like the debris of a rock slide. If I had to guess, I think this is the passage that leads to the cave high up on the island. When I turn off the headlamp, I can see how the light from above penetrates the still water. It is a relief to know that she wasn't in absolute darkness.

Because I know my mother was here. I felt it as soon as I surfaced.

I slip back into the water, turn my light on and aim it down. The pool is only about ten feet deep. Movement near the bottom catches my eye. At first, I think it's seaweed, but when I dive down and reach for it and pull it to the surface, it's cloth. It's ragged, ripped, with tiny shells growing on it. It could just be a piece of garbage that found its way in here. Or maybe it was once part of a summer dress worn by a young woman the night she went to a party.

I dive down again, moving slowly so I don't stir up silt. It takes a few dives, letting my eyes travel slowly across the rocky bottom, and then I find it. Caught on a sharp piece of rock, something catches the light of my headlamp. Carefully, I dislodge it and bring it to the surface: the other half of my necklace.

I swim back to the rock. My hands are shaking and I'm wearing gloves, but I manage to get the zipper opened enough that I can reach in and grab the necklace my grandmother gave me. Taking it off over my head would involve removing part of my suit and I can't risk it in here, so I tug and the old chain breaks. I wrap the silver chain around the tarnished chain of my mother's, putting the two half hearts together. Now, she can be held by both her mother and me, just as I am held by her and my daughter.

I swim to the center of the pool and drop the two necklaces, the completed heart, into the water.

Then, using the rope as my guide, I pull myself back to the people I love who wait for me on the surface.

ACKNOWLEDGMENTS

Many years ago, I was sitting in a coffee shop in Vancouver when I stumbled across a news article about a father and son who were both serial killers. Two of the father's victims had been a young couple who he'd picked up from the side of the road when their car broke down. He killed the man by luring him behind his truck to help adjust the load, then he held the woman captive for several hours before killing her too. As I was reading this, a woman came into the coffee shop with her daughter. Something so ordinary, so unspecial. But as I watched them, I realized that had that young woman lived, she might be doing exactly what this woman and her daughter were doing, but for something as meaningless as being in the wrong place at the wrong time. Instead, her sudden and violent ripping from the world would ripple outward for years to come. And her life—her possibilities—had been reduced to a sentence in a newspaper.

From there to here, these characters have lived with me for a long time. Along the way, many other people have helped me by offering their trust, their creativity, and their knowledge.

The story started as a play, so first a heartfelt thank-you to the actors and directors who entered that early version of the story with me and brought these characters to life. In Toronto, Shari Hollett, Jim Annan, Allan Hawco, Jason Jazrawy, Kimwun Perehinic, Clare Preuss, Birgitte Solem, Paul Tedeschini, and Brendan Wall. In Columbus, Ohio, with Available Light Theatre, Matthew Slaybaugh, Alex Beekman, Acacia Duncan, Michelle Schroeder, and Ian Short.

A huge thank-you to my agent, Victoria Marini of High Line Literary Collective, who understands the line I'm trying to walk as a writer and has championed this book from the start. And to my amazing editor, Loan Le at Atria, who said yes to going on this publishing ride a second time and, once again, has brought her sharp eye and thoughtful self to these pages to make them what they are now. And to the team at Atria: Natalie Argentina, Liz Byer, Libby McGuire, Lisa Nicholas, Kate Nintzel, Debbie Norflus, Jolena Podolsky, and Dana Troker. That you are reading these pages now is because of the unseen work they have done and for that, they have my deepest gratitude.

Perinatal or Postpartum Mood and Anxiety Disorders (PMADs) can include anxiety, depression, OCD, postpartum psychosis, and PTSD. They impact one in five birthing people, and can happen in pregnancy and after giving birth. My reason for writing about them is somewhat personal—the identity shift in becoming a parent was the most profound and complex experience I ever had and mental health is intricately woven into that. A huge thanks to my friend J. M. who shared her story of postpartum struggles with me. It takes tremendous bravery to reveal the darker parts of yourself. Her story is one of resilience and love. She also introduced me to The Motherhood Center in New York City. (https://themotherhoodcenter.com/) Their website, blog, and webinars have been an excellent resource in the writing of this book.

Doing research for a book often involves sending your friends messages that say, "do you know someone who . . . ?" My friends came through, and for that I have the following thanks to add: To Evelyn Gama, LCSW, who works with parents who are struggling with PMADs, thank you for talking to me about some of the ways they can manifest and how the approach to care has changed from the early 1990s to now. To Gerard McCarthy, retired Commander of Major Crimes Bureau (Suffolk County Police Department), for walking me through the first stages of a missing persons case. To Molly Booth, Public Defender, who gave me insight on the steps of a murder trial. To Dr. Zachary McClain, MD, who talked to me about the physiological effects of near drowning experiences and offered his guidance on appropriate medications for managing epilepsy in children. And to my uncle, John Fawcett, for answering my out-of-the-blue phone call to talk about boats. Any errors in this story are entirely mine.

To my early readers Kristen Bird, Allison Buccola, Sabrina Thatcher, and Michelle Maryk, thank you for your feedback and support. First drafts can be lumpy awkward things and it takes a generosity of spirit to see the story that wants to come out.

As always, a huge thank-you to my parents, Barry and Sheila Fawcett. And finally, to my husband, Sean Lewis, who is a writer himself and understands this roller-coaster ride better than anyone, and to our son, Eamon, who completes my heart.

ABOUT THE AUTHOR

Before writing books, Jennifer was an award-winning playwright and cofounder of the theater company, Working Group. Her first novel, *Beneath the Stairs*, was also published by Atria. Born and raised in Canada, she spent a decade living in the Midwest before settling in the Hudson Valley. *Keep This for Me* is her second book. Visit her at www.jenniferfawcettauthor.com.

ATRIA BOOKS, an imprint of Simon & Schuster, fosters an open environment where ideas flourish, bestselling authors soar to new heights, and tomorrow's finest voices are discovered and nurtured. Since its launch in 2002, Atria has published hundreds of bestsellers and extraordinary books, which would not have been possible without the invaluable support and expertise of its team and publishing partners. Thank you to the Atria Books colleagues who collaborated on *Keep This for Me* as well as to the hundreds of professionals in the Simon & Schuster advertising, audio, communications, design, ebook, finance, human resources, legal, marketing, operations, production, sales, supply chain, subsidiary rights, and warehouse departments who help Atria bring great books to light.

Editorial
Loan Le
Natalie Argentina

Jacket Design
Danielle Mazzella di Bosco
James Iacobelli

Marketing
Jolena Podolsky

Managing Editorial
Paige Lytle
Shelby Pumphrey
Lacee Burr
Sofia Echeverry

Production
Liz Byer
Beth Maglione
Lisa Nicholas
Jill Putorti
Erika R. Genova

Publicity
Debbie Norflus

Publishing Office
Suzanne Donahue
Abby Velasco

Subsidiary Rights
Nicole Bond
Sara Bowne
Rebecca Justiniano